THE ROCKING STONE

OTHER BOOKS BY JILL RUTHERFORD

Cherry Blossoms, Sushi and Takarazuka Seven Years in Japan

Secret Samurai Trilogy

The Day After I Won the Lottery...and Other Short Stories

Tama, the Extraordinary Cat

www.jillrutherford.co.uk

THE ROCKING STONE

Jill Rutherford

Little Wren Press

Published by Little Wren Press 2018
© Gillian Rutherford 2018

Gillian Rutherford asserts the moral right to be identified as
the author of this work.
This novel is a work of fiction based on historical fact. The
names, characters and incidents portrayed in it are the work
of the author's imagination. Any resemblance to actual
persons living or dead are entirely coincidental.

ISBN 978-0-9569679-8-5

A CIP catalogue record for this book is available from the
British Library

Little Wren Press, 27 Old Gloucester Street,
London, WC1N 3AX UK

This story is fiction based on the way of life of my much missed and loved grandparents

PROLOGUE

I picked up the newspaper from the doormat and sat down in my armchair. I opened it up to the headlines unaware of the shocks to come.

PONTYPRIDD CHRONICLE

23 August, 1973

BODY FOUND IN WELL

A skeleton was found this week at the bottom of a disused well on The Graig, Pontypridd. With the remains was a Miners' Federation Card dated 1920 in the name of Dudley J. Mallow. Anyone who has information about this person is requested to contact the police.

I sat up so suddenly and with such force it was as if a spring had been released in me. My breath caught in my throat and my heart and stomach lurched so hard it was like a physical pain.

Dudley?

After 53 years?

My mind threw up an image so lifelike of that foul, wicked man that I started to shake all over.

So, he had been dead all these years. My life would have been a different one if only I'd known. And now, even from the grave he had the power to destroy me.

And then it started again. That coil of hatred I had for Dudley curled itself around my body and through my veins and arteries like a poison. I couldn't let myself go back there, and yet, I couldn't stop my mind swirling in a vortex of old memories. I knew I had to find out what had happened to him and who had killed him. For, without a doubt, someone had.

But everyone was dead except for me. How could I discover the truth? There must be a clue in my life somewhere ... somewhere ...

I sat back and closed my eyes letting my mind go where it would with no censure or guidance from me. I found myself walking down a street as a child going back to the beginning of what made me the woman I became and shaped me to react to Dudley in the way I did.

CHAPTER ONE

I walked down the street to our house. It was hot and I was tired after my day at school and I was dreading seeing Aunty Gladys who would be waiting for me. I couldn't understand why my lovely, gentle mother had such two awful sisters, and Aunty Gladys was the worst.

Opening the front door slowly I tried to ignore the staircase rising straight in front of me – and where that led to – and glanced quickly up the dim passageway into our brighter kitchen at the end. It was empty. That was the only room we lived in so I knew my aunty wasn't here. She'd have been sat at the kitchen table glaring at me through the open door. I sat down at the table and waited. I couldn't understand it. Either she, or my father if he wasn't on shift, or my Aunty Irene would always be there to give us our tea when Davy and me came home from school. I'd told them I was old enough to do it, but as Davy was only five, my father insisted on a grown-up being there. But that day, Davy had gone to a friend's birthday party straight from school.

As pleased as I was that Aunty Gladys wasn't there, because she was always nasty to me, I was worried about my mother lying ill upstairs. I knew she was dying because horrible Jane Jones from across the street told me with relish. 'My mam told me your mam is dying of the consumption', and she stuck her tongue out at me. She was so spiteful she'd grow up with a wart on the end of her nose. But I wasn't absolutely certain what dying meant: something about heaven and hell and people

11

disappearing.

Our dad told us Mam was very ill, but was doing her best to get better and that we should help her all we could. For Davy and me, that meant we had to stay quiet, easier for me than him. I didn't tell anyone about horrible Jane . . . because, well, maybe my dad didn't know.

I sat at the table and took my school book out. We'd been learning about Alfred the Great that afternoon, and I wanted to read more about him, but I could hear my mother coughing and moaning. Where was Aunty? I didn't like her, but I knew my mother needed her. After about half an hour I decided I had to do something. She was always given her tea when we had ours and she wouldn't know what was happening. It must be terrible being stuck up there all the time. Me and Davy were not allowed to see her in case we caught the consumption too. I hadn't seen her for two months and I missed her very much.

I crept up the narrow staircase, trying not to make too much noise on the bare boards as I knew noise hurt my mother in some way. I was nervous because I hadn't seen her for so long and I knew I was doing something I shouldn't. My hand shook as I knocked softly on the bedroom door and waited. I knocked again, louder this time and heard a faint voice. I turned the knob and peeked around to my parents' bed. It was dark in the room and a horrible, yucky smell hit me. I'd never smelt anything like it before. My mother was propped up on lots of pillows and when she turned her head and looked at me I gasped. Was this my mam? She was so thin and didn't look pretty anymore. Her lovely long, black hair hung like bits of dirty string. She looked like a ghost and scared me.

She stared for a while, as if she didn't recognise me. 'Kate?' she whispered. 'Is that you *cariad*?'

'Yes, Mam, it's me.' My voice shook and it came out as a bit of a squeak, so I took a breath and repeated it. 'Yes, Mam, it's me. Would you like a cup of tea?' Then I added, 'There's no one home but me,' in case she was wondering why I was there.

There was a pause before she answered and her voice sounded strange, not like my mother's, and she spoke slowly.

'Yes, my lovely, and bring one for yourself, let's have a chat. I haven't seen you for such a long time.'

I knew I shouldn't, but if my mam said it was all right, then it was all right with me. I think she was confused, had forgotten why she didn't see me and Davy any more, but my mam would never do anything to put me in danger. She loved me more than anything she always told me.

I made the tea but when I picked up the cups and saucers my hands shook so much I had to put them down again. I was afraid of the woman upstairs who used to be my mother.

I carried up the cups without their saucers and tip-toed across the floorboards and put them down on the old apple box which was stood on its end next to the bed and used as a table. My mother had made a pretty green cover for it with roses on. She was clever like that. She'd gone to sleep and I stood on the rag rug by the side of the bed and wondered what to do. It was cold in the room, and airless. I looked over at the window wondering whether to open it and saw the curtains tightly closed. I remembered then that light hurt her eyes and because the curtains were so thin, my father had pasted newspaper over the glass to help keep the light out.

A short while later, her eyes opened and she looked at me with love. I saw my old mother then, the one I knew and loved. 'Oh, Mam,' I said.

She smiled and pulled the bedclothes back, 'Come and *cwtch* with your mam, Katie love.'

I climbed into the high bed and tucked myself under my mother's arm. She didn't smell too good, like she needed a wash, but I didn't mind. 'You know your mother isn't well right now. I have to speak softly as I haven't much breath left in my lungs.'

'Yes, Mam, but you'll get better like I did when I was bad last year. I felt terrible and then I suddenly got better.'

She chuckled, a small, soft sound. 'You're a good girl. You're probably right. I'll get better suddenly. But I'm worried about you. Are Dad and Aunty Gladys and Aunty Irene looking after you well?'

I couldn't tell her how much I hated her sisters because it would make her worry. 'Yes, Mam . . . and Davy likes school.'

'That's good, my lovely, and how are you getting on at school?'

'I like it. That hasn't changed. I love to learn about new things.'

'Yes, you always were a questioning child,' she said, smiling.

I pulled away from her a little and leaned my head against the pillow, turning it so that I could see her face. 'When you were little, were you good at school?'

She looked at me, still smiling. 'Yes, I was. Like you, I loved school. I went until I was eleven.'

'What subject did you like the best?'

She coughed softly. 'Reading. I loved books. I used to teach my dad how to read in the evenings. He couldn't you see, he didn't have the chance to go to school.'

'Why not?' I asked surprised. 'Everyone goes to school.'

'Yes, now they do, but then only rich children were taught their lessons. For people like my father . . . well, there were no schools for him to go to.'

'No schools?' What did they do then? You know, about learning?'

'They didn't learn, they worked. He had to go out and work in the pit when he was little. She paused and smiled. 'He used to call me his "miracle girl" because I used to teach him how to read for himself. I taught him until I was fourteen . . . and then everything stopped.'

I waited for her to continue and then realised she had tears in her eyes. They had looked red and sore before, but now looked even worse. I gave her my hankie and asked, 'Why did everything stop? Did you live here then?' I was desperate to know.

'No,' she sniffed, 'we lived near the Albion Pit in Cilfynydd, my father worked there you see . . . but it's almost here isn't it, only about a twenty minute walk. And our house was just like this one: two rooms up and two down,' she added in a whisper.

She started to cough and couldn't stop. She picked up a

14

bottle with a wide neck and spat into it. It was half full of dark bloody-looking slime and smelt terrible. 'I'm sorry, Katie love . . . my lungs are full of this awful stuff . . . I have to get it out. It's horrible I know.'

Her breathing was strange and I didn't want her to worry. 'No. It's not horrible,' I said. 'If it makes you feel better, it's not horrible.'

She smiled again. 'Thank you, lovely, like I said, you're a good girl.'

I was desperate for the rest of her story. 'Think of your pictures, Mam,' I pointed to the two pictures on the wall opposite the bed. 'You like those and the sun will make you feel better.'

She looked over and nodded. 'I do. I like them very much; and you're right, they always make me feel better.'

'What country are they again, Mam? I've forgotten.'

'Italy, my lovely,' she said with a smile. 'The gardens are in a country called Italy, where the sun always shines.' She gazed at them for a long time. 'They're so beautiful and the sun is so warm looking . . . so different from cold, damp Wales. They belonged to my mother.'

'Where'd she get them from? Can we get more?'

She chuckled again. 'I don't know where she got them, they were always on our wall at home and she gave them to me when I got married. I treasure them.'

'Can we go there, Mam? This . . . Italy . . . you'd get better in all that sun.'

She smiled. 'It would be nice wouldn't it, but it's not possible right now. Maybe one day you can go. Always have your dreams . . . I had mine. Always have your dreams.'

I waited as she looked at the pictures, a small smile on her lips. Then, the question I'd been longing to ask, burst out of me. 'Tell me what happened, why did you stop teaching your dad?'

'Oh, that's a terrible story. You don't want to hear about that . . . it's not for little girls to know.'

'Please, oh please tell me. I'm not so little. I'm eight and a half now.'

She laughed her soft laugh again, although I couldn't see why it was so funny. She hesitated and finally said, 'Well, you will probably marry a collier one day, maybe it is best if you know the worst from your mam.'

Oh, yes. I wanted to know what the worst was, but I also wanted to stay cwtched up with my mam.

She looked at me and I could tell she was thinking about it. She asked me to pass her tea and took several small sips before giving the cup back to me. Finally, she said, 'I think I have enough strength to tell you this story, but I may need to rest from time to time, so you will have to be patient. I'll whisper, that will help.'

I nodded and tried not to show my excitement. 'I don't mind,' I said, I just wanted to know the worst, whatever it was.

She coughed a little and made herself more comfortable. 'One day,' she whispered, 'when I was fourteen, something awful happened in our village. I remember the date very well. It was Saturday 23rd June, 1894, just before four-o' clock in the afternoon.

'It was stuffy in our front room, so I opened the window to let in some fresh air. While I was standing there taking a few deep breaths, I felt a strange juddering, as if our house was shaking ... and then ... there was a huge explosion, and then another straight after.' She stared into space. I was afraid to say anything or move, so I just waited. 'It was so powerful, so big and out of place ... people in the street stopped talking, their babies stopped crying ... I swear even the birds stopped singing. I couldn't breathe. I remember that, not being able to draw breath. It must have been only for a few seconds, but seemed endless ... and then life came back in a mad frenzy with colliers running from their houses. Our street overlooked the pit and the sight I saw will never leave me.'

She started to breathe in short, shallow breaths. 'The top ... the top of the pit ... had been blown to pieces with bits of it floating in the air ... as if wood were matchsticks and iron as light as cotton. The men ran pell-mell down our street. Most

16

of them had hob-nail boots on and I can't get the sound of them out of my mind . . . even now, the sound of hob-nails puts fear into me.' She breathed noisily and I waited, although it was hard to keep questions from popping out of my mouth. I bit my lip to keep quiet.

'I stood there, unable to move as I watched them. Then the women came rushing out, all running as fast as they could, but I still couldn't move.' She stared into space for a long time and I took her hand and squeezed it, she didn't notice.

'My sisters . . . my sisters came into the room. "Come, we have to get to the pit", they said. When I didn't move they pulled me out of the room and I saw my mother standing there, white faced and shocked. I came to my senses then and we all ran out of the house and down the street to the pit trying to avoid others doing the same. For you see . . . you see, cariad,' she took a shuddering breath, 'our dad was working in the pit that day.'

I didn't know what to say, so I stayed silent, clutching the bedclothes for support as my mother seemed to be back in that other world I wanted to know so much about.

'It was the silence I remember the most. The pit was covered in coal dust. It was still falling when we got there, like black rain. And the . . . the smell of it turned my stomach . . . a burnt, damp, sludgy smell that I'll never forget. I still can't burn small coal, the smell is the same; I'd rather be cold.' She shivered.

I couldn't hold my curiosity in any longer. 'What happened then? Did you find your dad?'

She closed her eyes and got lost in that other world again. 'No,' she finally said, 'it was days before we found him . . . it was the worst pit accident anyone had ever known . . . two hundred and ninety men died that day and my dad was one of them.' She wiped her tears with my hankie.

'What happened then, Mam?'

'Oh, it was awful . . . so many people rushed there we had to be divided up. The relatives were allowed on the pit grounds, near the two shafts –' she looked down at me and said so quietly I almost didn't hear – 'that's where the men would be brought back up. The rest of the people had to wait outside the fence.'

'What did you do?'

'Wait,' she whispered. 'There was nothing we could do except wait. It was awful, that waiting. People were crying,' she looked into the space in front of her, breathing short breaths, I waited. 'We took our lead from our mother and stayed silent. We kept our feelings under control. It was the way my mother coped . . . with things.'

She wiped her tears as she got lost again in that other world. 'There was a lot of smoke coming up from the shafts – horrible, thick smoke that almost choked us.' She shook her head from side to side. 'We had to wait for the smoke to stop before anyone could go down . . . it felt like a lifetime.'

She wiped her nose slowly and her breathing was noisy. 'But never mind about that, my lovely, people were very kind and women brought us tea and cake and bread. I remember that . . . the kindness of those women. But we couldn't eat or drink anything. Finally, a couple of men were brought up and they were alive. A puff of hope went around us, but the men died a short time later. Then a boy was brought up and the doctor said he would live. Another surge of hope went round.'

My mother continued to breathe noisily and I worried about her. I was wondering what to do when she came back to the present and looked at me with loving eyes. 'Oh, cariad, maybe it is better that you do not know, you're only a child. I don't want to frighten you. We should stop now.'

I was horrified. How could I make her understand that I really wanted to know the worst? 'Please, Mam, please tell me. I really want to know and I'm nearly grown up. Please.'

She sighed and looked at me closely. 'All right,' she whispered and I had a job to hear her, 'maybe you're right, but remember, it is not a pretty story, but it's our life here . . . it's the price we pay for being poor and working in the pits.' She coughed and paused. 'You'll find out soon enough that poor people always pay the price rich people demand. They don't care about us. Remember this story, for if you do marry a miner you could be doing the same thing I was.' She took ragged breaths and I waited again. 'Don't forget, my lovely, when this happened, I was only fourteen . . . but after it was over . . . I left my childhood behind and became a woman shaped by the mines . . . ruled by them . . . reliant on them . . . and hating them.' She looked at me to see if I had understood and I nodded.

'Yes, Mam, I understand,' although I didn't, but felt so grown up that my mother was telling me such things.

'Well, my lovely, will you pass me my tea again, I need a drink.' I passed her the cup and she drank in small sips until it was empty. I put it down on the table and snuggled into her again. She rested as I held her until her breathing was easier.

'Something like this is very hard to talk about. I've not talked about this to anyone else before . . . the memories are so real to me, even now, twelve years later.'

'That's before I was born . . . before I was me.'

She laughed, gently. 'Yes, that's right, before anyone knew anything about you. I never thought I would have such a lovely daughter.' She coughed. 'I'm proud of you, Kate, and I love you very much . . . whatever happens, don't ever forget that.'

I snuggled closer to her and never wanted this to end. It was like old times when we would cuddle up together and sing songs and play games. I missed her so much.

'What happened next?' I asked, full of curiosity.

'We continued to wait.'

Her voice was so quiet now I could only just hear her.

'Sometimes, bodies were brought up and women would cry thinking it might be their man. Hope went through us when someone was brought up alive. But mostly, the miners were dead . . . there were so many of them they had to lay them in the stables . . . they were empty you see . . . those lovely horses, over a hundred of them, were killed. Blown up or killed by the afterdamp. Poor, poor creatures, they deserved better . . . as did we.'

She blew her nose again and fell silent.

'What's afterdamp, Mam?'

She looked down at me. 'Curious child, but that's good. Find

19

out as much as you can about the world, there's more to life than Ponty and pits. Maybe your life will be different.' I didn't understand what she meant, but stayed silent.

She coughed and breathed heavily and took another rest. I took hold of her hand and squeezed it. It was cold, like ice. She took a shuddering breath and spoke slowly. 'Firedamp is a gas found in coal seams, it's always a danger because sometimes it explodes and sets the coal dust alight . . . and the afterdamp is a gas that comes from that and is very poisonous. It's a terrible thing . . . terrible. It will kill anything that breathes it in. That's what happened to my dad.'

'You found him then. When? When did you find him?'

'Oh, it was a long time after. We'd all been standing at the pit for days. It was all very slow. It was so difficult underground . . . it was awful above ground too as so many people had come to watch . . . I remember those people . . . I hated them.'

'Why, Mam?'

'They were terrible. People can be so cruel. They came just to look. To look at our misery, to see our loved ones brought up. They rushed when they saw a body being brought up, wanting to see all the–'

I looked up at her wondering why she'd stopped so suddenly as she took a shuddering breath and spoke very slowly. 'They were . . . *terrible* people . . . some say twenty thousand came and it was difficult for us to move through them when we needed to go to our homes for some rest. Some even got drunk – it was shameful. The breweries sent drays of beer and sold it as if people were at an entertainment.' She paused and when she spoke her whisper was fierce. 'I felt like pushing that beer down their throats and it was only because I was so well brought up and I couldn't shame my mother, that I didn't. But Maddy Thomas didn't have any such qualms. I remember her . . . poor Maddy . . . she took the mugs out of their hands and threw the beer into their faces shouting, 'Shame on you. Get out of here and take care of your own.' She paused. 'She got at least five of them before her sisters pulled her away. It was awful to see and I never liked people much after that: except

20

you and Daddy and Davy, of course.'

I felt my mother's body stiffen, she was so tense. We were silent for a while until I couldn't hold it in any longer.

'What about your dad? What happened?'

She looked at me, searching my eyes. 'I suppose I must tell you, you have to know the ending . . . but it is not nice.'

'I don't mind,' I said quickly, afraid she'd stop.

'Well, give me a moment to get my breath.'

'Yes, Mam. Will it help if I rub your chest? You know, like you do when I've got a cough.'

She laughed a little laugh, like a baby I thought. 'Oh, sweet Kate, if only . . .' She looked at her pictures again and sighed. She coughed and spat a few times.

She looked very serious. 'The men, Katie love, the men were laid in the hayloft of the stables and we families had to go and look at every one of them and try to identify our own. It was hard . . . so hard. I went with my mother and sisters every day, but we never saw him. We had to look . . . oh, God help us . . . but never mind about that.'

'What, Mam? Never mind about what?' I was itching to know. It was like a mysterious insight into the adult world.

She looked down at me and tears streamed down her face. 'No, I'm sorry my lovely. Some things are too awful to say. You'll be better off not knowing. Just let's say that one day, we went and we found him. We buried him. We lived without him. It was hard.'

'Is that why I don't have a grandmother either? It was too hard?'

She hugged me to her but it was so gentle it was almost no hug at all. 'My mother died a year later of a broken heart. She just couldn't carry on. She'd have been better off if she'd cried like so many of the women, but she kept all her feelings in. I didn't see her shed a tear. It's best to cry, Kate. Remember that, cry all you want, let that misery out of you . . . let those emotions out into the air and with luck, that air will kill them. An emotion out of the body is one less to cope with.'

Again, I didn't understand but I nodded and said, 'Yes, I'll remember.'

She coughed and spat into her jar again. I could see she was exhausted and I felt selfish but I couldn't stop myself. 'What happened? How could you live without a mam or dad?'

She smiled. I smiled back and our eyes locked in love. I felt loved and wanted and important because my mother was sharing bad things with me. I loved her more than I could say.

Her voice was getting weaker as I struggled to hear. 'We went into service, became servants. That's all we could do. I went to Cardiff and your aunties went to Brecon. They were lucky, they got work in the same house, but there was no opening for me, so I went to a big house in Cardiff.'

'What did you do?'

'I was young, so I had to work as the scullery maid. I washed up the dishes and cleaned pots and kept the kitchen clean. It was hard work, but I had a roof over my head and I had food to eat. I tried not to think about it too much . . . then I met your dad, and we got married. He was a collier in Ponty so I came back here to live. Then we had you and Davy to complete our family. I've been so blessed. So very blessed. Never forget that your mother felt blessed.'

'Yes, Mam, I'll never forget,' I said as I hugged her gently.

She closed her eyes and I could see she was asleep. I stayed there, cuddled up, not wanting to leave her. After a while, as I listened to her trying to breathe properly, I got worried about the time. My dad would be home soon. He mustn't catch me here, I knew that. I eased my way from under her arm and stood next to the bed as the cool air hit me like a slap. Tears filled my eyes as I looked at my mother. I picked up the cups and turned to look at her once more. I would remember this day forever.

I just got downstairs in time to wash the cups and put them away before my dad came in from work.

He was a small, thin man with a mop of black straight hair which he 'kept short for the pits'. He looked old: much older than last week.

'Where's your aunty?' he asked.

22

'She didn't come.'

'*What?* What do you mean? One of them has to be here when I'm on shift. You're too young to leave with mam like she is.' He looked around. 'Where's Davy?'

'He's gone to a friend's birthday party. I have to fetch him at five o' clock.'

He looked at the clock on the mantelpiece, 'Well, you'd better go and fetch him then. You didn't go upstairs to your mam did you?' His tone made me wary.

I didn't know what to say but the words came out as if it was not me speaking. 'No, Dad. I've been told not to.' It was the first big lie I had ever told him and I felt terrible. I was afraid my mother would get into trouble more than I was afraid for myself.

CHAPTER TWO

Three months went by and I hadn't seen my mother since our secret talk. I missed her so much. We knew she was at the end of her struggle and my mother's two sisters, Aunty Gladys, short in stature and temper, and stout with it and Aunty Irene, taller and thinner, but just as dour, had been in the house for hours. Neighbours came to the door saying, 'Oh, what a pity, can we do anything to help?' But I could see that they had excitement in their eyes, enjoying the drama of it, glad it wasn't their kin dying like this. People said you got the consumption because you were a bad person, or a dirty person, or any other horrible thing that took their fancy. I hated them all and I hated what was happening most of all.

My father refused to go to work that last week and he spent all his time with my mother and us, but mostly with my mother. Me and Davy didn't mind too much. Dad had explained how it was his last chance to spend time with her and how much she needed constant care. He cried a lot, which made Davy cry and I comforted Davy and my father comforted my mother, or did she comfort him like she did with me?

As we sat in our kitchen and waited I heard my aunties whispering to each other. 'Who does he think will feed his family if he doesn't go to work? Muggins us, that's who. Well, it will be bread and jam and that's that. And he's called the doctor too! The expense! Well, it won't stop her from dying.' That was the first time I realised they didn't like him, but I don't think Aunty Gladys liked anyone.

The thought of how my lovely mother could have two such witches for sisters kept going round and round in my head as Davy and me sat at the table, where we could see all that was happening. He was snivelling and frightened. Poor little Davy: I tried to comfort him, but he was like a dog who'd taken fright.

Then, as we were eating bread and jam for our tea, Davy and me looked up at the noisy footsteps on the stairs. Our father appeared with the doctor. 'Well, she's at peace now,' the doctor said as he looked around at my aunties and us. His gaze lingered on us. 'Her suffering is over, thank the Lord.' We looked down at the floor.

'Who will look after the children?' he asked.

'They'll go to my wife's sisters for a while. They'll help out,' my father said.

The doctor nodded and my aunties smiled sweet little smiles at him and when he was gone they glared at us. Davy looked up at me with pleading eyes and I put my arm around his bony shoulders and hugged him to me.

'The doctor's given me the death certificate,' my father said. 'I need some–' I thought he was going to burst into tears. 'I'm going down to . . . to register the death. I've just got time. I'll be back as soon as I can.' And he picked up his cap and was gone.

He'd left us! Left me and Davy with the aunties. The shock of that made me speechless. How could he?

My aunties went upstairs for a while and then Aunty Gladys came down. Davy and me were still sat cuddled up.

'Right, upstairs, both of you,' she barked. Davy and I were terrified and I shook my head, afraid of what I would see. But Aunty Gladys stood over us. I knew she ruled her house with a rod of iron and my mother had always warned me not to get on the wrong side of her. Davy was still snivelling. She folded her arms and waited. 'I haven't got all day, get up those stairs and say goodbye to your mother.' Davy and I looked at each other, terrified, but I knew we had no choice. I nodded, got up and took his hand pulling him up. He hung on to my hand tightly and I wanted to be brave for him.

We stood in the bedroom doorway and looked at our mother. She was lying on her back and the smell in the room was even worse than before. I felt sick and Davy snivelled even more. The bedclothes were drawn up under her chin and her eyes were closed. But there was something different about her. Her ravaged look had gone and she looked young, almost happy.

I felt a surge of happiness, she was better. 'Mam, it's us, me and Davy,' I said.

Aunty Gladys interrupted, 'She's dead you stupid child. Can't you understand dead? You'll never see her again. She'll never move again or speak to you again. She's ready to be put into the ground. Say goodbye to her.' She pushed us towards the bed and the smell got worse and I knew this person in the bed was not my mother, my lovely, pretty, happy mother, who had looked at me with such love.

'Kiss her then,' Aunty Gladys said.

Davy stared up at me with a look of horror. Aunty Gladys picked him up and moved him so that his face was near our mother's. 'Kiss her then, child, I haven't got all day.' Davy made an exaggerated smacking noise with his lips although I could see he didn't touch her but it seemed to satisfy Aunty.

'Your turn next, child.'

I didn't want her to pick me up and force my face into my mother's, so I took a deep breath and held it as I stood on tip toe and decided that, unlike Davy, I was going to kiss my mother. Touch her skin with my lips. I kissed her on her cheek and it felt clammy and odd, but I shut my eyes and saw my mother laughing and running over the mountain as we used to do together. When she didn't take me into her arms but lay unmoving, tears filled my eyes. I knew then what death was. She'd left us.

Aunty Gladys said, 'Right, your bag is packed, let's go. You're coming to live with me for a while and I have to get the tea ready for my own family. They won't take kindly to going without even though your mother has died.'

I heard her say to Aunty Irene, 'Don't forget you get to look after them in six months' time. I'm not having them a minute longer than I have to.'

'I know. Don't worry, we agreed. I'll take them in six months and then they go back to you for another six.'

'And back to you for another six,' she hissed. 'And don't you

26

forget it,' said Aunty Gladys, glaring at her sister as she had done to us earlier. 'Well, come on you two. Hurry up. Pick up your bag, I'm not a porter.'

How I hated her. My heart was breaking and Davy was crying in earnest now. I took his hand and picked up the bag and followed her into our new life.

'Is our dad coming to live at your house too, Aunty Gladys?' I asked as she marched us through the streets to her house. '

'Of course not,' she said. 'I've no room for him as well. He'll have to find himself some lodgings with a family.'

I tried to stop the tears welling up. So, no dad either.

And with that, Davy and I started our loveless life. We were farmed out between Aunty Gladys and Aunty Irene. There was never quite enough of anything to go round, especially food, and we got the least of everything; consequently, neither of us grew very big.

The houses around us were all built to the same design, grey stone and terraced, two rooms up and two down with a toilet at the end of the garden. They were so similar that I sometimes got confused as to whose house I was living in, but it didn't matter as they all treated me as a skivvy. I hated them all.

Aunty Gladys was the worst. She had seven children who she ruled with a rod of spite and a husband who got drunk regularly. She couldn't rule him so she turned on us every time he turned on her. Fortunately, Davy, being so young, and a boy, got off lightly in comparison and didn't have to do as much as me.

I did a lot of the cleaning, washing and worst of all, the emptying of the chamber pots. No one wanted that job and it was left to me. If I didn't do it, Aunty Gladys made sure I did. I learned what being a wife and mother in a mining town actually meant. The never-ending slog of day after day cleaning away the thick, heavy coal dust that settled on everything. Walls, doors and windows, inside and out, needed washing every day as even with the doors and windows shut the dust came in. It covered our food if we left it out of the cupboard and we breathed the horrible stuff into our lungs. We lived, breathed and ate coal dust and I knew no different.

I had to help her eldest, Alice, with the cooking. She was thirteen and hated it, and made me do all the peeling of vegetables and the cutting up of what little meat there was even though I was too young for such a job. The knife was too big for my small hands and I had many little scars on my fingers where the knife had slipped. One day, while I was cutting up a poor rabbit that one of the boys had trapped, Alice shouted, 'Stop that snivelling. What's the matter with you?'

I wiped my nose on my sleeve, sniffing loudly. 'It's still warm, and it's so pretty. I feel sorry for it. I don't want to eat it.'

'Good, all the more for me then. You'll do as I tell you, now hurry up and get that rabbit ready for the pot. If you cut its head off first, it wouldn't be so pretty.'

'I can't, Alice,' I said horrified. 'I can't cut if off.'

'Why not? It's only a stupid rabbit!'

'Please cut if off for me . . . please.' I wiped my nose again and she looked at me with disgust.

'You'll do as I tell you and if you don't, I'll tell my mother and she'll lock you up again. You don't want that do you?'

'Please, Alice. Please don't tell her. I'll cut it off, but don't tell her.' The fear of being locked in the shed again was worse than cutting off the head of the rabbit. The shed was cold and dark and full of bits of wood, sacking and newspapers waiting to be cut up for the privy. But the worst were the spiders, beetles and rats. The rats came in at night via the gaps and walked over me in the darkness. Some even nibbled at my flesh. If I screamed, no one came, but I screamed nonetheless as I hit out at them.

I lifted the knife and took aim at the rabbit's neck, but I couldn't look and closed my eyes as I brought the knife down with as much force as I could. But it was not enough to get through the poor thing's neck. Some of the blood shot upwards and hit Alice in the face. In a temper, she hit me as I was bringing the knife down again, eyes closed and somehow, Alice hit the knife from my hand and accidentally cut her arm. It was a bad cut and she screamed that I had tried to murder her. Aunty Gladys came running downstairs, saw all the blood, and believed Alice's story.

I was locked in the shed for two days without food or water and I don't think they would have cared if I'd died. But Davy did and he slipped me a piece of bread under the door but was caught and put in the shed with me. I was weak from hunger and thirst. I was so glad to have Davy with me, but sad for him. After he'd finished crying at the injustice of being locked in for his kindness, he encouraged me to think of nice things and we sang nursery songs and made up our own about toys and flowers; Davy loved flowers. He always had a good imagination. I don't know what I would have done without him.

It rained on and off and Davy and I cupped our hands under leaks in the roof and drank the water. It was slow work, but we had nothing else to do. Davy and I grew even closer during this time and he had a maturity beyond his years. I worried that he would not enjoy the rest of his childhood. He was too young to remember much about his life with our mother before she was ill and I was determined those aunts would not destroy him. Also, I was not going to let them destroy me. Each handful of rain, each raindrop I drank, settled in me and turned to steel. I was determined to live and survive this, just to spite them. They were my family and all I had, but I hated them.

I suppose it wasn't fair on them either. My aunts had lots of children of their own and didn't have enough money to feed them properly. Aunty Gladys had seven and was pregnant again. Aunty Irene had eight, the last two being twins. Life was hard.

The last thing they wanted was us. But it was expected of them, you looked after your own. If they didn't, it was the workhouse for Davy and me, and the shame that would bring on the family spurred them on to accept us into their homes, but my aunts and uncles couldn't gather enough goodwill to show us simple kindness.

When we went to school, Aunty Gladys would kiss all her kids as they went out the door, like a ritual, but she never kissed me. I made like it didn't matter. But it did. It mattered like hell.

I went to school and learned about Boadicea. I cemented that warrior Queen into my soul and her strength kept me strong. Her story of the battles she won against the Romans inspired me. I clung to her image, afraid that if I let go I'd be swept away by my family's cruelty.

Davy was luckier. Our father must have become aware of our situation and after about a year he managed to find a widow with no children to take in one of us for a fee. But she couldn't cope with two children, she said. Of course, our dad chose the boy to get the best treatment and Davy went to live with Mrs Dawson. I was left to my relatives.

But that's not being fair on my father. He did his best and worked hard but I knew he didn't have the money to pay for both of us. The life of a miner was a poor life. I never stopped loving him. None of this was his fault.

'How are you Katie, bach?' he'd ask when we saw each other.

'I'm fine, thanks, Dad,' I'd say. Just that. And he accepted it. I didn't want to worry him or risk complaining. He might stop liking me.

My father met us every Sunday afternoon at Davy's lodgings. Mrs Dawson always gave us bread and butter and tea, and once a month, we had cake too. Those meetings kept the hope alive in me that I could have a better life, like the one I'd had before. Then, one fateful day over our tea, when I was twelve, my father cleared his throat and directed his voice towards the tablecloth. 'I've got something to tell you.' He glanced up at us and then back to the white, clean tablecloth with the yellow roses embroidered onto it. He fixed his eyes on a rose. 'This is difficult for me to talk about.' He cleared his throat again. 'I'm not one to talk about my feelings.' He fiddled with the spoon on his saucer. 'I know,' he said, still talking to the rose, 'you loved your mother very much. I did too. No one can take her place.'

He wiped some tears with the back of his hand. 'But it's been four years since she went to that better place in heaven . . . and . . . well . . .' He cleared his throat again and said, very fast, 'How would you feel if I got married again and you had

30

a new mother?' He looked at us then, his eyes pleading. 'We could all live together again, you know, not like before, nothing can be like before, but well, it would be better than this, don't you think?'

I felt hope surge through me. Could this really be happening? I could leave the aunties? Davy jumped up and shouted, 'Yessss! Yes, yes, yes.' It was so unlike him for he was usually so quiet.

I'd learned that hope is always taken away, so I held myself back, but of course, I wanted it as much as Davy, anything to leave the aunties and live with my father again.

'Is she nice, Dad? I asked. 'Who is she? Do we know her?'

'You don't know her, cariad, her name is Miss Mason. Miss Anne Mason and she's from Tonypandy. She's a very nice woman. Would you like to meet her? We can meet next Sunday afternoon if you like?'

Hope surged in me again. My excitement bubbled over and I laughed. 'Does she have a family, Dad? Did her husband die?' I wanted to know everything about this woman who could be my saviour.

'No, Katie love, she's never been married before, but she's looked after her elderly parents for years.'

'Will they come and live with us too?' I asked, feeling worried about living with strange old folk.

'No, they died last year, and then we met and . . . well, liked each other. I hope, well, I hope you will like her too.'

'Oh, Dad,' I said, laughing again. 'If you like her, then so shall we.'

'Yes, Dad,' Davy agreed, 'if you like her, so shall we.'

And that's how it happened. How my life changed from one of misery to one of joy. Aunty Annie, as we called her, was a big, plain woman who had laughing eyes and a bun at the back of her head. Her thick brown hair was her crowning glory and I liked her and grew to love her. I was saved by her and became human again.

CHAPTER THREE

After they married, my father rented a terraced house in a street near his pit, it saved on bus and train fares. The house had running water out the back near the privy, and Aunty Annie emptied the chamber pots. When I offered to do it, eager to be in her good books, she said, 'You're too young for such a horrible job, Katie dear, your time will come soon enough when you'll have to do it and you'll hate the sight of them.' I could have kissed her – and did.

She took over the running of the house and refused to let me help with any housework. I think she must have guessed how I was treated because she was always cold to my relatives. But I wanted to help her and it made me feel wanted. I so desperately wanted to be wanted. She was a wise woman and could see my need and gave me some easy jobs to do. Washing up, sweeping the front and back and making her a nice cup of tea when I came in from school. Minor things, so different from before, but they made me feel useful. Sometimes she'd ask me to help her with something and Davy would jump up and say he'd do it. Bless him. He used to say, 'You've done enough, Kate. I'll do this.' He might only have been nine years old, but he had an old head on his shoulders and it was his way of showing me his love. I felt blessed.

We hadn't been long together when Aunty Annie asked me a question. We were sat at the kitchen table, just the two of us, drinking a cup of tea. 'Will you come to church with me every Sunday, Kate? I know your father and Davy are not keen on going, but it's been my life, and I'd like you to have the benefit of the Church behind you.'

'Oh, yes please, Aunty,' I said. I was so happy to be included in her life I didn't care what we did. I began to love Sundays and my time at church. It was a refuge to me, something that took me out of ordinary life and into a promise of something better. The minister told us that God would look after us if we looked after him. If we were good and true, nothing could harm us. I believed it absolutely.

Aunty Annie was a great reader and belonged to the library. One day, as we were drinking some tea, she noticed me glancing towards her books which were piled up on the edge of the table. 'Do you like books? She asked.

'I . . . I don't know,' I stammered.

'What do you mean, you don't know? she asked, softly.

'Well, I've never read one, not a real book I mean. Just the bits of books we read together in school . . . and then . . . well . . .'

She remained silent, waiting.

I took a deep breath, ashamed. 'I can't read them very well. I . . . I get lost . . . don't know how to read some words.'

'You can't read?' Her voice was so soft I hardly heard it.

'Y . . . yes, I can – a bit – but not as well as some of the others in my class.'

I could see she was horrified and I felt more ashamed and hung my head.

'Why can't you read well?' she asked as she leaned towards me and put her hand over mine. 'What happened? she asked ever so softly. 'Don't you learn at school? You're twelve now, you should be reading quite well.'

My mouth went dry. 'I think . . . well . . . I did read well, Aunty, when I was younger. We read together at school and I liked it.'

'Did you read with your Mam?'

I shook my head. 'No, my Mam nor Dad, they never read anything. But Mam, well, she used to tell me and Davy lots of stories she made up. We had lots of fun doing that.'

'Yes, I see,' she said slowly. Your Mam was a good woman; I can see that, Katie love. And if you read well when you were younger, that means you stopped learning after your mam died, is that right, lovely?'

I thought for a moment and nodded. 'I suppose so.' I felt a few tears prick at the back of my eyes.

'So why do you think that was?' she asked as she squeezed my hand gently.

I shrugged, and Aunty didn't say anything, just looked at me kindly. I had to tell her the truth. 'I . . . I think it was because I was too tired to concentrate. I loved school, I really did, Aunty, but . . . I couldn't stop thinking about food as my belly rumbled and I was cold an' tired an' miserable.'

It was all too much for me, her sympathy and compassion, it was something I was not used to and it tore at my deep inner fears. I couldn't stop the tears and she moved her chair next to mine and took me in her soft arms and hugged me close.

'Come and cwtch,' she said just like my mother used to. 'Come and cwtch, my lovely, there's a good girl, let your Aunty Annie take away the pain. I'm bigger than you and very strong, give your sadness to me and I can throw it away. We don't need it do we?'

I loved her more than I thought possible – almost as much as my mam.

We were silent for a while. 'I think it's time to enrol you in the library. Would you like that?'

She was still cwtching me and I had a job to contain the excitement that surged up. I wanted to jump up for joy, but knew I would be disappointed, like always, so I squashed my hopes down. 'I don't know,' I said quietly, looking at the table, embarrassed and uncertain. 'It's . . .' I looked at the table again, afraid to speak.

'What is it, my lovely?' she asked, stroking my hair in that reassuring way she had. 'Tell your aunty.'

My heart was beating hard. 'Well,' I forced out, 'it's very posh . . . only very clever people go there.'

There was a pause. 'Who told you that, lovely? That's not true. Look at me. I belong to the library. And I'm not posh am I?'

'No, but you were a teacher and you're very clever,' I blurted out.

She laughed. 'Thank you, Katie. It's true that I was a teacher before I had to look after my parents, but if you think I'm clever then I think you are too. So we're even. Tell me true now, I don't want to force you to do things, but would you like to join the library and read books at home? There are lots of different kinds of books . . . different worlds and thoughts, different lives. I'll help you with your reading. You'll come on in no time. What do you think?'

I could hardly breathe. 'Is it possible?' I whispered.

She smiled and nodded. 'Yes, of course – if you want it.'

'Really?' Tears filled my eyes.

She stroked my hair again. 'What else is the matter?'

I was so afraid of her answer I breathed deeply to gain courage. 'The . . . the library building is so posh, the poshest in Ponty . . . can . . . can someone like *me really* go there?'

Aunty didn't say anything so I risked a peek at her. She was looking at me in a different way. 'What did those awful relatives do to you?' she said, more to herself, than to me. Then her looked changed and she took my face in her hands and smiled at me. 'Yes, my lovely girl, *you* more than anyone else in the whole of Ponty deserves to and can join the library. They will welcome you with open arms.'

So, we went to the library; such a simple thing. Aunty filled in the form for me and signed it and I was given three tickets with my name on. I felt very important, but couldn't take my eyes off the woman behind the counter who looked very severe and wore such good clothes she frightened me. But Aunty Annie told me I was just as good as her and not to worry. We would work on my reading until I was so good, I could enter the library with pride.

We started the reading lessons in the evenings with the books she chose for me. *Treasure Island, Black Beauty, Alice in Wonderland, Little Women.* Oh, the magic of them. New worlds opened up. They were my escape. I even read about my saviour, Boadicea and confirmed my warrior queen image of myself. But whereas she was strong and confident when under duress, I went quiet and withdrawn. But inside, like her, I was strong. Those aunties had tried to break my spirit, but with the help of Boadicea and Aunty Annie, they wouldn't succeed. If anything upset me, I'd stab it to death with my sword.

I made great progress in school after this and always had my head in a book. My reading had caught up with the others and I enjoyed school once again. Davy, however, was having trouble. He was an intelligent boy but didn't seem to be making a lot of progress.

Over breakfast one morning as I ate my bread and dripping, reading my latest book, Dad asked him, 'Why don't you read books like Kate does? It might put a smile on your face.'

'I hate school. I'm not going,' he grumbled.

'You'll go and do as your told,' dad said in his no-nonsense voice that we knew we had to obey.

But Davy persisted. 'But why do I have to go? I don't learn anything.'

Aunty Annie and I looked at each other, but didn't say anything. 'What do you mean you don't learn anything?' dad asked more gently. 'Come on now, mun, tell your dad. What's happening at that school?'

Davy put his head down and nibbled on his bread, looking miserable. Aunty Annie put her hand on our father's shoulder. 'Matt,' she said, 'I'll take Davy to school this morning and have a word with his teacher. Maybe we can understand more after that.'

'No!' Davy jumped up. 'No, don't come with me. I'll go. I'll go now. I didn't mean it. I love school really.'

We looked at each other in amazement as he shot out of the door, picking up his jacket as he flew past us.

'I'll go and see his teacher after school,' Aunty Annie said. 'There's something not right.'

'He's being bullied,' dad said. 'I'll bet that's it. Boys will be boys you know. It happened to me too. Tell you what, I'll teach him to fight. It's about time he knew how to take care of himself.'

'Well, let's just wait, Matt, until I've seen his teacher.'

'What about you, Kate, have you seen him being bullied?'

'No, Dad, I'd have said something if I had. He's not popular I know that much, he has one friend he plays with, but Davy's a quiet boy. He doesn't mix well.'

'And how about you, lovely?' Aunty Annie asked. 'How do you get on with your classmates? You always tell me you're happy at school now.'

'I am, Aunty,' I said quickly. 'I love learning and school. The others call me a swot, and sometimes they tease me, but I stick my tongue out at them and tell them they're just jealous. They usually leave me alone.'

Dad nodded. 'Mm, I suppose girls are not as nasty as boys can be.'

'Don't you believe it,' Aunty Annie said. 'I was a teacher, remember? Girls can be just as horrible as boys.' She pulled a face and we all laughed.

'But seriously, you are all right at school? No one is bullying you?' she asked.

'No. I've got my friends.' I smiled. 'I'm fine, Aunty.'

Later that day, Aunty spoke to Davy's teacher and told us she thought him a weak man who just wanted a quiet life. Not one she would have chosen to teach Davy. But we were stuck with him. She said he was bad at discipline, she'd seen it before, she knew the signs.

'Well, that settles it,' dad said. 'I'll teach Davy to fight; that should sort things out.'

Davy was horrified. 'I don't want to fight. I hate fighting.'

'But you can be happy at school if you can beat those other boys. They'll leave you alone.'

But Davy ran out of the house saying he refused to fight.

The next day, he came home from school with a black eye and a split lip. He said he had 'tripped', but Aunty said that some of the boys from his class had seen her talking to the teacher, so they probably had a go at Davy.

'Right, that's it then. Come on lad,' our father said, 'out the back and let's start our fighting lesson.'

Davy didn't object this time, but still looked really miserable.

Aunty Annie and I thought Davy might be miserable because he didn't do as well as the other boys in class. I knew his reading was as bad as mine had been so we decided to encourage him academically while my father concentrated on the physical side of it.

Every evening, I read little stories to him and when we came towards the ending, I'd put my arm around his shoulders and we'd read it between us. We'd puzzle over words we didn't know and tried to guess their meaning. Later, as he grew more accustomed to it, he started to read bits to me. His eyes sparkled as he read out the words. He was beginning to enjoy himself.

It was after we'd finished reading *Robin Hood* that Davy said, 'I want to read my own books, can I go to the library too?' Aunty Annie and I kept our faces impassive. It was what we had been working for, but we didn't want him to suspect.

'Of course, my lovely,' Aunty Annie said. 'Let's go together tomorrow after school and I'll enrol you in the library. You can choose your own books then.'

Davy never looked back and his reading skills overtook those of his classmates. But that made him even more unpopular and they called him a swot. He kept on practising his fighting with our dad, and one day he came home with a black eye and a bloody nose, grinning from ear to ear. 'You should see the other boy. I thrashed him good and proper.'

So although Davy never really fitted in, never became 'one of the boys', he gained respect. My father enrolled him in a boxing club and, much to Davy's surprise, he enjoyed it. He got respect and attention so he worked hard at it and got stronger. His muscles grew and looked like buds spurting out from the thin sticks of his arms and legs. Some of the men at the club thought he had some talent and could make a career as a flyweight. Davy became even more enthusiastic with all the positive attention he was getting.

Our dad's attitude to Davy changed with his fighting success and one day, he took it into his head to insist that Aunty Annie give Davy the best food, including meat – when we had meat that is – plus larger portions of everything.

'He has to grow more, Annie love,' he would say, 'give him the best food.'

'But, Matt, you need it. You can't work down the pit without good food in your belly. You'll get ill, and then where would we be – on the parish, that's where!' Aunty used to get so indignant it made me smile and I tried hiding it by looking down at the table, but Davy always looked crestfallen.

'I can't eat his food,' he said to me one day as we walked to school, 'it's not right. I'm taking the food out of his belly. He needs it more than me. I don't know what to do, Kate. How can I stop this happening? I feel so bad about it.'

'He loves you, Davy. Be proud of that.'

'Oh, I am. I'm very proud of it.' He looked dejected.

'What is it?' I asked gently.

He was silent for a while and I didn't force him. 'I . . . I always feel . . .' he kicked at a small stone and sent it flying in front of us, 'I let him down.' He kicked the stone again. 'He's such a strong man. I can't be strong like him. I can't make myself grow.'

'That's why he wants you to have the best food.'

'I know,' he said, kicking the stone really hard. 'I *know*, Kate. But I feel like the food gets stuck in my throat as I watch him eat his vegetables while I eat vegetables *and* meat. His meat.' He ran on ahead then, afraid his classmates would see him in deep discussion with his sister. You usually ignored your sisters in their world.

He worked it out though. He just stopped eating the meat. He ate all his vegetables and one piece of the meat and then he gave the rest to our dad. 'Here, Dad, I'm full. You eat this for me, please.' He'd empty his plate onto our dad's and walk out of the house. Our dad had no choice but to eat it or waste it, so he ate it.

This went on for weeks and seeing that Davy would not relent, our father accepted the best food. Davy had that kind of a way with him. Soft and gentle, nothing direct, but he got his way more often than most by his subterfuge.

CHAPTER FOUR

Life was uneventful for a couple of years, calm, happy years. When I left school aged fourteen, Aunty Annie and my father were adamant that I wouldn't go and work in the pits. Many girls and women worked as surface workers, sorting coal, oiling machinery, emptying trams and goodness knows what else. It was hard, physical work enough to spoil a body. Fortunately, Aunty Annie had an acquaintance at church who owned a dress shop in town. She was looking for an apprentice seamstress and Aunty suggested me. I loved sewing and had even designed a few of my clothes. I only had to see a dress on some fashionable lady to be able to draw it and make a pattern. I went to see Mrs Coombes and got the job. I would be apprenticed for four years.

I was frightened and unsure. It was a posh shop, the kind of place where people like my family didn't go. It was a place for managers' and solicitors' wives and daughters – the people who lived on The Avenue and in the big houses on The Common. Those of us who lived in the two-ups and two-downs never went into such a shop; we went to the market stalls to buy our clothes. But I packed up my insecurities and did my best.

I made friends with another girl who was a seamstress there. Edie was the same age as me and lived in Maes-y-coed which was a little step up in social status from the Graig where we lived. She was fun and we hit it off straight away. Mrs Hanse, the seamstress was old and kind. She must have been at least fifty when I went to work there and Edie and I used to laugh at her old-fashioned ways, her wrinkles, of which there were plenty, her grey hair and her barrel-like middle. But she was a kindly soul and we hid our disrespect from her – or at least, I think we did.

Meanwhile, Davy was nagging our dad. Most children left school at twelve because their family needed them to work to earn extra money, but Davy and I were lucky and we were able to stay until we were fourteen. Dad had been promoted to fireman in the pit, and this gave him more wages and job security, which the ordinary miner never had. A fireman is in charge of safety in the pit and is a very responsible job.

From the age of twelve, Davy was always pestering dad to let him leave school and go down the pit. He wanted to give up his boxing too and concentrate on the pit. I couldn't fathom it at all.

'Davy, boy, listen to your dad now. The pits are hard and dangerous. You have to be very strong to work there.'

'I am strong, Dad. I box every week and train hard. I'm strong now. I've got good muscles and can beat any boy my size and even bigger. I can start as a boy doing easy things on the surface, sorting coal, tram oiler, picker, winder, labourer and things like that. Women do these jobs, I've seen them, so I don't see why I can't too.'

'No, you can't and that's the end of it. I've spoken and I don't want to hear another word about it. You stay on and work hard. I'll not have you in the pit.'

Davy sulked, but stayed on at school. He had no other choice.

*

Dad was in his early thirties when the war started. One evening, when I had my head buried in a book and Davy was out, Aunty Annie said quietly to him, 'What are you going to do, Matt? We're at war now. You're not going to join up are you?'

'What makes you think that?' he asked.

'Well, so many men are going. Mrs Thomas from over the road, her husband joined up yesterday. Oh, Matt, I don't want you to join up.'

'Well, I've been thinking it through and reading the papers. They say miners are of more value working in the mines, getting the coal out for the navy, rather than going off to fight.

The skill of the miner is valued at last, Annie. Those in charge are realising what a good job we do and how much they need us.' He tapped his pipe on the grate and packed it with tobacco, taking his time. Aunty kept on with her sewing but I could see she was only pretending, and I kept my head down, pretending not to hear.

He lit his pipe with a quill made of newspaper and puffed a few puffs. 'I love the mines, Annie, you know that.' He paused and I sneaked a look. He was looking at her quizzically, and she was nodding, looking concerned. 'Well, with your agreement, I don't want to do anything you don't agree with, I thought, well . . . I thought I'd stay in the pits.'

'Oh, Matt,' Aunty said as she got up and kneeled in front of him, 'I'm so happy. I don't want you to go away.'

I looked up at them and they didn't even notice me as Aunty hugged him and put her head on his chest. She started to cry. He looked up and saw me staring and winked at me. I smiled and we shared a secret moment of intimacy. I did love my dad so.

Aunty recovered herself and looked a little embarrassed. She stood up. 'Well, that's that then, thank goodness, I'll make us a nice cup of tea.'

'I'll be of more use here than fighting,' he said to her as she busied herself with the tea. 'I'm not a trained solider but I do know my pits – and it takes a lot of knowing to mine a colliery.'

The pit was my father's life, more than we were in a way. He loved us and provided for us, but his priority was always 'his men' and their welfare. We didn't see much of him and he wasn't prominent in my or Davy's lives. I suppose he thought he didn't need to invest any more in his family than food, shelter and education. Our emotional needs didn't cross his mind. We were provided for and his men needed him and that was what mattered to him. He was always fighting for improved conditions and getting compensation for men injured or for their families if they had been killed. Everyone loved my dad, including us. I suppose there was not enough of him to go round. He did what he thought was best.

For us youngsters, the war seemed so glamorous at first, all those young men going off to war looking happy and dapper in their uniforms. But then we started seeing them return home without legs, or arms, until finally, almost nobody returned. Killed in action the local paper said. And I for one, started to wonder about war and why we were fighting. We also had food and fuel shortages. There wasn't enough coal for us as it was all going to the navy. The coal that was brought up just a mile away from our house was transported hundreds of miles away while we shivered. But it was a sacrifice we were all prepared to make.

But it wasn't long before we realised that the war was a godsend for us in the valleys because the government took over control of the mines from the owners and upped the wages to a living wage and shortened the hours. Something the miners had been fighting to get for years and never achieved.

'Here you are, Annie love. Another big pay packet. Don't spend it all at once, put some aside for a rainy day. Those sods, the owners, will lower our wages when the war is over and they get control back. You mark my words, the bastards.'

I knew my dad hated the owners; most of the men did. They were greedy and only interested in profit even at the cost of lives – as long as it wasn't theirs. It was a them and us mentality on both sides.

I was doing well at the shop and the war increased our workload. Because of shortages, we started to make more clothes ourselves to sell in the shop. That's where I learned to design clothes on a budget. Material was in short supply and fancy things almost impossible to get hold of. Everything went to winning the war. Manufacturing went to produce warm uniforms instead of making pretty clothes for women. Practicality was the fashion of the day. But the valleys prospered and so did our shop.

Once a week, after work, Edie and I would go to the theatre to watch the turns at the Clarence Music Hall. It was very glamorous with all the singers, dancers, jugglers and comedians. We enjoyed the sing-along to the songs which lifted our spirits.

It was good, innocent fun.

*

At fourteen, Davy finally wore dad down and went to work in the pit and within three months had his first accident. He was grading coal above ground, sending the best coal one way and the rest graded into house coal and slag. It was a simple accident. He slipped on the wet ground at the end of his shift, overbalanced and fell over hitting himself against a moving tram. He broke his collarbone and right arm and was concussed. He was off work for two months and like a bear with a sore head until he got better. And then, to our father's astonishment and anger, behind his back, Davy returned to the pit as a miner's assistant. Boys often helped miners underground, passing them equipment and generally helping out.

'The work's too dangerous boyo,' our dad said. 'I don't want my son working underground like me. I had no choice, but you – I'm giving you a choice and you throw it back at me.'

But Davy was adamant he wanted to go underground. I think he had some strange idea of mining, or maybe he was attracted to the camaraderie that existed between miners, I don't really know, but he only lasted a few weeks before he was back home with a broken ankle, black eyes, and a ricked back.

'It was dark. Honest, Dad, I couldn't see a thing and I was so keen to do everything well that when my collier asked me to pass him his mandrel quickly, I rushed in the dark and fell over the tram rails. I'm so angry with myself. But I want to work in the pit, Dad. Really I do.' His little face was all puckered up and earnest. It must have been hell for him to be trapped into his small body, because although he was now stronger physically, he was still small. He never grew more than five foot and had the same slim build as me. He was like a delicate bird. We both were, but it was harder for him, being a boy.

'The work is too dangerous for you, son,' Dad said. 'You've had two accidents already and if you have another one you'll be looked on as bad luck. No miner will want to work with

45

you. It happens sometimes, this bad luck with one person.'

'I know I'm little, and believe me, I wish I wasn't, but it doesn't stop me working. I can work, I want to work.'

Dad sighed. 'I'll talk to the manager about you. Maybe he can suggest something safer for you. But there's no more going underground, son. I'll not have it.'

Soon, Davy was sent to look after the slag tips. It was a solitary job. When the coal had been sorted, what couldn't be used was graded slag and no good for anything. It had to be got rid of and the easiest way was to dump it in any open space near the pit. It was dumped on until it resembled a small mountain – a black, soggy, depressing monument to coal. They got so tall they strung up wire ropes on pylons high in the air, leading from the pit face to the tip. Every few yards, buckets were hung from the wires, filled with slag at the pit, and transported to the top of the tip where men like Davy were waiting, standing alone to make sure the buckets emptied all the slag and in the right place.

It was a monotonous, boring job, but Davy loved it. He loved the isolation, he told me. And the views down the valleys. Even in the wet and cold of snowy winters, Davy would be there up on top of the latest tip he was looking after. He earned a lot of respect by doing this job, so maybe that had something to do with his liking it too. It was generally believed that there were ghosts up there and many a big solid man working in the twilight thought they saw a ghost. Some would run down to the safety of the ground as if the devil himself was after him and refuse to go back. But Davy never did. He stayed put and walked slowly up and down the tips in the dark, working away with his torch and if he was ever scared, he never told me.

I was so pleased for Davy. He had finally found something he could do and I was getting on very well at the shop. I had been promoted and was now a fully qualified seamstress and was in charge of Edie and a junior and I loved every day. No two days were the same with alterations and new designs to make patterns for. We made wedding dresses, bridesmaids dresses and lovely clothes for the guests too. The shop prospered and the staff got a modest wage increase.

Edie had a boyfriend called Reg. He was strong on pubs, beer and fags. After a date with Edie he used to drop her off at home early so that he could go to the pub, 'for a quick one'.

'You should find yourself another beau, Edie,' I said. 'He doesn't treat you well.'

'I know, but there's something about him other boys don't have.' She laughed and winked at me, poking me with her elbow.

'Oh, you! You're hopeless. Well, on your head be it,' I said laughing.

'Come on, Kate, don't be so po-faced. It's about time you found a nice boy. You're nineteen now, you'll be over the hill before too long and no boy will want you.'

It was a sore point with me. 'I have boyfriends. They are, well, they're just not the right ones for me.'

'You're too fussy. No boy will ever live up to your ideals. Come on, Kate. You can't be an old maid. What will I do when I marry my big lug and my best friend is an old spinster?'

I tried to laugh it off, but she was right. I was fussy. I was popular with the boys, they thought me pretty, but I didn't reciprocate the feeling. I couldn't get enthusiastic about them and it was starting to worry me. Was there something wrong with me? Would I ever find my Mr Right? I wasn't sure I ever would.

CHAPTER FIVE

Aunty Annie and Davy had not been getting on as well as usual over the past year or so. The war had ended and when Davy became eighteen, he thought he was grown up and resented her interference. She wanted to know where he was going, what he was doing, and it rankled with him. It all blew up unexpectedly, but then, in my experience, major ordeals always blow up unexpectedly.

Davy had made a new friend, Rhys. They were the same age and had started to stay out late drinking in the more disreputable pubs and Davy came home drunk on many occasions. Then things started to change and Davy became secretive but at the same time, he was bubbling over with excitement. He was hiding something.

'What are you up to, young man?' Aunty would ask. 'There's something afoot, I can tell.'

'Nothing, Aunty,' Davy would invariably reply. But he became more secretive and his eyes shone like polished jewels.

One Sunday morning Aunty Annie and I were at church as usual and Dad was at work. He always worked Sundays as that was the one day the pit was closed and he and his assistant could go underground and check everything was as it should be. They checked for gas too and it always took a long time. He was very thorough.

Aunty and I returned home earlier than usual as she wasn't feeling well. Normally, we would have gone straight to the kitchen, but as it was a Sunday, we went straight to our parlour, the room we kept best for Sundays – and we stumbled into a scene that was to change us all forever.

Davy and Rhys were on the floor in front of the cold

fireplace, naked and 'doing things to each other,' was the way Aunty described it.

Aunty and I froze in the doorway. 'My God,' she said quietly, 'so that's how it is.'

The boys froze. The horror in their eyes was pitiful.

And then Aunty turned her back on them and instructed me to do the same. 'Get yourselves decent you devils incarnate,' she hissed. I could hear them moving about in haste. I heard Rhys whisper, 'Those are my underpants.'

Finally, Davy said, 'We're decent now, Aunty,' in a shaky voice.

We turned around and the look on both their faces was of shame and embarrassment. Davy looked at Aunty and then at me and then down at the floor.

'What's going on, Davy?' I asked. I couldn't understand it. It was bad enough doing it outside of marriage with a girl, but two boys? I'd never heard of such a thing. My confusion must have shown in my face as Davy looked up at me again with pleading eyes. He said nothing.

Aunty drew herself up to her fullest height and ordered Rhys out of the house. 'Now!' she yelled, as Rhys stole a look at Davy. I'd never seen Aunty like this before. She was scary. Whatever it was that they were doing, I knew it was bad.

'Don't go,' Davy pleaded, looking at Rhys.

The look between them was something I had never seen before. It was full of love . . . intimacy . . . apology . . . a plethora of emotions and feelings that made my heart ache for them. Whatever it was between them, I knew then I wanted to experience it too. To feel such a way for another person was something I had not been prepared for, not dreamed possible. And here was Davy, my younger brother, showing such things for another boy. I was shocked and envious and didn't know what to do.

'Out!' Aunty yelled.

I saw Rhys mouth the words, 'I'm sorry,' to Davy as he walked reluctantly to the door. I stepped into the room so that he could pass while Aunty stood unyielding, looking straight ahead. 'You never set foot in this house again,' she hissed as he went out of the door.

Davy looked stricken, and I knew then what it looked like to have a broken heart. He couldn't hide it, probably didn't know how. Maybe Davy's heart and spirit had not been broken as badly as mine. He could still love and that gave me hope for my own feelings. All these thoughts went through my mind in seconds and I pulled myself together to face the now, not what might be in the future.

Davy continued to stand in front of the fireplace. The room was small and we were all uncomfortably close together.

'Well. What have you got to say for yourself?' Aunty barked.

'Aunty, I . . . I . . . can't . . . .' Davy stumbled over his words. He looked at me with pleading eyes, but I couldn't help him this time. I had always looked after him but now, with this, it was a Davy I didn't know or understand.

'Out with it, boy,' said Aunty, 'what have you got to say for yourself?' Her voice was cold and authoritative and Davy crumpled onto a chair with his head bowed, looking at his feet, he took a breath that went deep and shuddered.

'Aunty,' he whispered, and I had to struggle to hear him, 'I can't help it. I love Rhys and he loves me. I know it's wrong and we tried not to, but we just have to. That's all there is to it. We just have to.'

'Rubbish, boy, there's no have to about it. You just don't do it that's all. Life is not for your enjoyment, it's about duty to your family and respectability in the community. And people don't respect two Nancy Boys indulging in their perversity. It's disgusting, that's the last you'll ever see of Rhys Richards. I forbid you to see him again.'

Davy looked at her with such loathing I thought he was going to strike her. 'You can't tell me what to do, I'm eighteen. I can join the army at eighteen. I'm a man now.'

'And I'm telling you that, by law, you are not a man until you're twenty-one and it's me and your father who are responsible for you until then. I'm telling you to pull yourself together and do the right thing. Cut off all ties with that Rhys, he's a bad influence on you, and whatever you do, don't tell your father.'

'I won't stop seeing Rhys. I can't stop seeing him.' His voice was pleading and he looked like a whipped dog who didn't know what to do to make it better.

'Well you can't stay in this house if you continue to indulge in such disgusting things. I have to live here with my neighbours, so does Kate and your father.'

'Aunty,' I'd found my voice at last and I touched her on the arm, trying to calm her, 'I don't mind if it's what Davy wants. I don't want him to leave.' I couldn't imagine my life without Davy in it. He had been part of me forever. We were joined together by something more than just blood. We had helped and encouraged each other. 'I don't know what's happening. Can't we stop all this and be calm?'

'No we can't,' she said harshly. 'Davy has to realise what this kind of behaviour means. It's against God and nature. It's not something I can tolerate. I'd almost prefer it if he were a murderer.'

'Aunty,' I shouted, 'how could you? Davy's not a bad person. He's . . . he's Davy, that's all. He's my brother. I don't understand you or what Davy feels, but is love that bad? Love is love after all.'

'How dare you!' retorted Aunty. 'One man loving another like . . . like that . . . is not love, it's just disgusting.'

'It's not! It's not!' cried Davy. 'It's beautiful and I can't help it, neither can Rhys. It's how we feel. I'd rather die than give him up. I mean that, I can't give him up.'

'Then you'll leave this house right now, young man. I'll not have someone like you in my house a minute longer.'

'I'm going. You'll never see me again, not if I see you first.' With that, Davy picked up his shoes and ran out of the house. I ran after him and caught up with him outside the front door as he struggled to put them on.

'Oh Davy, come back. Please. She'll calm down. You can't leave me. What will I do without you? Please for my sake, please come back and apologise to Aunty.'

'I can't. I'm sorry, I just can't. You don't understand.'

'No, I don't. Don't you care about us anymore?'

'Of course I do. It's not about that. But what I feel for Rhys is more powerful than anything. I don't understand it, but please believe me I have no control over this.' The neighbours' curtains twitched and a few looked out and seeing us in earnest conversation, quickly moved away. Davy saw it too, and he ran off down the street. I wished that we lived in the posh detached houses on The Avenue or up The Common, with their long front gardens separating them from the world around them. But for us in our terraced houses built straight onto the street, we had no such privacy. We knew who was rowing, cheating, wife beating, loving or just existing – it was the only entertainment many people had.

I hoped people would think it was just a family row. And that's what happened and there were no adverse comments. This was usual in our world. I told people that Davy had gone to live with his friend's family for a while because of a disagreement with his aunty. Everyone understood that, no more had to be said.

I found out that Davy had gone to live on the other side of town with Rhys' family in Coedpenmaen Road. It was less than a half hour's walk away but it could have been in Timbuktu I felt so isolated from him. He didn't contact me and that hurt me deeply. It was as if our life together had meant nothing. He could have got a message to me without Aunty knowing. Had he abandoned me? What had I done to deserve such treatment? Anger towards him kept me away, but after a couple of months worry drove me to go and see him, to check he was all right and to find out what was going on. Aunty had gone into herself and was no longer the jolly person she used to be.

Coedpenmaen Road is a long road of small terraced houses, just like every other street in Ponty, the only difference being in the long length of the street. I found the house and knocked on the door. Davy answered and looked resigned when he saw me.

'Davy, I must talk to you. Can I come in?'

'No, Kate, let's go for a walk, it's better.'

He picked up his jacket and shut the door behind him and I followed him at a trot. He might have short legs, but he could move apace.

'Let's go up the mountain,' he said as he turned towards me. 'I can talk better up there.'

He was immaculately dressed I noticed as I followed him. Since he had grown up, he had taken to being really fussy about his clothes and always looked like he was going to church in his Sunday best. Even going off to the pit his working clothes were always washed and ironed and were smart. It was a thing he had. I wondered if he ironed all his clothes or was it Rhys' mother.

We walked for quite a while, gradually climbing. The mountains surrounding Ponty are not too high and the one behind Davy's new home is rather soft, curvaceous and comforting. We climbed to the very top and Davy finally sat himself down with his back against a dry stone wall and a view over Ponty in the distance. It was the first time I'd been up here and the town itself was on our left. It was an impressive view with the bowl of the valley stretching out before us as if a giant of old had come along and scooped out a handful of earth leaving a perfectly level bottom where the town was now built and the river flowed and the trains puffed. The Graig led on from the town, ever upwards. I'd never seen it from this angle before. It looked a lot smaller than I'd imagined it would. From this distance, the continuous streets of houses looked like children's toys rather than real places. I felt like I could pick them up and rearrange them. Surprisingly, it looked rather dull and cramped and I had a job imagining all the thousands of people who lived there. I felt like a god as I looked down and a feeling of power crept up on me as if I was somehow superior to the life that was teeming below me. I'd never had such a feeling before. We were also sat in a slight dip which continued down the mountain in a line. It pointed straight to Davy's new home and I wondered if that was why he liked this spot.

'It's a wonderful view, Davy. No wonder you like it up here.'

He remained silent as put his elbows on his upraised knees

and his head in his hands and started to cry. I didn't know what to do so sat next to him and put my arm around his shoulders. We stayed like that for a long time, with his gentle tears flowing. He cried quietly, but then Davy always had. He seemed to gain some control and wiped his face with his clean, white hankie.

Finally, he said, something so matter of fact that the effect was like an unexpected thunderclap to me. 'You know he's dead, don't you?'

'What? What do you mean?'

'Rhys, he's dead.'

I couldn't speak, I just stared at him. Eventually, I whispered, 'No. No, I didn't know . . . I'm so very sorry.' I put my hand on his arm and he didn't shrug it away.

We sat in silence for a while. 'How did it happen, Davy . . . can you talk about it?'

He didn't speak at first and I thought he'd shut me off, until he murmured, 'I'll try. But don't look at me please, just don't look at me.'

'I won't, don't worry, I promise.' I could understand his not liking to be looked at when he was upset. I was the same. I sat up straight and looked out over the town.

He took a shuddering breath. 'Rhys worked in the pit as you know, but not the Albion like Dad, he worked at the Lewes Merthyr. It happened only a week after my row with Aunty . . . after I ran away from you. I went to Rhys' house and his mother, Mrs Richards, took me in. She's a good sort and said I could stay there for a while if we didn't mind sharing Rhys' room. It was perfect for us. We were very happy, but tried not to show it to Mrs Richards. We didn't want another row like the one with Aunty.' He sniffed. 'He was my life, Kate, you realise that, don't you?'

'Yes, Davy, I know he must have been very special because you don't make friends easily.'

'Thank you, I'm glad you understand.' He wiped his eyes and blew his nose again. 'I'm sorry but I'll have to say this very quickly. It's the only way I can say it.' He took a deep breath and looked down and talked to the grass below him. 'He went off to work as usual one morning and never came back. He was killed in an accident underground. There was a cave-in on the section he was working in, no one else was hurt, but Rhys took the full force of it and died underground. It happens a lot, maybe a pit prop gave out, or there was water above that no one knew about, or the roof there was just weak. Anyway, it happened and killed Rhys. He died instantly, that's all I have to cling to. I don't know what to do or think, I've been crying ever since.' I put my hand on his arm but he shrugged it off. 'Mrs Richards is very good to me and she told me that I can stay lodging with her for as long as I like. She said to take Rhys' room. She treats me like a son. She says that I am her son now that Rhys is dead. I like her Kate, and I like living with her and Rhys' sisters. She told me that I am the man in the house now, because all her men have been killed in the pits. I feel like I belong there, it's funny but true. I feel so close to him when I'm with her. They treat me with respect, like I am a man. Not like at home where Dad and Aunty treat me like a boy still, and a silly one at that.'

He looked up and across the valley. 'She calls me cariad, just like she called him and every time she calls me that I feel loved and wanted, and valued.'

He blew his nose noisily and took another shuddering breath. I'd never heard Davy talk like this before. It was a revelation.

'Don't think badly of me, please. I know it hurts you and I don't want to do that, but things are all changed now. I can never go back home to live. It's just not possible. Dad came to see me a few weeks back.'

'He did?' I was astonished. He'd not said anything.

'He did. And it wasn't a nice visit. He asked me when I was going to realise that what we'd done . . . I'd done, was wrong and to promise never to do anything like that again. I told him I could not deny my feelings for Rhys, not under any circumstances. He got very angry and told me that I was no son to him if I didn't repent.' He looked at me and his tears welled-up. 'Is love so bad? Oh, Kate . . . and Aunty looked at

55

me with such loathing that day. I can never forget that look. I can never forgive her.'

I fidgeted and tried to decide what to say. I'd found out something about Aunty and was unsure whether to share it with Davy. Finally, I decided that it might help him to look at Aunty in a different way. I said, very matter of factly, as if it was nothing, whilst all the time knowing it wasn't. 'I think I know why she looked at you like that.'

'I don't care. I can't forgive her. It's like a lump of hate inside me. There was always something not quite right between us and she looked at me in a funny way sometimes. It always unnerved me.'

'Well, just listen, let me tell you and you can judge for yourself. When you left the house that day, Aunty was crying and was deeply upset. I tried to calm her, but she just cried the more. I thought that it was strange that she should take on so. There were so many tears. Finally she said a strange thing. She said that if she could give up her great love for the sake of her family and respectability then why couldn't Davy? I asked her what his name was and she whispered, "Margery," very softly, but I heard it. She got all flustered and asked me, "What did I say then, Katie love, I can't remember." I told her that I didn't hear her. She looked relieved and said she was going to bed with a headache and rushed upstairs.'

I looked out over the valley and Davy remained silent. I wasn't sure he understood. 'I think she felt about another woman what you feel for Rhys, but gave her up for respectability and family. She was angry with you for putting yourself before your family. To her that was unforgivable.' I glanced at Davy, unsure of how he was taking this, but he was just staring straight ahead, his face expressionless. 'I wonder what went on in her life before she married our father. We don't know, do we?'

He turned and looked at me. 'How do you feel about all this, Kate? Do you think it is disgusting?'

I was jarred by such a direct question and didn't quite know how to answer, so I decided on honesty. 'I'm sorry, but I don't know. I've never thought about it before you and Rhys. I don't understand it, but I love you. I just don't know what to think and what's worse, I can't talk about it to anyone. So I've decided not think about it. Just carry on as usual. I'll pray for you both.'

'Don't do that,' Davy bristled. 'Don't. Just don't.' I looked at him in amazement.

'Why not? It can't do any harm.'

'I don't want your pity. I'm sorry, but that's what it would be. You don't understand and that's all there is to it. I can do my own praying, thank you.'

I was shocked and hurt. 'I'm . . . I'm sorry, I didn't mean to offend you.'

He was staring ahead looking furious and I was fighting the tears that were welling up. In the silence, he looked at me and his face turned from one of fury to one of love. He took hold of my hand. 'I'm sorry. I really am sorry, I never wanted to hurt you, I'll never do that on purpose, you know that . . . you're my big sister. We've always looked after each other.'

I nodded and the tears came. 'And I still want to look after you,' I sniffled.

'Oh, Kate, thank you. But you know it's impossible, don't you. We're all grown up now. We have to live our own lives and . . . well, all I know is that I want to stay with Mrs Richards and her family. Can you understand that? They've welcomed me and being with them keeps me close to him. I'll see you now and again. Ponty's not a big town.'

He looked out at the view again. 'If I'm honest, and I always want to be honest with you, I've been unhappy at home for a long time. Dad treats me like a boy still and one that needs his strength and protection. Well, I'm not a boy. I'm a man. A young man and I can make my own decisions. What do they know of me? We never speak to each other . . . you know, really speak . . . say what we mean. It's all platitudes and keeping the peace. Oh, I know Aunty was good to us when we first lived together and I'll always be grateful for that but she still treats us like children. We have to move on with our lives. We can't live in the past.'

I put my arm around his shoulders and gave him a kiss on

the cheek. 'There, that's from the past. Do you remember I always kissed you goodnight when you went to bed?'

He nodded. 'Of course,' and I could see a little smile on his lips.

'Well, that's for then and from now on, we'll be like grownups. We can shake hands when we meet.'

He laughed. 'You could always make me laugh.' We looked at each other and he turned serious. 'But you do understand me, don't you?'

It was my turn to nod. 'Yes, Davy bach, I'm trying my best and I am beginning to see it from your point of view, but I'm still unhappy about the whole thing.'

'I know, and I'm sorry.' He stood up and I struggled up too. He held out his hand and we shook hands solemnly and then smiled at each other.

'Oh, Katie, Katie, I shall miss you.' And with that, he bounded down the mountain like a goat: surefooted and light. He turned around and waved. I waved back and brushed the tears away and made my way more slowly back down to the town.

I couldn't force Davy to come home and I couldn't force my father and Aunty to accept him again. Goodness knows what Aunty had told my father. I wasn't privy to it, but he told me he never wanted to speak of Davy again. 'My son is dead,' he shouted at me when I mentioned him. 'Don't mention his name in this house ever again.'

CHAPTER SIX

It's surprising how small things can change lives: a silly accident, a chance meeting, an unexpected glance.

It was a beautiful summer's day as I walked slowly home from work enjoying its warmth. I was lost in thought as I started the long haul up the Graig hill. As I passed an alley on my left, an urgent whispering and giggling penetrated my thoughts and then a movement caught my eye. I turned my head and saw a young man had a girl pressed up against a wall. She was laughing and encouraging him, running her hand up and down his back and pulling him closer, kissing him deeply. She broke off and saw me looking and her eyes turned scornful. She must have read my mind for I was thinking, trollop! What a disgusting way to behave in broad daylight.

She called out, 'What you lookin' at Little Miss Madam?' The man followed her gaze and our look held. I was shocked by the effect it had on me as my breath caught and my stomach flew up into my throat and I started to shake. I looked away quickly, but his image had burnt itself into my memory. His black hair, a little too long, curly and unruly - had she been running her hands through it? Unreasonably, the thought upset me. His strong body was slim but muscular – a miner I thought. He had a way with him and my reaction scared me. I'd never experienced anything like this.

His eyes bored into me and to my mortification, he walked away from the girl and came up to me. I didn't know what to do. I wanted to run, but was rooted to the spot.

'Hello,' he said. His voice was softer than I thought it would be. He must have seen something in my face, because he added, 'Sorry, didn't mean to upset anyone, just having a bit of fun.' I could smell beer on his breath and backed away a bit. He noticed, and looked at me intensely, his eyes softening as he looked into mine.

The girl grabbed his arm. 'Come on, Tom, leave her, she's nothing to do with us.' But he continued to stare at me. I turned away and started to walk up the hill again with that look of his still burning in front of my eyes. I was feeling confused and flustered – and I said to myself, his name is Tom.

I'd had a few boyfriends, well, enough to know that this boy was different. Was it his eyes? They were just eyes – brown, and I preferred blue. Was it his black hair? But most of the boys here had black hair. Was it his curls? I didn't like boys with curls. Sissy-looking for a miner I thought.

He wasn't particularly tall, and I liked tall men. He was muscular – as a miner would be, but I liked more sensitive men, like my brother Davy.

My last boyfriend was a nice boy, but we'd never done lots of kissing – even in private – as they were doing in broad daylight. My boyfriend was always trying though; it was me who wasn't interested. That's probably why he gave me up in the end. But seeing those two in the alley had stirred something deep inside me.

The Graig was small enough for me to bump into him quite regularly after that first meeting – or was he seeking me out? He always said, 'Hello', even though I ignored him. He frightened me. It was the first time I'd met someone who attracted me so.

We both lived on the Graig so that gave us something in common. It was a poor person's place although it wasn't a slum, far from it. The people who lived here were fiercely proud and housewives kept their houses spic and span with their doorsteps well scrubbed with carbolic soap and vinegar. But it was overcrowded and because the Graig was built from the floor of the valley to half way up the mountain-side it was very steep, making walking up and down the Graig Hill difficult, especially with shopping.

The streets are so narrow and closely packed you could hold a conversation with the people living opposite without leaving your house and many of the women did, standing in their doorways, watching their children playing or just looking for company. The Graig was made up of rows of identical terraced houses, built in tandem with the opening of new mines. Ponty itself had a dozen or so big mines with new ones opening up constantly. The town had grown so fast it was called the 'Wild West of Wales' and the builders had no time for niceties in their design. Most houses were basic and a mirror image of their neighbour. As their tenants would be uneducated poor folk moving here from all over, wanting to improve their meagre lot, each house was built as fast and as economically as possible.

I have a fanciful mind and always thought of those streets funnelling off the Graig Hill as being like a marching band. All dressed up in the same uniform, striding on relentlessly in step, playing the same tune of grey brick houses and black slate roofs. An occasional missed note here and there as a pub or a church was built, a squiggle on the ends to get around natural hazards, but soon going back to the same old tune of terraced houses. On they marched, upwards and outwards, eating up the mountain and icing it over with concrete and brick.

I bumped into him once when I was with Edie. He said, 'Hello', and smiled as he walked by, but neither of us reacted.

'You want to watch that boy,' she said, 'he's got a reputation for liking the girls too much. He's always got a different one on his arm. He's fickle and too good looking by half. Take my advice, stay away from him, Kate. I know you're twenty-one and almost over the hill and desperate, but you don't want to be another notch on his belt.'

'Oh, don't be silly,' I said, all indignant. 'I have no intention of getting to know him.'

She looked at me and grinned. 'But he is lovely, though. I wouldn't say no myself.' She laughed as she added, 'You know, just a quick fling.'

I laughed too. 'Oh, Edie, you're hopeless, and your husband would have a thing or two to say about that.'

'Well, I do love my big lug, but you know . . . a girl can

dream.'

I did like Edie, she always made me laugh. 'Well, it's just as well you're married already.'

She laughed again. 'True, I'm just joking, but if I was single, well, a boy like that's okay for a girl like me, you know, fun loving and don't take things too seriously. But for you, well, you're different – you're serious, not his sort at all. But he likes you. I can see it in the way he looked at you. Be careful, Kate. That's all I'm saying.'

*

I was walking home from work not long after this. It was my half day and it was hot again and the two bags of shopping I was carrying drew the sweat from me. My arms were stretched and I was tetchy walking up the hill. As I approached one of the houses that fronted the hill, the door opened and a boy shot out, heedless of safety. Nearly all front doors on the Graig opened directly onto the street, and most people stopped to look before stepping out, but kids, well, they're all the same, especially the boys. 'Sorry, Missus,' he shouted as he ran past me. I put my bags down to take a rest and recover from the shock of nearly being knocked over. My fanciful mind took over and I thought, if he had knocked me over and I fell backwards, I probably wouldn't stop until I came to the bottom of the hill under the railway bridge. I turned to look. It was a long way down. As I turned back I looked up and saw Tom walking down towards me. My heart raced uncomfortably and my nerves tingled. Flustered, I picked up my bags to cover my nervousness.

'Let me carry your bags for you. I'm in no hurry,' he said as he took them from me before I could say no.

I started to tremble. This boy was having an effect on me that no one else ever had and I didn't like it. I didn't want to encourage him.

'What's your name? I'm sure it must be a beautiful one.'

I glared at him.

'Sorry,' he said with bravado, 'girls usually like that kind of talk.'

'Well, I don't.'

'You've got nice hair. I like long hair and yours is so wavy, it's lovely.'

I glared at him again. 'I'll be sure to get it cut tomorrow.'

We walked on slowly and in silence and Edie needn't have worried, I didn't want a Jack-the-lad boy like him as a boyfriend. I'd seen where that led with other people. I wanted better.

But he wasn't to be put off. 'I'm Tom Mallow, by the way. I've lived in Ponty all my life, but never on the Graig. Me and my mam and two sisters moved here about a month ago. I'm really glad we moved here now I've met you. Where do you live? Can I walk you home?'

'I'd rather you didn't,' I retorted, trying to take my bags off him.

'Now, now, don't be like that,' he said, laughing and holding on to the bags. 'Come on mun, play fair, I'm not that bad am I?'

I didn't answer.

'What do you do, Kate?'

'How do you know my name?' I was angry and I let it show.

'Oh, come on. A man can ask about a girl he likes, can't he?'

'No. Not this girl you can't. Give me back my bags and go on your way please.'

'You don't like me do you? Why not?'

I was really angry now. Didn't he ever listen? He was the kind of man I'd seen turn into selfish husbands with no respect for their wives or children: the kind that never takes no for an answer from a woman. I didn't want anything to do with him.

And then, he stopped and put down the bags and turned to me and took my hands in his before I realised what had happened. My hands tingled in his and a wave of excitement shot through me. I was confused and didn't know how to behave. I looked into his eyes and saw he was triumphant.

That did it. I had to put an end to this. This boy and I would go no further. I had to be cruel, it was obviously the only way to get him to understand.

'How dare you! And you're right. I don't like you. You're big headed and think you can do what you like. Well, not with this girl you can't.' His hold had slackened and I pulled my hands free and went to pick up my bags, but he beat me to it.

'You're an exciting woman. I like that,' he said, straightening up.

'Well you can like away, I am no fool and I'm not interested in fools.'

'You think I'm a fool?' His look was hard.

It was obvious he was not well educated, so I decided to use the extra learning Aunty had given me. I dredged up some words from books I'd read, words I didn't normally use. 'I think you are a disrespectful, antagonistic, philanderer,' I said to him before I stormed up the hill, feeling pleased with myself. There, that should shock him into dislike.

But he just laughed as he struggled to catch me up. 'Oh, I like it,' he yelled loud enough for anyone to hear. 'She's a walking dictionary.'

I stopped dead and turned and slapped his face. 'Go back to your trollop. She's about your level.'

I stormed up the hill again without a glance and turned into my street. I realised then that he still had my shopping and I worried what I would tell Aunty Annie. She'd be furious. But I wouldn't go back for shopping. I'd rather die first.

I'd promised to go to our church at six o'clock to help Aunty Annie polish the silver. She'd gone to visit her relatives in Tonypandy and we agreed to meet at the church. So, a few hours later I left home to meet her. The church was directly opposite the turning for my street and as I approached it I saw someone sitting on the pavement in front of it. My heart leapt into my mouth as I realised it was him. He stood up and leaned casually against the wall. My bags of shopping were on the pavement beside him. I had no choice and couldn't turn back so I ignored him as I walked passed and went into the church.

Fortunately, Aunty Annie arrived before long and we started our polishing. I didn't mention anything about Tom, but then, to my horror, the door creaked open and there he was.

A silhouette in the doorway with the sun setting behind him, looking for all the world like some angel come down from heaven.

He walked inside and closed the door and sat down in one of the back pews. He didn't pray or anything like that but just sat there and looked sad. The vicar came in and started to talk to Aunty. They looked over at Tom. 'Who is that young man?' the vicar asked Aunty. She shook her head, 'I don't know, do you, Kate?'

I couldn't lie, especially in church. 'His name is Tom Mallow, that's all I know.'

'Could I ask you a favour,' the vicar said. 'I need to talk to your Aunty about something important, can you go up to him and welcome him to the church. Just a friendly hello and hope to see you again, will do.'

I swallowed my pride for the sake of Christ. This was his house after all. As I walked reluctantly towards Tom, I rehearsed what to say, but was totally thrown by seeing tears in his eyes.

Before I could say anything he said, 'Do you have a father?'

'Yes. Yes, I do,' I found myself answering.

'My father died recently, that's why we moved here.' He blinked some tears away and turned his head so I couldn't see his face.

My good manners came to the fore, I felt obliged to respond. 'I'm sorry. Did he have an accident?'

'No, not an accident . . . deliberate . . . someone wanted him dead.'

I was shocked. 'What do you mean?'

'He was in the war see, a soldier . . . and those . . . those . . . *Hun* got him . . . the gas got him too. He couldn't walk properly. Useless for anything he was. He came home and had to walk on sticks and drag his legs and then he couldn't even do that as he had no breath and had to be wheeled around in an old pram. Humiliating! It was so humiliating for him. And for us . . . we couldn't help him you see, couldn't make it better. What could we do? What could I do? He took it bad. He just up and died one day. Couldn't take it no longer see. That's why we moved here.'

I knew he meant that they'd moved to the Graig because it was cheaper than where they lived. The Graig was the cheapest place in Ponty. I wondered about his family, but didn't ask.

'I'm sorry,' I said again, trying to fathom this strange boy.

'I got a job at the Maritime. It was better for me to change pits. My dad's pit had too many memories . . . present and past.'

'Where was that?'

'The Albion.'

My stomach flew up to my mouth as I stifled a gasp. Memories of my mother telling me of her father dying in that awful disaster flooded my brain. Whenever anyone spoke of The Albion Pit it had the same effect on me. I couldn't help it. But I didn't want him to know.

'. . . we lived near it in Cilfynydd, see,' he was saying. 'He worked there until they laid him off – him and hundreds of others. It was a bad time, too many miners chasing too few jobs. They put the wages down and people like my dad, decent men who wanted a fair day's pay for a fair day's work, were thrown out and replaced by others desperate enough to work for starvation wages. He was out of work for a long time, well like so many of the men, and then, when the war started, my mother persuaded him to join the army.'

'But they were crying out for miners then to replace the young men who'd joined up. Why didn't he stay?' I could have bitten my tongue off. It was no business of mine.

But he didn't seem to mind. 'Well, he joined up as soon as the war started, before they knew so many miners would be needed to stay. My mother was struggling to feed us and he'd get a shilling a day in the army. So he went to fight. He was too old really. He was forty, but they took him because he'd been a soldier before, when he was a young man. Experience I suppose.' He had his elbows on his knees, looking at the floor. 'My mam, she's so upset.'

I didn't know what to say to him and we sat there in silence for a while. 'She wouldn't have sent him to fight,' I said, 'if she'd known how awful things would be.'

He glanced up at me. 'No, I suppose not. But we didn't know, we all thought the war would be over in a few months. We didn't know it would be so awful and go on so long. How could we? We believed what we were told. She blames herself. She's upset all the time.'

'But your dad didn't have to go. It was his decision too.'

'We've been telling her that, my sisters and me. I don't know what to do.'

I heard footsteps coming up the aisle and looked up and saw the vicar striding towards us. Tom saw him too and got up. 'Sorry, I didn't mean–' And then he rushed out before the vicar got to us.

'Is he all right?' he asked.

'I don't know,' I replied as I looked down and saw my two bags of shopping. I was so confused by this boy. He was good to his family, but too casual about the wrong kind of girls. But why should I care? He was nothing to me. And he was a miner. All my life, I'd been surrounded by miners. I didn't want one for a husband. But in reality, I knew that, for someone like me, from my background, there was little else in Ponty. But it didn't stop me dreaming of marrying an educated man who worked in a nice, clean office . . . a clerk . . . an accountant . . . but most definitely, not a miner.

All my efforts to try and put Tom off had the opposite effect to the one I wanted. It spurred him on even more. He started to show up at church every Sunday, in his best suit, his hair all neat and tidy, and as if that wasn't enough, he always wore a flower in his button hole. When we left the church he gave it to me with an exaggerated bow and a twinkle in his eye, but it made no difference, I still refused to go out with him. I learned later that he used to pay old Mr Forbes, who loved his garden, a penny a flower every Sunday morning.

Tom introduced me to his mother one Sunday after service and I was surprised that this new member of our congregation, so haughty and private, was Tom's mother. She was a proud woman, regal, with a straight back and her head was always held high. The opposite of what I thought his mother would be. Even though some called her haughty I grew to like her as we passed the time of day after church sometimes. She told me she came from Somerset originally and she still had a faint burr to her words which I found attractive.

Tom had been coming to church for about three months and I was despairing of him ever giving up. One day he arrived late and was with another man, who I took a dislike to on sight. His carrot red hair with a will of its own, and his small, too close together eyes gave him a menacing look. But it was his assured cockiness and obvious desire to be unpleasant that really turned me against him.

At the end of the service, Tom came up to me as usual and presented me with his flower. The ginger man followed him. 'This is why you've taken to coming to church is it?' His voice was mocking. 'Introduce me, Tom, to the beautiful and charming young lady.'

Tom looked agitated, and tried to elbow him away, but finally, resigned to it he said, 'This is my brother, Dudley.'

'I didn't know you had a brother,' I said to Tom, perplexed. He'd never mentioned a brother. I was prevented from saying more when Dudley took my hand and kissed the back of it. I'd read about this in books, although I'd never known it done in real life before. But I did know that in books, they didn't press their lips hard into your skin and caress it with their tongue, which is what Dudley had done.

I was furious. How dare he! This man was trouble. I felt Tom's anger mounting. He had never tried to kiss me in any form, he had more respect for me. But I didn't want to cause any trouble at church, so I decided to ignore Dudley. 'Thank you for the flower, Tom, it's lovely,' I said as I walked away from them hoping this man would take the hint. But he wasn't that kind of man. The next Sunday, he was there with Tom and his mother, and, to my dismay, he had a flower in his buttonhole too. At the end of the service, he rushed over to me and presented it with a great flourish. Tom came then and saw what he'd done. He went pale, but I said to Dudley, all prim and proper, 'No, thank you, Tom always gives me a

68

flower, I only need one. Please find someone else to give it to.'

Tom and I exchanged our first look of understanding.

That was the start of a scheme of pestering by Dudley. He always hung around waiting to walk me to work, or back home. He wouldn't take no for an answer. Tom, as much as he wanted to be, was not my boyfriend and I had managed to keep him at bay without too much trouble, but I was having great difficulty with Dudley. While Tom was at work, Dudley made a nuisance of himself. He didn't have a job, I don't know what he did for a living, but he always seemed to have money. He'd smile at me and offer some trinket or sweets. When he did this, I noticed that his smile never reached his eyes.

I had no qualms about telling Dudley how much I disliked him and to stop bothering me. But he took no notice. In the end, I had to ask my father to have a word with him. It did no good, he carried on as before. In the end, it was Dudley who finally made up my mind to accept Tom as my boyfriend. He made Tom seem like a perfect gentleman and I knew that Tom hated him as much as I did. So to get rid of Dudley, I started to walk out with Tom. I knew my feelings for him were getting stronger by the week and the more I tried to shut him out, the more I thought of him. Deep down, I realised I was in love with him but I wouldn't admit it. I was scared of the power of my feelings. And I still had my dreams of marrying a professional man.

I knew there were lots of rows between Tom and Dudley but I didn't know the extent of them until one day Tom came to meet me as usual on our Wednesday evening date. We always met at the foot of the mountain and walked up together. It was raining and I was sheltering under my umbrella and when Tom dipped under it, I saw his black eyes and purple, split lips.

'Oh, you poor thing, what happened? Did you have an accident in the pit?' I asked, putting my hand up to his face. He winced before I touched him and I put my hand down quickly.

He had difficulty in speaking. 'It was that bastard Dudley,' he spat out. Spittle ran over his oversized lips and he wiped it away none too gently. He took a deep breath, as if he'd forgotten to breathe. 'He refused to stop trying to see you, and I told him that if he did it again I'd beat him up.' He wiped the spittle away again. 'He laughed in my face, Kate – and I'm sorry for the bad language – he said . . . "Try it you bastard. I'll see anyone I like and you'll lump it. I kissed her before you and I intend to fuck her before you."'

I gasped and took a step back, shocked to my core.

'That did it. I snapped. I pulled him out into the back garden and laid into him. He's a good fighter, but he didn't have my fury and I was determined to kill him.' He stopped as if he'd just realised what he'd said. He wiped the spittle away again. 'I'm sorry, Kate, but that's how I felt. After a few minutes Mam arrived and started screaming for us to stop but that spurred him on to get even more vicious. I couldn't let him win, Kate, it would have been like giving up on you. I hit him with such an almighty blow to the nose that he fell like a stone and I kept kicking him when he was down. I couldn't control myself. All those memories of the awful things he'd done to me . . . and what he said he would do to you.'

He stepped out from under the umbrella into the rain and looked up at the sky, getting soaked. I was so shocked I just looked at him, not knowing what to think.

He took another shuddering breath. 'Years of living with him. Putting up with his nastiness. It all came out. All I could see was your beautiful face and his ugly one leering at you. Finally, my mother lay down on top of him, which meant that if I kept on kicking him, I'd be kicking her too. She begged me to stop. She said if I killed him then she would lose me to the hangman.'

He fell silent, looking up at the grey sky, letting the rain soak him. I was afraid to ask if Dudley was dead.

'He's in the hospital. He'll be in for a few weeks they said.'

I stared at the man I had come to love and realised I didn't know him at all.

His lips began to bleed and he looked beseechingly at me, like a child asking for forgiveness. I'd put my hand over my mouth and was clenching my jaw so hard it was hurting.

'My God, Tom,' I whispered from behind my hand. 'I know he's awful, but to nearly kill him?' I walked away from him then, not knowing how to react. I was in deep shock. He ran after me and asked for my forgiveness saying – and I'll never forget it – 'Don't you know how much I love you and worship you? There'll never be anyone else. Don't you know that?'

'I . . . I don't know anything right now,' I mumbled. 'I need some time to think.' I remember his look of despair. And I don't think I ever loved him more.

*

A few days later, Edie and I were walking through town, Edie pushing her daughter, in her pram, and the late evening sun shining down on us as we window shopped. Taff Street was our main shopping street and was built narrow, like our valley. The grand Victorian buildings on either side were built closely packed and the sun was only able to penetrate along the street when it was low in the sky. It looked its best then. It was the place to be and to go, the height of sophistication for the valley people to come to. We were proud of our town.

Everyone in Ponty seemed to know about 'The Fight' as it had become known. To put Dudley in the hospital notched up Tom's standing among the men. It had the opposite effect on me.

'I don't know what to do about Tom,' I said.

'Well, you've had enough time to think about it. It's quite simple. Do you love him?'

'I don't know. What's love anyway?'

'Well, you'll know it if you feel it. You're hopeless.' She looked at me, curious. 'Look, do you tingle when he touches you?'

I nodded, embarrassed.

'Mm, I see,' she smiled. 'And does he make your stomach turn over and your heart beat stronger and do you want to touch him?'

I nodded again.

'And do you like his personality? Does he make you laugh?

71

Do you trust him?'

'That's just it. How can I trust him when I know of his reputation with women, and now, what he did to Dudley?'

We'd come to Weston's, which sold good mackintoshes and umbrellas, the kind we couldn't afford. But we liked to look just the same.

'I like that mac,' Edie said, pointing.

'It's lovely,' I said without seeing it.

'Well, you should make up your mind soon. It's not fair dangling him on a piece of string like you do.'

'The thing is, if I'm honest, I *am* attracted to him. In fact, I've never been so attracted to anyone before, but, well, I'm not sure what he's like inside, you know, his real character. Oh, I just don't know.'

'But he's changed, hasn't he? He goes to your church every Sunday, gives you a flower. For goodness sake girl, what more do you want?'

'Yes, but . . . oh, I don't know . . . I've seen so many bad husbands who are all over their wives at first and then change and treat them like items, things to use. I always told myself I would never have a husband like that.'

'You think he'd be like that then?'

'I don't know. Can he really change?'

'Well, he practically killed his brother for you. That's proof, isn't it?'

'It's proof that he has a violent side to him.'

'Oh, Kate. You want too much.'

I looked at her reflection in the shop window, ignoring all the umbrellas and waterproof clothing, and thought for a while. 'Is it bad to want too much? Surely, low expectations get you nothing except struggle and sorrow.'

'Now you're sounding like a poet. Oh, come on, Kate. Give him a chance. If it was me, I would. He's the catch of the town, so many girls want him he could have his choice. But for some reason he's fallen hard for you. Sorry, I don't mean that the way it sounds, but, well, maybe I'm speaking out of turn, but I think you should give him a chance. He doesn't have a reputation for fighting in town, so it could be that it's as he said. Dudley finally pushed him too hard. It could happen to anyone, in the right circumstances, don't you think?'

'I'm not so sure about that, I don't think I could fight someone or feel such hatred for someone that I'd want to kill them.'

'Well, I could,' said Edie in consternation. 'You're sometimes too good to be true. Be a bit human sometimes.'

'What do you mean by *that?*'

'Look, Kate, you're my best friend, we've known each other for a long time, but sometimes, you can be cold, like you don't have any feelings at all. Give yourself a chance. Let Tom back in, after all, you can always give him the push again.' She laughed, which made me remember why she was my best friend. She could always put me in a better mood and see the funny side of things.

But it didn't really help me any because I was still dithering about Tom when his mother asked to speak to me after church one Sunday. I knew that Dudley had recovered and that he hadn't pressed charges against Tom – his mother's doing I think – and Dudley had stopped coming to the church, so at least he'd learned that much.

We left Tom to go home alone and Mrs Mallow and I walked together to the end of Graig Street and down the long, widely spaced steps into Madoc Street. I didn't say anything. It wasn't my place, but I was anxious and the continuing silence made me nervous. We walked along as far as the ridge. The ground fell away here and was too narrow to build on, so it was left natural with a fence to stop anyone falling down into the street below.

She stopped me by putting her hand on my arm. 'It's breaking Tom's heart to have bad feeling between you. Can't you give him another chance, Kate?'

I was taken aback. I'd expected her to have a go at me and was shocked that she wanted me for Tom. That was the first time she'd ever said anything about our relationship. I clutched the top of the fence and looked out over the roofs of the street below.

'How can I, Mrs Mallow,' I said speaking into the void in front of me. 'He was so violent against Dudley. I'm . . . well, if I'm honest, and I feel I have to be . . . then I have to tell you that I'm afraid – afraid that if he can do that to Dudley he can do it to others, even me.'

'No! No, Kate. Please understand he's not like that. The fight was totally out of character for Tom. You have to believe that. It was the accumulation of a lifetime of bad feeling between him and Dudley. It was Dudley's fault.' Her breath trembled as she whispered, 'Lord, forgive me, but I have to make you understand. It was . . . my fault. Everything has been my fault.'

'Your fault? What do you mean, Mrs Mallow?'

'Kate, promise me this will go no further. If I confide in you, please keep my shame to yourself.'

CHAPTER SEVEN

She looked up at the sky as if the answers were to be found in the grey, heavy clouds.

I was astounded. 'Yes. Yes, of course I'll keep your secret.'

She took a deep breath. 'Let me explain. Did you know that Tom is my adopted son?'

'Your adopted son?' I repeated stupidly: stunned. Tom had never mentioned it. 'No,' I whispered. 'No, I didn't.'

Her knuckles were white as she clutched the top of the fence. 'Dudley was a very difficult child. It pains me to say it, but he had – has – a cruel streak. His father and I despaired of him. But he was our son and we did our best with him. Then my best friend died in childbirth. Tom was that child. His father died about two months later in an accident at the pit. Some people said it was a strange accident which shouldn't have happened and that maybe he'd committed suicide. I know he was broken hearted and couldn't even pick Tom up and cuddle him. I think he thought of Tom as killing his wife.

'I took Tom to live with us, temporarily I thought, but after his father died, I just kept him and he became mine. My husband was quite happy about this as he'd grown to love Tom too. We had our two girls who were as unlike Dudley as they could be. We loved them and Tom. He was such a happy baby, never any trouble, unlike Dudley who'd been a bad-tempered baby and had turned into a spiteful and selfish boy. No one liked him, including, I'm sorry to say, us. It was really difficult to love him. Please believe that.' She looked at me, pleading for understanding.

'Oh, I do, Mrs Mallow, I know Dudley a little and I disliked him on sight. There's something about him that's unnerving.'

She nodded. 'Dudley was five years old when Tom came into our family and it really put Dudley's nose out of joint. All his hate went onto Tom and it's really hard for me to admit, but I failed Dudley. I gave all my love to my other children, including Tom, and ignored Dudley. I let him do what he liked as long as he didn't cause problems for me.' She paused and looked out over the rooftops for a long time and I didn't dare speak. 'You know . . . if I hadn't seen his bad-tempered face and red hair covered in my blood and attached to my cord, I wouldn't have believed he was mine. He came into the world in a temper, with a chip on his shoulder and it grew with him. It hurts me to say so, but he's as selfish and nasty as they come. I should have given him more attention and tried to help him be a nicer boy, but it was easier to ignore him and love Tom. He was always my favourite, even though he wasn't mine in reality. He was mine in every other way.'

I was astonished at her candour but unsure of what she expected of me. She made me feel like an equal to her and I did my best to act like one.

'You're too hard on yourself, Mrs Mallow, I'm sure you did your best.'

'Thank you, I tried, I really did, but I don't think you appreciate what trouble I had with Dudley. He was bad enough before Tom came into our lives but that was a turning point for him and made him worse. As they were growing up they fought all the time, and it was always Dudley who started it. He tormented Tom.' She opened her handbag and took out a hankie, so clean and perfectly ironed, and shook it out before dabbing the tears from her eyes and putting it neatly back. 'Tom didn't retaliate often. He took a sensible view and ignored him as much as possible. Tom was always like that, gentle and kind. That was his nature. He was just like his mother.'

I noticed the pride in her voice.

'But his attitude infuriated Dudley and he made my other children's childhood very difficult when it should have been a happy time.' The hankie came out again and she blew her nose.

'Let's walk a while,' she said, turning towards the way we had come. As we slowly climbed the steps again she stopped to take a breather. 'I was ever hopeful that Dudley would grow up and get some sense, but he didn't change at all. He went to work in the pit when he left school, but he hated it. Hated the hard graft and having to rely on others for his safety, and if I'm honest, the other men didn't want him down there. His attitude was all about himself. He wasn't a good man to have to rely on.' We started climbing again. 'When he was eighteen he signed up for the army saying he couldn't wait to leave and he'd never come back to us again. I can't tell you how relieved I was. It was like being given a gift of peace and every day was like Christmas day after that.'

We fell silent as we reached the top of the steps into Graig Street again. It was the last of the streets at this end of the Graig before the mountain took over in its natural, unruly state. 'Let's climb up a way,' she said, and I followed her in silence trying to avoid the sheep droppings and tufts of coarse grass that could easily trip you up. The mountain loomed bulbous with the grass flecked black from coal dust. I didn't really want to climb it in my Sunday best, but follow her I did. She was Tom's mother after all, and I wanted to find out about Dudley.

As we climbed the air became cleaner, but not by much. It depended on which way the wind blew. You had to climb right up to the top to get cleaner air, but most people were too tired or busy to make the trek. After ten minutes or so, we came to a flat rock people used as a seat. There was no one else around and we sat down and kept the silence. I knew better than to disturb her. She seemed to be wrestling with some memories and I wondered if she was trying to decide how much to tell me. With her pride I knew it must have been difficult for her to talk to me about these things. I felt privileged that she was confiding in me, and thought that she must love Tom very much to be helping him in such a way.

I looked at the backs of the houses and rooftops marching down the hillside. They were grey and dark but strangely comforting. I started to get a little chilly and shivered and I think she noticed for she suddenly said, very quickly, as if she was afraid of it, 'He was dishonourably discharged from the army a year after the war finished.'

'*Dishonourably discharged?*'

I could see she was trying hard to keep tears at bay, so I said, gently, 'Why? What did he do?'

I had to struggle to hear her. 'He was too difficult for the army. They said his character wasn't suitable soldier material. He was always getting into fights and volunteered for any duty that might involve some bother or other. It came to a head after a fight he started left the other soldier badly beaten and on the critical list in hospital. It wasn't the first time, and he'd been warned apparently, but to no avail. He just carried on being the same . . .' she took a deep breath, '*horrible* person he's always been.' She sighed deeply, fingering the hankie in her hand. 'Poor Dudley,' she whispered. 'No one wants him. Not even the army.'

'How long had he been in?'

'Seven years in all. Of course, the army wanted him throughout the war, I'm sure he was a fearless fighter, he even won some medals. Then, after he'd been thrown out, he turned up on our door demanding to live with us again. The children had grown up and there was simply not enough room. He would have had to share a room with Tom and that was out of the question. I had to think of Tom's welfare.' She hesitated. 'I'd believed him when he said he wouldn't come back. It was a great shock to see him again. His father and I decided that he would have to go into lodgings and we arranged for him to go and live with a miner and his wife in a nearby street. They had no children and the man was big and powerful, he could take care of Dudley and his ways. Strangely enough, he seemed to like it there. He respects strength I suppose. Anyway, he always comes to us for Sunday dinner. Quite frankly, I wish he wouldn't, but he insists, saying he's part of our family. I'm trying so hard, but he makes it very difficult.'

She didn't speak as she dabbed her eyes and turned to look at me. 'You see, it was shortly after Dudley returned that my husband died. He'd been injured in the war and he was in so much pain he had to go to Rookwood Hospital.'

'That's in Cardiff, isn't it? For soldiers injured in the war?'

'Yes. He'd been shot in the spine and he had great difficulty in walking until finally, he couldn't walk at all. But he struggled on bravely. I was proud of him. He was a good man, he deserved better.' Suddenly, she broke down into heaving sobs and her body convulsed uncontrollably. She was living on the edge of her tolerance and I felt Tom had good cause to be afraid for her.

I felt useless and just sat there as she cried herself out. I didn't dare put my arms around her shoulders, although I felt that was what was needed. She should have someone to lean on but I was so busy stifling my own emotions that I knew I wasn't the one to help her. I couldn't. I wasn't capable.

'I'm sorry,' she said as the sobs subsided. 'I try to be strong for my family, especially Tom, who fusses about me all the time, but I'm not feeling strong. I'm sure Dudley coming back hastened my husband's end. Oh, it's all so unfair!' she shouted. 'I can't take much more.'

She looked up at the sky again and I felt she was on the edge of a scream. I'd never seen anyone in such a state and I didn't know what to do. So we sat there. The two of us: Mrs Mallow trying to gain control of herself and me, shocked and unsure.

'I watched him, you know,' she blurted between sobs. 'I watched him die a painful death. He used to scream with pain when he needed another dose of morphine. But there wasn't enough to go around all the men. They had to ration it out. Oh God! So much suffering. He was in the hospital for three months before he died. It was awful to watch. I tried to help him. Go there every day, hold his hand. You see . . . I loved him very much and I blame myself for sending him off to war. It was all my fault – like Dudley was all my fault.'

'Oh, it wasn't, Mrs Mallow, it wasn't. You're too hard on yourself.'

She looked down at her lap, blew her nose and took a deep shuddering breath.

'We had to move to the Graig after my husband died, and

oh, God help me, Dudley moved here too. He found himself lodgings nearby and still comes to Sunday dinner.' She stared ahead, lost in thought and the look of anguish on her face told me all I needed to know.

She grabbed hold of my hand. 'I don't want to see any more suffering in my family, please, for me, please see Tom. Let him talk to you and explain why that stupid, *stupid,* fight happened and let him explain about Dudley. If, after you've heard his story, you still don't trust him, then at least he'll know there's no hope for you two. That's all I'm asking. Just give him a chance. I've never seen him so smitten with a girl before. You'd be good for him – not like those tarts – sorry; I didn't mean to say that.' She hesitated. 'He needs a nice, decent girl, like you, Kate.'

Her tears subsided. She'd gained control once more although little tears escaped from her eyes, a light shower escaping from the storm inside her. I couldn't really do anything but agree to meet Tom after church next Sunday.

CHAPTER EIGHT

That Sunday, the sun shone. It was warm and the buzzing of the insects felt reassuring. Tom's face had healed and we were both in our Sunday best but walked up the mountain none-the-less. The tufts of grass were soft underfoot and as long as I avoided the whimberry bushes their ripening berries didn't stain my shoes. The incline of the Graig Mountain is deceptive and I felt the climb in my calves. I was glad when we reached the rocking stone: two large slabs of stone with their legs embedded in the mountainside while their bodies sat flat and naked exposed to the dirty air. They lay one on top of the other, not quite fitting together, and when I was a child it took six of us jumping at the same time to cause any slight movement to the top stone, but Tom and I didn't attempt any such frivolity. He took off his jacket and put it down on the rock for us to sit on. We sat in nervous silence for a few minutes. Tom was sitting with his knees up to his chest, clutching them as if they would fall off if he didn't. He was looking out over the town as if it was the most interesting sight he'd ever seen.

Picking at a thread in my dress, I took a deep breath and said the one thing that I'd promised myself I wouldn't talk about. 'I haven't seen Dudley since your fight. He avoids me now, so at least something good has come out of it.' I could have kicked myself. Why was I talking about Dudley?

'I'm glad,' he said, still looking out over the valley. 'I told him if I ever caught him near you again I'd kill him.'

'Tom, please don't talk like that, it upsets me.' I picked more strongly at the thread. 'I don't like violence, it frightens me.'

He looked down at the rocking stone. 'I'm sorry, but it's the only way to make him stay away from you. I don't mean this to sound rude, but you know he only wants you because I want you, don't you?'

'What do you mean? Surely he can get girls for himself. I've seen him with a girl on his arm many times.'

'Yes, that's true, but they're girls of a certain type, they seem to like his temperament, his little bit of danger. They find it exciting or something. But nice girls – like you – won't go near him. He's always fighting around town, outside the pubs and things. But that's what he's like. He likes to spoil things for people.'

We fell silent again. It was now or never. 'Your mother said you'd tell me about your childhood and how things were between you and Dudley.'

I saw his body stiffen and he took a few deep breaths.

'Yes, you need to know,' he said, looking straight ahead. 'This is difficult, but if you're to understand about Dudley and me then I have to tell you as much as I can. How it's always been.' He rubbed his hands over his face as if he'd walked into a large cobweb. 'My mother told you some things I think.'

'She told me that Dudley was always fighting with you, causing trouble between you, but she didn't go into detail.'

'Yes, well, she's right, he made my life hell. I . . . I don't know where to start.' He looked anguished.

'Why not at the beginning?' I suggested gently. 'What do you remember first?'

He looked out over the valley. 'Well, I remember when I was about six and my mother saw bruises all over my body one bath night. Dudley was always tormenting me, pinching me and thumping me. I didn't say anything to anyone, just said I'd fallen over or something, because if I told, he just became worse. But these were big bruises, much more than usual and when she asked me how I got them I remember crying and it all came out. Dudley got a hiding and was sent to bed without his tea. That night, when I went to bed – we had to share the same bed – he put his pillow over my face and almost suffocated me. I really thought I was going to die.' He was silent for a while.

82

'I'll never forget the panic of it. I tried to push him off, but he was too strong for me. He told me that tell tales got what was coming to them and one day, he just might have to kill me. And so it went on. It was like torture.'

He stared ahead and I waited patiently, afraid to break his thoughts. He sighed. 'But never mind about all the details, you get the picture, don't you?'

I nodded. 'Yes, Tom. I'm sorry.'

'Then when I got bigger, I was able to give as good as I got, but I don't like fighting so I tried not to. It was only if he went too far that I had a scrap with him. Boys fight, Kate, it's a fact, and boys in Ponty do seem to like a scrap and sometimes it's difficult not to get involved.'

'Yes, I know.'

He looked at me for the first time. 'He always wants to be the top dog and control people, especially me. He said his life was perfect before I came into it.'

He smiled a little. 'He was the only son with two sisters, he was top dog, but suddenly, he was pushed aside in favour of this little bundle of sunshine – me!'

I laughed and it broke the tension somewhat.

'But seriously, Kate, he loves power, even if it's against a dog or a cat, he'll do his best to rule them and torment them. Being pushed into second place by me made him angry and he gets very nasty and violent when he's angry. That's just the way he is.' He fell silent and took a deep breath.

'Take your time, Tom, there's no hurry.' We smiled at each other in a tentative way.

'It all sounds so stupid now. I mean, lots of boys fight. But Dudley was different. Oh, how to make you understand . . .'

'Just tell me simple things, things you remember.'

'Well, it didn't help we shared a birthday,' he said after a while. 'So there was always a double celebration. He hated that and said I had ruined his birthdays forever. When we were kids he refused to celebrate them. Mam would bake a nice cake and put icing sugar on it as a special treat, but he would throw his piece into the grate. One year after everyone had sung happy

83

birthday to us, he picked up the cake and pushed it hard into my face. My father jumped up and smacked him one round the head in no uncertain terms, but he ruined the party and that was his aim. It's always his aim, to ruin things for everyone, especially me.' He looked at me, unsure.

'Go on,' I encouraged, 'you may as well tell me everything. I want to understand.'

'You're a nice girl, Kate.' He looked into my eyes. 'I can talk to you.' Then he went all shy and looked down at my hands resting in my lap. He put his hands out to touch them and his were shaking. He hesitated and then stroked the back of my hands, very gently. 'I've not talked like this to anyone before. It's nice, I like it. You have beautiful hands, so small and perfect.' He looked at his own. 'Not like my great big miner's hands, all rough and chapped and calloused.' He looked down at the rock again, embarrassed.

I took his hand and squeezed it encouragingly. 'Go on, Tom.'

'Well . . . you know, Kate . . . sometimes it's . . . it's best not to say too much. It's not good to know about some things. You're a nice girl and these things are vile. They're vile to me, and I'm a miner. It takes a lot to upset a miner. I can't tell you anymore, it's not suitable. And truth is, I don't like to say such things. He looked up at the sky. 'I think he's mad. He doesn't think right. Not like a normal person.'

I was shocked. 'Is it that bad?'

He looked into my eyes. 'Oh, yes, it is that bad. He's a nasty, nasty person.'

'Do you know why he's like that?'

'I wish I knew. Our mam thinks he was born like it. You know, some people are well, just like that I suppose.'

'Do you think he has some bad feeling about himself, deep down inside and he's afraid people will find out? I know a boy at my school who was like that and one day he just burst out crying instead of fighting and cried for a fortnight so his mother said. He never did come back to school. His parents moved to another village, for his sake, I think.'

'Could be, who knows what goes on in his mind, but I doubt

it. I never saw Dudley cry. Quite frankly, he's done so many horrible things to me, I don't care. I can't see him any other way but as my enemy. I tried when I was younger to be nice to him, in fact I was always trying to be nice to him and that threw him into an even more violent temper.'

'I don't think anyone is wholly bad,' I said, sounding pompous even to myself. 'There must be *some* good in everyone,' I added, trying to redeem myself.

Tom bristled and I realised I'd said the wrong thing. He looked me straight in the eye. 'You take too much notice of church,' he said harshly. 'Let me warn you now that it's dangerous to think like that about him. If you give him any rope he'll take advantage. Always has and always will. He has a selfish heart and no pity for others. I can't think of anything that would change Dudley – not even love. He's not capable of it.'

He looked embarrassed and I couldn't help wondering if Tom had been changed by love – love for me?

'What I'm trying to tell you is that Dudley is a devil. He made my life miserable just for spite. And the thing about Dudley is that it never stopped. I had to always think Dudley. Whatever I did I'd have to take action to avoid him. It dominated my life. I should have given him what for years ago, but I didn't and that encouraged him. I'm not a coward. I can fight and stand up for myself, but not every day, every hour of every day. Our mother wanted peace in the house, so I spent as much time as I could out with my friends. I tried to avoid him and not rise to any of his taunts. It was hell. I could never relax or enjoy anything because if I did, he would find a way to spoil it.'

I squeezed his hand, trying to encourage him. I felt his suffering.

'I was so glad when he joined the army. But now he's back he's worse than ever. I don't know what happened to him in the army but he's become even more unbearable, if that's possible.'

His eyes filled with pain. 'I hope you can see why I lost my temper with him so completely when he said he was going to kiss you and . . . and . . . well, all the years I'd suffered at his hands flared into that moment and now I know I'm capable of killing someone. I nearly did kill him and I'm not proud of that. But at least it has finally told him that he must not go near you anymore. He's stayed away from you, hasn't he? He's not bothered you since?'

'No. He's not been near me. If he sees me in the street he looks the other way or turns round and walks away, making a big point of it in my opinion. He frightens me.'

He looked down briefly and then into my eyes. His own were pleading as he cupped his still shaking hands gently around my face. 'He won't dare bother you, not now. Telling you this has been hard but I hope you can understand why that fight happened and why I lost my temper.' He searched my face. 'You're everything to me. You know that, don't you? Can you look upon me in a good light? I'm not a monster, I'm not violent. He just pushed me too far.'

He put his hands down and looked out over the valley again. 'I've changed, Kate. Can't you see that? I know I was a Jack-the-lad as you put it. As I grew up I became popular with the girls, they liked me and well, I was flattered, what man wouldn't be.' He looked at me. 'I'm a man, Kate, I like girls and I had a good time with them, but as time went on, I felt there was something . . . well, missing. But I didn't know what to do about it, so I didn't think too hard, but the feeling kept growing. Then I saw you that first time in the alley and I knew it was you who was missing from my life. I just knew it.'

My heart beat harder. Was it the same for him? 'How did you know . . . how could you know . . . with just a glance?'

He smiled. 'Oh, Kate, I knew. I knew because my stomach turned over and I started to tingle, my knees went weak. It was like being hit by something hard. My whole being wanted to know who you were, where you were from, about your family, your likes and dislikes. I wanted to know it all. I couldn't see any other life for me but one with you. I had to get to know you.'

So, it had been the same for him. The same shock of meeting, like being hit by something hard, he'd said. Was this something

86

neither of us could control?

'But you were not easy to know and I was shocked, truth be told. You were the only girl I was really interested in and you didn't want me. I didn't know what to do, how to behave. I made many mistakes but I didn't give up. I couldn't. The power of you was too strong.'

'But that's the danger, isn't it? You wanted me and I didn't respond, it became a challenge, but what happens if you get me? You might find that, over time, you don't want me. That you tire of me like you tired of all your other girlfriends. You don't have a strong reputation for loyalty, Tom. And when you've got me, you'll find out that I'm no one special – I'm just me. I worry that you've built me up into someone I'm not. Put me on a pedestal. You might be disappointed with the passing of time.'

'Never! I'll never be disappointed in you. I've grown to know you and my feelings have deepened, grown bigger and stronger. No, Kate, you're wrong. I've changed. My life – the only life I can see for myself – is with you. Oh, what do I have to do to make you believe in me?'

He fell silent. 'Be honest with me. If there's no hope for me, then tell me now. Rejection will be preferable to this torment of loving you from afar, wondering if you could ever feel the same.'

Something had changed in me. I felt closer to this man than to anyone else I'd ever known. I was beginning to understand him. See inside him and I liked what I saw. Liked his honesty, his struggle to tell me, his determination to tell me, to make me understand.

The tension in his body was so strong I thought he might snap and I realised he was afraid to look at me, afraid of my answer.

I took his hand in mine and linked our fingers. I tried to speak but nothing came out. I squeezed his hand hard, trying to say through action what I couldn't say out loud. He turned and looked at me. He caressed my face so lightly I almost didn't feel it, but it sent shivers of desire through me I didn't know it was possible to feel. I wanted this man and I now understood the meaning of that.

'I love you, Kate. I love you so much. I'd die for you.' We gazed into each other's eyes. 'I'm just a man in love with the most beautiful girl in the world and I want what's best for her, and I want to keep her safe. Oh, please see me as I am, see the goodness in me. We can all be pushed too far in the right circumstances. It was just my time to be pushed over the edge by Dudley.'

He looked at me with such love and I knew Tom was mine and mine alone. I felt the same about him. I caressed his face and our eyes locked. Everything around me disappeared as I was sucked into a bubble of love. It was a magic moment, one I'll never forget. It was almost worth living to have a moment like that in your life.

As we looked at each other I fancied a thread was growing, a spider's web of love was developing and as we searched each other's eyes it grew stronger, weaving its silken threads, linking us, so soft and strong I felt they would never break. They would just stretch when we were apart and contract again when we were together.

'I can't live without you. Marry me, Kate. I'll always be true to you. There'll never be another woman for me. I'll do my very best to give you all the things you want. Oh, Kate, I do love you so.'

The last bit came out as a sob. He had changed. It was time to acknowledge that. He'd practically killed a man with his bare hands to protect me.

I wiped my tears away. 'It's time for honesty, Tom. I love you too. More than I ever thought I could love anyone. The answer is yes. Yes, I would be honoured to be Mrs Thomas Mallow.'

He looked shocked and took a ragged, deep breath. His eyes filled with tears and that set me off again. We both cried and laughed at the same time. Not deep cries, just gentle ones that come from too much emotion building up inside. He gently kissed my wet eyes, then my forehead, cheeks, nose and chin until he came to my lips. The feel of his lips on mine, the gentle pressure of them opened a floodgate of desire inside me. I put my hands behind his head and drew him to me. He responded instantly and before I knew what was happening I was experiencing my first passionate kiss: deep and long. It sent me to a place I had never been before and I knew then what people meant by passion and desire. We lay down on the rock without thinking of what we were doing and I swear that if we had been lying on something soft, we would have had trouble in stopping. As it was, that Welsh granite bit into me like an angry dog. It bruised the back of my head, my shoulders, elbows and heels. The pain of it brought me back to real life and I realised that we were in a public place where kids played and which could be seen by the people living below if they had enough interest to peer upwards.

'Tom. No. We mustn't. Tom. Please stop.' He groaned as if the air had been knocked out of him and rolled away from me.

'This damned rock is hard. I wished we'd picked a comfier place.'

I laughed softly. 'I'm glad we picked here. There's no telling what would have happened if we'd been comfortable.'

He rolled back towards me and propped himself up on his elbow. 'That's what I mean,' he said, his eyes shining with love and desire. 'Wouldn't it have been romantic to have sealed our love like that?'

I kissed him lightly on his lips. 'Oh, Tom, I don't think so, I believe in keeping yourself pure for your wedding night. I've been brought up to that. I'm not one of your loose women.'

He sat up rigid. 'Oh, Kate, I'm so sorry. I didn't mean . . . sorry, no, I didn't mean that at all. I wasn't thinking of them. I was thinking of us. Oh, God, what a fool I am. Now I've offended you. Please, please, believe me and forgive me, I really didn't mean–'

'Shhh.' I caressed his face lightly and I was pleased to see it made him shiver.

'I want to save myself for our wedding night,' I whispered, 'that would make it really special, don't you think? I know you've had other girls before, I'm not daft, but I'm pure and proud of it. I've always dreamed of a fairytale wedding. Of being with my husband on our first night together, discovering the mystery of love.'

'Mm,' he smiled. 'It's a lovely picture in my mind.'

'It's up to us, isn't it? We can make our wedding whatever we like. It depends on our thoughts and feelings. We can save each other for that special time if we want to. And I want to. Do this for me, lovely Tom, it means so much to me. The fruit would be so much sweeter.'

I saw the love he had for me. Like a magnet it drew us to each other again. 'Of course,' he whispered. 'Of course. Anything you want. I'd do anything for you. You know that.'

We kissed again, gently and deeply. It was all we needed. It silently sealed our pact. We were one and understood each other.

*

Over the next few months I was feeling carefree and happy, so confident in my life to come. I loved Tom passionately. I laughed at my worries about something not being 'normal' about me. I just needed to meet the right man. Tom was it, I had no doubts. He was very respectful to me and never tried to push himself on me as I knew other boys did to their girlfriends. It was common knowledge that men wanted to make sure their girlfriends could get pregnant before they married them, for your security was your children. They looked after you in old age. You didn't want a barren wife. Many brides went up the church in white with a seed in their bellies. But Tom wanted us to wait too, to make it special.

I'd put my arms around him and cuddle him to me. It always gave me a thrill to do that, to feel his strong body so close to mine. He'd tell me over and over how much he loved me and kiss my face, neck, hands, over and over. I loved it. He was my Tom and I could be myself with him. No more pretence, no more Boadicea spirit. I didn't need it with Tom. He was my Boadicea now. I thought I would burst with happiness. Tom too.

We saved hard and developed an easy way with each other.

We regularly walked up the Graig Mountain to be alone. We walked up high, where the grass was green because the coal dust couldn't get that far up. The only other creatures were the sheep and a few stunted trees struggling for life with the same tenaciousness as we people who lived below them. It was on one of these walks, with bread and cheese and a bottle of water in Tom's pockets, that we came to understand each other even more deeply.

We climbed up, stopping to kiss every so often. I took his hand and said, 'I love your hands, they're so strong and capable.'

'And calloused and rough,' he laughed, 'and guaranteed to have arthritis and turn blue.'

'Yes, that too, but when we're married, I'll get your bath ready at the end of every shift and clean and massage your hands with soap and cream.'

'Mm, sounds like heaven. Will you clean and massage other parts of me too?'

We burst out laughing. 'Of course, my lovely Tom. Anywhere and everywhere.'

We walked on upwards, taking ourselves further away from the world and into one of our own making, keeping the silence of the air around us.

We came to our favourite spot where one of the few trees struggled for life. It was gnarled and kept small and bent from the wind but it provided some shade on hot days. We sat with our backs to the dry stone wall which gave us a view over the valley and the town, but we weren't interested in the view.

I put my arm in Tom's and hugged him to me. He turned and kissed me gently and it soon turned into passion as was the way with us.

'I can't wait for our wedding night,' Tom said, grinning. 'Oh, my, what a night it will be.'

'Well, it won't be long now,' I replied, stroking his cheek. 'Can I be honest?'

He looked alarmed. 'Always. You know that.'

I continued stroking his cheek. 'I'm . . . well, I'm frightened, you know, about it all. I know you have experience – men always do – but I haven't.' I hesitated.

'What is it?' he asked gently.

'I know what the girls all say – I've heard some stories I can tell you –' I laughed nervously. 'Well, um, what I'm trying to say is . . .' I lost my nerve. 'Oh, it doesn't matter. It'll all be all right I'm sure,' I said as calmly as I could.

He moved away from me a little so that he could see into my eyes. 'Kate? What's this about? Why are you frightened? Tell me. You know you can tell me.'

I looked down. I should have kept my mouth shut and just hoped for the best. Now I had to explain myself and I found it difficult.

'Come on, sweet, sweet Kate. No secrets now, mun. You know that. Please tell me. I'll help all I can.'

I took his hand in mine and ran my fingers over the calloused lumps and bumps. 'I'm being silly, I know, but, well, I'm a miner's daughter, I know what men look like. I helped my mother to bath my father when he came home every day from the pit. Got the bath out in front of the fire, warmed the water ready for him.

'I helped my aunties too, with their husbands, scrubbing the coal dust out of their backs, scooping water over their heads, holding the towels out for them. I know the mechanics of . . . you know . . . men and women.'

Tom nodded, looking serious. 'Yes, like all our women, but what's this about, Kate? What's worrying you?'

'And I know what happens on wedding nights, my friends and neighbours who are already married have made sure of that.'

Tom took my hand and squeezed it.

I looked down at the grass. 'I'm worried about whether, you know, whether I'll disappoint you . . . how I'll feel . . . the unknown I suppose. Some say it is incredible, like nothing else and others say, well, it's all right for the men but women get a rough deal. I don't know what to think.'

'Oh, Kate,' he said instantly, 'look at me . . . look at me, please.'

As embarrassed as I was, I looked into his eyes. 'You mustn't listen to them. You and me, we're nothing to do with them. You can never be a disappointment to me, no matter what. You know that.'

I made an effort to smile.

'Will . . . will you be gentle with me?' I whispered. There, I'd said it. The one thing I really wanted from him was to be caring and gentle. I'd heard so much from girls who'd said it was slammed into them and they had no chance to feel anything except pain and bemusement, that men were beasts when it came to lovemaking. I didn't know anything about that side of men. I wanted it all to be so perfect. But I couldn't tell Tom all that.

He smiled. 'Katie, my love, my soon-to-be-wife, how could I be anything but gentle with you? I'll be as gentle as a butterfly, as soft as a feather. I'll treat you like a precious peach in summer. One false move with a peach and it bruises and goes bad.'

I laughed. Tom could always do that, make me laugh. 'You've been practising on peaches?'

He laughed as well and then he caressed my cheek. 'I'll never hurt you, in any way at all. I guarantee it.'

I kissed him lightly on the lips and hugged him close. We lay down then and wrapped our bodies around each other. 'I can't wait either,' I whispered.

Later, when we'd gone as far as was decent, we pulled apart before we couldn't. We lay on our backs and looked up at the blue sky and watched the fluffy little clouds fly by.

'It's my turn now,' he said.

'Your turn for what?'

'To share my secrets.'

I turned over on my front, snuggling my head into his shoulder, putting my arm around his middle. 'And I will be as gentle as a butterfly and as soft as a feather too.'

He laughed gently. 'I have dreams, you know. I might only be a miner, but I have dreams.'

'Go on,' I encouraged him. 'Tell me. Don't be embarrassed,

not with me.'

'Ah, yes, embarrassed. But, no, you are right, not with you. Let's sit up,' he said moving smoothly, fluidly and gracefully: my Tom.

We sat side by side against the wall. 'See that view over by there, Kate.' He pointed over the valley and the town. 'It's lovely. Even now, it's lovely. Even though it's covered with houses and roads you can still see bits of the original valley. See how lovely it was before coal was discovered. I think about that a lot. How lovely it was before and how we miners go down underground and hew out the coal. Cutting nature out of her home. Making holes. It's not natural. It's not natural at all. And it's a hard life, as you know. And I wonder why we miners have to do that. Do that horrible job. And get injured and ruin our health and sometimes even die, just to earn a living. It's the right of all men to earn their living without risking death or injury every day.'

'You've never said anything like this before.' I said, surprised. 'Don't you want to be a miner?'

'If I'm honest, no, I don't. Like I said, it's not natural. It's my dad's fault, I suppose, although he didn't have any choice either, but if you are born to a miner you become a miner. If you're born to a white collar-worker, you become a white collar-worker, sitting in a nice, warm, safe office, using your brain instead of your brawn.'

He put his knees up and hugged them; an action I was beginning to understand was his way of coping with things that were difficult to say.

He stared out over the valley. 'I have dreams of better things. I do think about it a lot. Sometimes I hope I can get better work, but I'm not educated. I can't do anything but manual work. It's too late for me, but well, for our children.' He looked at me. 'I want better things for our children, Kate. I don't want any of them to be a miner.'

I caressed his arm. 'What do you mean by better things?'

He picked at some grass, making a big show of being interested in it. 'Well, um,' he cleared his throat, 'education.

94

That's the thing, see. You have to be educated to get better jobs.' He looked at me. 'I've never said anything like this to you before, but, well, you're educated, you educated yourself. I admire you very much for that. You know far more than me. And I want that for our children.'

He turned right around so that he was facing me. 'Can we do that? Can we educate our children – give them ambitions beyond the pits? I couldn't bear a son of mine to be a miner.' He shook his head. 'I just . . . I just couldn't bear it.'

I could see the earnestness in his eyes and it touched my heart. I smoothed his hair back from his forehead and kissed him lightly. 'You are a surprising man sometimes, do you know that?'

He raised his eyebrows in question.

'That's just what I want for my children too. I never thought I'd hear you say something like that. It's made me so happy. And I agree, it's too late for us, but for our children . . . oh, what an ambition. Thank you, Tom. For being so . . . so ambitious,' I said, laughing.

He was smiling from ear to ear. 'Thank you. Thank you, Katie bach,' he said so softly I almost couldn't hear him. 'I knew you'd understand . . . but, well – don't tell anyone else about it. You know, my mates. Thing is they don't think like me. They talk of making mining safer for their sons to go underground. They think that miners who want out are traitors to their trade. We're a proud lot. It takes a lot of courage to go underground every day. They'd never understand, that's why I haven't been able to talk to you about it before. But I knew you would understand. Knew you were different to other girls. I knew you were the one for me.'

I kissed the palm of his hand and held it to my cheek. I couldn't stop smiling. I looked into his eyes. 'I think it's my turn to be honest now.'

'Oh?'

'I'm proud of you. Proud of your ambitions, I misunderstood you when we first met.'

'No,' he said, looking anguished. 'Don't say that. It was my fault. I put pleasure before anything else. I can see that now. I was young and like so many, I didn't think. But I do now, Kate. I do think now.'

We kissed for a long time.

Later, as we were eating our bread and cheese, I said, 'Tom?'

'Yes,' he said, smiling, pulling off a chunk of bread.

'As we're being honest, can I ask you something? It might sound strange, I mean, coming from a miner's daughter and all, but well, I don't really know what it's like underground.' I chewed on my cheese, pondering. 'Whenever I asked my father he said it's not a suitable topic for nice young girls like me to know about. But I'm about to be your wife, and I think it would be helpful to me to understand what it's like exactly. You know, to be able to help you with it, make me a better wife.'

He laughed.

'Why are you laughing?'

'Because I'm so happy you want to know. I've never thought about it before. Come to think of it, my dad never talked of being underground so I suppose that's right, we don't talk about it, to our families at any rate.'

He kissed me gently on the lips and gazed into my eyes. 'Well now, let me think. I've never described what it's like before.' He screwed up his face and put his hand over his forehead, pretending to think. He always tried to make me laugh.

'Come on Tom, tidy now. Tell me tidy, please.'

'All right, serious it is then. Well, it's dark. I mean pitch black. You've never seen such blackness. It's solid and it always surprises me when I find I can walk through it. I think I'm going to hit a wall, but it's a wall of nothing except space. We have our lamps, but they don't give out much light and often blow out unexpectedly, taking God with the light and leaving us in the blackness of the devil. Me and my mates, we call it the devil's blackness.'

He looked up. 'Look at this beautiful sky. I always marvel at it when I come up off shift because, below ground, it's cramped and dirty and wet . . . with midges biting you. Can you believe that? Who would have thought that you'd get insects underground? And up here it's all light with wonderful skies, even grey skies are wonderful. Nature's such a marvellous thing.'

He pulled a silly face and kissed me lightly on the tip of my nose and as he did so, said, 'Rats!' I jumped and screeched a little, which was the effect he wanted.

'Rats run around us and although my trousers are tied around my ankles, I have nightmares about them running up them and biting my bits.'

I laughed.

'Oh, it's all right for you to laugh,' he said smiling, 'but it's awful, it really is. And I don't care who knows I'm scared of the rats. They'll eat your food if it's not in your Tommy tin and they'd take the spit out of your mouth given the chance. They're devils. Do you know how long a rat's tail is?'

I shivered but couldn't suppress my smile. 'No, Tom, but I think you're going to tell me.'

'Well, they're long. That's all. Just long. And strong. You don't want to get a whip from a rat's tail. And it's hot down there too. Air comes down a shaft which is enough for us to breathe easier, but not enough to cool the air around us because men's and horses' labour heats up the air and the sweat just runs down us.' He ran the back of his hand across his forehead as if reliving the heat. 'Sometimes it's so hot it's almost unbearable. I've never known such heat above ground.'

'Never? Even on a summer's day?'

'Never! But then sometimes, it's so cold down there. It depends on the weather and no two collieries are the same. Each one has different drawbacks . . . but mostly, I suppose, it's the top that's different. You have to adjust your way of working. In some mines you have rock above you and in some it's clod. You have to put up a post, to support the roof, every yard for clod and that's time consuming. There's some that thinks rock is safer, so you don't need to put in as many supports, but that rock can crack without warning and come down on top of you. Better to put posts in both I do say. It's slower but safer although that gets us into trouble with the management who

97

want faster and faster work. But many of us keep slow and steady and put in the posts, clod or rock. It is dangerous work, we all know that, us miners more than anyone.

'I was underground with Dai Davies one day, he was older than me and had lots of experience, he was working just a few yards away when, without warning, the top gave way and a huge chunk of rock fell down on him. It took us ages to get him out from underneath and he left his brains for the rats. They had a good day that day, those rats.'

He stared out over the valley and I didn't disturb his mourning. He took several deep breaths. 'The bosses are always pushing us harder and wanting to pay us less for more work. They don't care about us, there are always more men waiting to take our place, they keep us like cattle. They use us men just for profit knowing there's always another unemployed bull waiting his turn to prove himself when one of us working bulls fall.'

He fell silent and I waited.

'Then there's the gas. That blasted firedamp gets into you. You don't know it's there until it makes your head swim. You can't smell it. And if it goes up, maybe with a spark from a mandrill if you hit a rail by mistake, then up you go and maybe take your mates with you.'

He looked angry and I smoothed his face and kissed him calm.

He lifted my hand to his lips and kissing it tenderly, whispered, 'And then there's the ghosts!'

'Ghosts?'

'Yes, real ones, I mean. I've seen a few and so have many of my mates. Men are killed underground all the time and if there's been an explosion or a roof fall, we just can't get them out, or there's nothing left of them to get out. They're trapped forever. They haunt us down there.'

'How do you know they're there?'

'Well, you know when you're there. There are strange noises and lamp lights where there shouldn't be, and feelings that run up your spine and make you shiver for no reason. The air goes cold. Oh, they're there all right. It's a hard life. I think that's why your father doesn't want to talk about it. He doesn't want to worry you.'

I was still holding on to Tom's hand and realised that I knew so little of the deep feelings of this man I was soon to marry.

He wrapped his hands around his knees and stared into the distance. 'Like I said, I do hate being a miner. I really, really do hate it. If I could do something different I would. When I get in that cage to go down into the blackness below, all us men crammed in so tight we're cocks to bums, that's when I hate it the most. Speeding downwards fast and your stomach goes up to your throat and your ears pop and although the brake man engages the brakes half-way down, we still hit the bottom with a hard bump and it takes me a while to get over my fear that one day we'll hit the bottom too hard and end up with our knees pushed up into our hips. Then, when we get out of the cage we have to walk out to our working places. It could be a mile or so, bent over, crawling sometimes in low seams, in water, the dust already in my mouth, knowing its going into my lungs, that death is getting a tighter hold of me every day.' He shivered.

'I never knew you felt like that, Tom,' I said as I put my arm around his shoulders, hugging him to me. 'Oh, you poor, poor thing. It must be awful. And to have to do it day after day. Oh, Tom. Maybe we should think of another job after all, you know, even if it means less money or moving away.'

He was quiet for a while. 'Trouble is, it's a bit late now. As you know, my sisters have moved with their new husbands to Canada, God forbid. So you see, I can't leave my mother, not now. And she won't leave Ponty. Says she cannot abandon my father in his grave. She visits it every week. She feels so bad he died.' He looked out over the valley. 'And anyway, would it make any difference?'

'What do you mean?'

'I had a cousin who went to Stoke-on-Trent to work in the potteries. It was just as bad there, he said. And there's little work there for an unskilled man, just like there's little work here. But I do have a skill, Kate, I'm a miner and as much as

I hate it, at least I can earn enough to keep my family. If we moved away, then who knows what would happen and we'd have no family or friends around us to help us. The grass is not always greener.'

I pondered his words. 'You're right, the grass is not always greener somewhere else. We could end up much worse off than here, and as you say, we'd not have family and friends around us.'

'If I . . . if I shared something else with you, you wouldn't laugh, would you?'

He looked so earnest. 'No, of course I wouldn't,' I answered, gently.

'Well, then, I . . . I sometimes think that all we miners do is create holes. You know, when the cage reaches the bottom, we get out and walk into a hole we've created. We follow it to the end and then extend it or make new holes. By the end of the day, or year, or a lifetime of mining, all we leave behind are black holes. Chip it out, load it up into trams, look at the hole you've created and make it bigger or move on to create another one. Sometimes, the coal seems to be incidental, it's the creating of holes that becomes the important thing, for me anyway. It's like a competition with myself. How many holes can I make this week? Or can I increase the size of this hole anymore? Is there enough coal left to make a bigger hole? I get obsessed with the hole.'

He looked embarrassed, as if he'd shared too much with me.

I took his hand and squeezed it anxious to reassure him that I understood. 'You're like a poet, Tom. I love the way you think about your holes.'

'I know it's daft but . . . it's how I feel. There's not much joy down there, well, none at all if I'm honest. We have the camaraderie of our mates, the support of each other, that's special, but we eat our food with black, sweaty hands and drink our tea from Tommy tins, knowing that we are washing that damned coal dust down our throats. We only take a short break, there's so much pressure to get the coal out in large amounts that we have little time to rest.' He turned to look at me. 'I know I'm ruining my body. But I'll do it for you, Kate, I have someone I love and who loves me, I'd do anything for you.'

'Oh, Tom.' I stroked his hair. 'I think I love you more each day that passes.'

We kissed. 'But I worry, Kate. I worry what might happen. I see the older men, too injured to work anymore, and they have nothing. On the parish it is for them and their families. They can't work with their lungs ruined or backs broken, or eyes blinded. Whatever it is, the mines did it to them.' He stroked my cheek. 'But that's not going to happen to us, is it? We'll be different. Won't we? We'll be different.'

I hugged him. 'Yes, Tom. We have each other. We'll be different.'

CHAPTER NINE

The plans were all laid for the wedding. We would marry on August 6th 1921 and Edie would be my bridesmaid and a friend of Tom's would be best man. I'd visited Davy and invited him and he agreed to come. 'And I wish you all the happiness in the world. Just don't sit me near Dad or Aunty and I'll come with pleasure,' he said. He didn't forgive easily and I always thought his life could have been much sweeter if he could. But that was just how he was. He was still living with Rhys' mother, Mrs Richards, and looked contented. He was smartly dressed in the latest fashion in his wide trousers, waistcoat and his tie was securely in place. He always wore a tie, even indoors, and his jacket hung on a hanger behind the door. He was a fastidious young man with high standards. I was proud of him.

Then, four months before our wedding, Tom called round with bad news. He knocked hard on the front door and came in like a bear with a sore head. 'We're out on strike,' he spat. 'Can you believe that? Out again! Those bastard owners should be shot. Should be made to go down the mines and hew that bloody coal for themselves. Then they'd change their tune. No doubt about that.'

'Calm down,' I said. 'So they've decided then, the vote went for a strike. Sit calm now and tell me what happened.'

He sat on a kitchen chair with a face like thunder. 'I was hoping we could sort this out without a strike.' He shot out of the chair and began pacing. 'God knows how long it might last.' He swung around. 'I know it's the right thing to do, but we're too weak to have another long battle. We're all practically starving now, what's it going to be like when we're on strike again? I know we have to fight for our rights, but not now.'

He sat down on the chair again and looked up at me. 'Not just before our marriage!'

I kneeled in front of him and took his hand. 'But we can still get married. What's to stop us?'

He looked at me as if I were dim. 'Simple mun, we won't have any money. That's what will stop us. We have so little now we'll starve if we go on strike. We can't justify spending all this money on our wedding now. We'll need every penny.'

'Well we're not exactly spending much and we can cut back even more. I've already got the material for my dress so all I have to do is make it, that won't cost anything except my time. We can cut back. Everyone will understand. I think we can go ahead.'

'I think so too,' said Aunty Annie, who'd been sitting quietly in her armchair next to the empty grate. 'You shouldn't let anything get in the way of your happiness. We've been out on strike before and I dare say we will again. If we don't fight now, then the owners will get richer and we'll be so poor we won't have enough food to keep the men fit enough to work in the sodding mines.' She almost never swore and looked so embarrassed and indignant that I almost laughed, but didn't dare.

I poured some tea and we all sat quietly lost in our own thoughts. I knew Tom was right. We were too weak to have another strike. We'd been striking for years, terrible strikes, long battles and riots in Tonypandy and the government called in the troops: awful, unbelievable times. We were not the enemy, the mine owners were, but the government couldn't see it, or didn't want to see it. They were supporting their own kind after all. The fact that the owners treated us worse than animals was neither here nor there to the government. A miner's life was worth £18 in compensation to his widow, while a working horse killed underground was worth £40. Says it all. So many miners killed while working because of the owners' insistence on more and more coal being extracted in less and less time. And instead of rewarding the harder work with more wages, they cut them. Families were starving all over South Wales.

'All this has come about because of that damned war,' Aunty Annie said quietly, into her teacup.

Tom shot her a look of distain. 'How can you say that? We had good times during the war when the government took over the mines. We got paid well to get that coal out and to the ships. Best coal, South Wales coal is,' he added puffing himself up. 'It was good times.'

'Yes, maybe,' she said, sipping at her tea. 'I know the war depended on our coal for victory, we've been told often enough. But if it hadn't been for the war, we might have won the battle against the owners by now; but they are digging in with a vengeance now they have them back.

'And that's not right,' exploded Tom. 'They have no right to take us back to where we were before the war. No right at all.'

'It was a boom time, all right,' Aunty said, 'but in my experience, all things that seem too good to be true are not true. They come to a sticky end. The boom time has collapsed like a pile of cards.'

'That's the whole point. That lily-livered Lloyd George doesn't want to be lumbered with coal mines when the economy is collapsing. We miners are too much trouble,' Tom said, proudly. 'That's why he gave them back before the potato got too hot to handle and now the bastards have slashed our wages and safe working practices and we're right where we were. It's not right. I know it's not right, but I say it again, we're too weak for another strike.' He rubbed his hand over his face. 'The price of coal has collapsed with the economy and that's going to make them even more determined not to give way to us in any way. We'll be daft to strike, mun. Daft.' He picked up his cup and drank the rest of his tea down fast and burped.

'Another cup, Tom?' I asked sweetly, trying to diffuse the atmosphere.

He ignored me. 'That bloody Lloyd George should be shot,' he said. 'Traitor to the miners, that's what he is. Those bloody owners said they would lock out any miner who didn't agree with the new terms, and that's all of us really.' He looked dejected. 'Me included, whatever I think.'

'Matt agrees with you,' Aunty said. 'He's down the pit now, checking it's all closed down safely. You know how thorough he is but there is nothing you nor he nor any of us can do to change it. The strike's been called.'

Tom stood up with his back to the room, looking out of the window. 'You're right. Nothing we can do about it. Sorry, I do get carried away sometimes.'

'Don't apologise,' Aunty said, 'I understand and agree with you. But take my advice, calm down about it. Plan for your wedding and let the world take its course. It always does you know, whatever you try and do.' He turned and she smiled at him and he smiled back. He liked Aunty, said she talked sense.

So, Tom and I decided it would not stop our wedding, whatever happened we would wed as planned. We were young and could live on hope and optimism. We had each other.

The strike ended after three months. We lost the fight and the feeling of anger and frustration in the valleys was all-consuming and festering. I despaired but was determined not to let it spoil our day. But I vowed to myself that if ever I met a mine owner I'd spit in his eye. He'd deserve it.

CHAPTER TEN

The day started ordinarily enough. Idle tittle-tattle over breakfast until it was time for my father and Aunty Annie to take the train to Tonypandy. They were going to the funeral of one of my father's old friends who'd had the misfortune of being in the wrong place at the wrong time as a tunnel collapsed at his pit. I'd decided to stay at home as I didn't know him or his family and was looking forward to a rare day to myself. It was three weeks before our wedding and I'd already given up work because Mrs Coombes, the owner, had already started a new girl. I would have preferred to have stayed on until the last because of the wages, but she couldn't afford to pay for two of us.

I was putting the finishing touches to my wedding dress. Mrs Coombes was a lovely lady and she had given me enough white satin as a wedding present to make the dress, together with some salmon pink satin for Edie's dress. I'd finished Edie's. She was to wear a traditional A-line dress, fitted under the bust to hide her six-month pregnancy. It didn't do to have a pregnant bridesmaid, even if she was married.

I'd designed the dresses myself, checking magazines at the library for the latest fashions. I was feeling very proud and a little bit smug about it. Hems were fluctuating, but I decided to finish my dress just above my ankles to show off the white satin wedding shoes a cousin had lent me. Aunty Annie had made me a lace cap which would sit low over my forehead in the new style. I wanted to look fashionable and for Tom to be proud of me. Aunty Annie cut my long hair short in the new fashion (she was good at hairdressing and did all the family) and as I had a natural wave, it suited me very well. Tom loved it, which pleased me.

I made sure the kitchen table was clean and swished the dress out over it and checked it over. I threaded my needle to make a start on the hem when there was a knock at the door. We never locked our doors except when we went to bed, so whenever you went calling you just knocked and walked in, usually shouting, 'Hello, anyone at home?' So, when I looked through our open kitchen door and down the passageway to the slowly opening front door I didn't think too much of it except that it was an annoyance because I wanted to finish my sewing. Everything changed when I saw who was behind that moving door. I saw his red hair first and then his grinning, freckled face.

'Kate, my darlin',' Dudley called out as he pushed the door open wide and stepped into our passageway. 'All alone are we?'

I clung on to my sewing as if to a lifeline and started to sew as if it would protect me. 'What do you want?' I demanded.

My insides were shaking. I knew he was up to no good, it was written all over him.

He grinned, self satisfied, walking towards the kitchen. 'That's no way to talk to your almost brother-in-law, is it? Be welcoming now. I've just come to wish you good luck on your wedding to Tommy boy.'

'I don't need your good wishes. Please leave right now,' I said, cursing my shaking voice.

'Oh, come on, Kate. Let's have a little smile from you. You know you like your lovely Dudley, don't you?' He leaned against the door frame. 'I just saw your father and aunty going into the station all dressed up in their best black. Where are they off to then?' I didn't answer and kept on sewing furiously as if those stitches could sew him up too, making him harmless.

I could smell him from the doorway; cigarettes, beer and that stale unwashed smell men often have, like a dank riverbed. He came into the kitchen slowly, like a cat. 'Please go away, Dudley, I don't want to talk to you and I don't think it's right for you to be here.' I sounded pompous, even to myself but I couldn't help it.

'Right!' he shouted, making me jump as anger flashed in his eyes. 'You talk about right! How dare you talk to me about what you think is *right*. You always were a stuck-up bitch with your high-and-mighty attitude. Never running after the boys like a normal girl would, going to church and clutching your Bible like a shield. Well, I'll tell you, Little Miss Stuck-up, I was in the army for years and fought in the war, I'm used to destroying protective shields. Oh yes, I know a trick or two you'd never believe.'

I was so frightened I accidentally jammed the needle into my finger and jumped.

'That's right, give yourself a fright. It's practice for what's to come.'

'What do you mean? Get out of here now. Tom would be furious if he knew you were here.'

'Tom' he snarled. 'Let's not forget about *dear old Tom*.' He stood in front of me, very close. His genital area was level with my face and I could detect a sour smell coming from it. My stomach churned again. By this time my fear had grown into a panic. 'If you try to hurt me, I'll scream and the neighbours will hear.'

'You try doing that, Kate my darlin', and I'll kill you. Don't think that I won't. I've killed many a man, woman and even child when I was in the army. It's nothing to me, but I'd rather you lived so you can tell *dear old Tom!*

'We had an argument last night, Tom and me, and when I accused him of poking you to his heart's content, he got angry and let slip that he's never touched you. "Kate's not like that,"' Dudley said in a mocking voice. 'Oh, Kate's not like that,' he repeated in a sing-song imitation of Tom's voice.

'Fuck that,' he said. Then, his attitude changed. He became soft and gentle and sweet, as if he was talking to a baby. 'We'll have to educate poor old Tom won't we, Katie darlin'? Let's show Tom how much his perfect Kate loves it – how inside she's just an animal, lusting after a male. Come on, Katie my love. Come to the top dog, the leader. I'll show you what's what.'

He grabbed my arm and pulled me up from the chair and threw me down onto the floor as if I was a rag doll. He pulled his braces down and started to undo the buttons on his trousers. I shot up off the floor and made a run for the front door but he was fast and pulled me back into the room. He put his arms around me and pressed himself into my back. He started to kiss my neck and caress my breasts. I tried to get away but he had a vice-like grip. He turned me around and I managed to get my hand up to his face and scratched him down his cheek. He yelled and slapped me across the face. It almost knocked me out and he caught me as I fell backwards. The violence seemed to calm him and he became gentle.

'Now you sit there, Katie love, while your Uncle Dudley makes himself ready. Don't move, because if you do I might just hit you hard enough to kill you, and you don't want that do you, Little Miss Religion? It wouldn't look good for your father and aunty to come back to find you naked and dead on their floor.'

I was shaking uncontrollably as I sat there stunned from the blow, and could do nothing. I tried to concentrate my mind on looking for a way out and realised I would have to reason with him or hit him very hard on the head with something heavy. I looked around the room and saw the poker sitting in the grate. But he saw my eyes move and followed my gaze.

'Oh, no you don't,' he said as he picked it up with the other fire irons, opened the back door and threw them out.

He glared at me with eyes full of anger and I realised he saw me not as a woman or a human being, but as something to despoil. I knew then that he hated me and would have no hesitation in killing me if he had to.

'I'll show you and your lovey-dovey Tom what life is all about. It's about the strongest and the fittest surviving. I'm going to fuck you, Kate, before your wonderful Tom gets the chance. I'm going to take your virginity around my cock and fuck you with it. I'm going to shoot out a son for you, Kate, and after you're married and Tom thinks he's a father, my little brat with red hair will squawk out of you like a miniature me.

Oh, what a revenge! A son of the Mallow family but fathered by the wrong son. Oh what sweet joy.' He looked up to the ceiling and put his hands on his hips and howled like a dog in heat.

He grabbed me again and pushed me through the door and up the stairs. He opened a bedroom door and seeing it was my parents' bedroom, closed it again and tried the other one. 'Your room!' he said as he pushed me into it. He ordered me to undress. I had to try and get away, it was my last chance. In a sudden lunge, I pushed him away from me with all my might and caught him unbalanced. He went over and I turned to run but he caught hold of my ankle. I tried to kick out, but he had a strong hold and I fell over too. I hit the floor boards hard and saw stars.

He struggled up and stood over me, hissing, 'I'll spoil you if you don't do as you're told. I'll ruin your face, punch it, slash it, make it so ugly that your wonderful Tom won't want to marry you and it will be a reminder forever of this day. It's up to you, Katie my love. This either remains our secret or all the world will know.'

'You wouldn't dare. It would mean that you would be caught and put in prison. You wouldn't want that.'

He laughed: a strange baying sound I'd never heard anyone make before. 'Oh, Katie my darlin', I'd be long gone before you became conscious and I know how to get out of this country. I'd be happy to flee from here, no one could get me. You don't think this is my first time, do you? You simple-minded girl. You know nothing.'

I was now certain that I couldn't stop him so I decided not to give him the satisfaction of seeing any fear in me. It was obvious that's what excited him. So I shut my emotions off as firmly as a water tap, turned the handle hard, dripped a few drips of uncertainty, and then knew that this was the only way. I was not powerful enough to overcome him. He knew all the tricks. He'd said this was not the first time he'd done something like this and I believed him. My only weapon was to not give him the satisfaction he craved by making me a quivering mess.

110

'Take off your clothes,' he demanded.

When I didn't respond straight away, he shouted, 'Now!'

There was no option. Survive this, or be disfigured for life or killed. I had to protect Tom and our life together. So, in those last minutes of my innocence, I quietly and without fuss, took off my clothes as he had ordered, and put them neatly on the chair near my bedside. I did this slowly and deliberately, as if nothing was amiss and I could see it infuriated him. I got on the bed and lay down looking up at the ceiling.

He undressed.

He raped me then: viciously, degradingly, humiliatingly.

The body being violated was no longer mine but a lump of flesh that had become unfeeling and no longer human. It was being despoiled. But I refused to let him pollute my mind too. I had to remain sane and calm if I stood any chance of surviving this.

Finally, he stopped when he emitted a cry of what I assumed was pleasure. The weight of his body crushed me, his chest suffocating me as he lay across my face. This brought me back to myself. He was heavy and smelt of stale sweat and dirty skin and lying under him was like a life sentence. Seconds seemed like hours and minutes like days.

Finally, he moved off me and looked down at the sheet and let out a yell of pure pleasure. I looked down too and saw a splattering of blood there and knew enough about wedding nights and virginity to know that mine had been well and truly violated. 'That's got him,' he said triumphantly. It was the only time I ever saw his eyes smile.

He picked up his watch and looked at the time. 'Get dressed,' he barked.

I tried to get out of the bed but felt ripped apart as if someone had pulled out all my joints and pushed them back in. My personal parts were agony but I wouldn't give him the satisfaction of seeing the effect he'd had on me so I pulled myself up and dressed with a much dignity as I could. I felt a welt on my face. Oh God, what was I going to say? I knew I had to keep this a secret from Tom as he would kill Dudley if he knew. I didn't want that. I wanted Tom for my husband. I didn't want him to hang for Dudley.

'Get downstairs and make me a pot of tea, girl,' he instructed me.

I had no choice and I went downstairs as best as my aches and pains would let me. I saw my wedding dress still laid out over the table in all its virginal whiteness and all that represented. I started to shake violently as the implications of what had happened flooded through me anew. A wave of sobbing broke free in my throat as I heaved and tried not to make a sound to alert Dudley. With my hand over my mouth, trying to swallow down the sobs, I picked up the dress. I didn't want to remind Dudley of my wedding to Tom. I laid it almost reverently over a chair in the front room and bit down the sobs again as I forced myself back to the kitchen and put the kettle on.

I was making the tea as he came down, thankfully fully dressed and sat at the kitchen table. I put the teapot on the table with some cups and saucers and I was shaking so much they clattered fit to break.

'Got a touch of the shakes, Kate, darlin'. I know a great cure for that.' His hands went to his trouser buttons again. Oh no. Please, no.

The thought of going through it again: the humiliation, the pain, the degradation. No! I couldn't let him do that to me again and to hell with the consequences. I didn't care anymore. A raw animal violence rose up inside me as I realised everyone has a snapping point where all common sense is lost. Nothing else existed except to get that man out of my life. It was my turn to be brutal now.

I made a grab for the teapot, and before he could react, I pulled off the lid and threw the boiling hot tea over his hand which was resting on the table. He jumped up and swiped at the teapot. It fell into the grate with a clatter.

'You bastard. You fucking bastard,' he screamed as he staggered around the kitchen.

I ran into the pantry and picked up the kettle which still had boiling water in it. I brandished it in front of me. 'That's enough,' I yelled. 'There'll be no more because I swear, I'll throw this over you.'

He gave me a look of pure hatred.

'I don't care if Tom knows,' I said. 'Do your worst. I won't let you ever come near me again . . . and if you tell Tom, I'll tell your mother exactly what happened. How depraved you are.'

'Don't you dare fucking tell her,' he roared, out of control. 'You tell my mother and I'll shoot another little Dudley bastard into you, anytime I like. You'll never get away from me – or the threat of me. All Tom's children could be Dudley bastards. Remember that girl, and hold your tongue.'

I understood now what Dudley was like deep down, what he was capable of and why Tom almost killed him. I also knew that I was capable of killing someone.

But I'd also discovered something more. By chance, I had found out that he did have some humanity in him, a weak spot: his mother.

'Get out,' I yelled, 'before I throw this boiling water over you.'

I could tell by his face he was in agony, and to my utter relief, he picked up his jacket and stormed past me to the front door. As he opened it I shouted, 'You come near me again, I'll kill you. I swear it.'

He turned and looked at me with such loathing. 'You just try it, sweet darlin'. You'll be as successful as you were in keeping your virginity. Let's do this again, Katie, let's do it many times until you get married and Tom won't know what's happened when he gets his little virgin with sexual knowledge. He'll know you're not a virgin, darlin'. Tom's been around. He'll know.'

I rose up to my full height, and said through clenched teeth, 'I swear to God . . . you . . . you bastard,' I yelled at his back as he went through the door.

He turned in the doorway and winked at me. 'Oh, more than that, Kate, much more than that, I'm a fucking bastard, as you well know.'

He closed the door gently behind him and his words hung in the air and stayed there.

CHAPTER ELEVEN

As the door closed behind him, I threw myself at it and locked it. I knew it would cause suspicion if someone called round, but I couldn't risk him coming back. I got myself to the kitchen, sat down hard on a chair and started to shake uncontrollably. My stomach heaved and I ran outside to the privy and was violently sick. Later, as I kneeled over the toilet bowl, retching bile, I wanted someone to say, there, there, everything will be all right. But I only had me. Only I could do this. Women through the ages had coped with rape, so I'd better too.

I tried to pull myself together – knew I had to – because my future with Tom depended on me coping. My father and aunty would be back soon, they must have no inkling anything was wrong. But it was hard. I called on my childhood friend Boadicea and her strength helped somewhat. At least she took my mind off what I was doing as I cleaned everything up in an unfeeling daze, as if it wasn't really me. I was desperate to wash Dudley off my skin, but knew I had to clean up first in case my father and aunty got home early. I washed the cups and saucers, cleaned up the splattered tea from the grate and was thankful we had an aluminium teapot. It was dented, but serviceable. I'd have to think up an excuse. I put the pot and cups and saucers very carefully into the cupboard as if my care would make things better.

Next, thankfully, I could attend to myself. I didn't want the comfort of hot water on my skin: cold water was the only thing that could expunge Dudley from my body. I stripped off and stood in front of the cold water tap outside. I washed and swilled myself over and over. It was like a religious act and with each wash my resolve tightened and gripped my heart. My life had been ruined. Where was God now?

I went upstairs and changed my sheets, cursing loudly. I could smell him on them. I opened the window wide to get his vileness out. Because the window was open, my curses softened into whispers and I soon found I felt calmer if I didn't curse him at all. I decided there and then to close him off, to close off what had happened. It was like a shutter banging down inside me and I wrapped up all my emotions, put them in a little bag and drew the drawstrings tight. Maybe I would let them out one day, but for now, it was the only way I could survive what I had to do. I must never give the slightest hint of what Dudley had done to me. I still loved Tom. Tom was not Dudley. Tom was my future. We had discussed the children we would have, how well they would do at school, all those things lovers plan for their future lives. Our banns would be read this Sunday at church. We would be there in our Sunday best, proud and happy. Oh God! I wasn't sure I could do it. How was I going to get through this? I drew the drawstrings on my bag even tighter, and pulled myself together and got on with things. Cope with what I could bear and cry silently for what I couldn't.

I filled our big washing bucket with water and put it onto the stove to heat up. Meanwhile I washed my virgin blood out of the sheet and thrust the sheet in the bubbling water. I felt like I was boiling Dudley away. His poison was being diluted. I had enough sense to know that I mustn't let him spoil the rest of my life, but I also knew that he would never do it to me again. I would rather hang for murdering him than suffer the bastard again.

When I'd boiled and scrubbed the sheet clean, I put it upstairs in my bedroom to dry, I couldn't let aunty see I'd washed it as she'd want to know why. My head throbbed and my body ached and I was still shaking. A deep lassitude overtook me and I realised all my resources were spent. I was too weak to face my father and aunty. They'd instantly know something was wrong. So I did the only thing I could do and went to the only place that was mine: my bedroom and my bed. I unlocked the front door and then left a note to say that I had a severe headache and had gone to bed and to please not disturb me. I apologised for not getting their dinner ready and asked them to take care of themselves. It would have to do, I couldn't do anything else.

I made the bed with fresh linen, undressed and put my clothes into the washing pile. I would have to wash them tomorrow. Wash that filthy man out of my clothes tomorrow because I was exhausted. As much as my body resisted getting into that bed again, I knew I must. I forced myself into it, trying not to think about what had happened there. I almost vomited but held control, knowing there was nothing left in my stomach. I lay down hoping for the oblivion of sleep but my thoughts were as violent as Dudley's actions had been as I relived how stupid I'd been in the past: how naive. I'd been brought up on Jane Austin and gentle, romantic books and thought my wedding night was to be treasured. It would be full of stars, excitement, love and tenderness and the next morning I would wake up a fully fledged woman with the knowledge of the world now in my head by osmosis. I would have a generous, tender and perfect husband because I had been a generous, tender and perfect virgin wife. But it was nothing like that now and I had been denied the chance to find out if it ever could have been.

And what if I was pregnant? Could you get pregnant from so much hate? I'd always thought pregnancy came from love, that you couldn't have one without the other and then I remembered my relatives. My Aunty Gladys and Aunty Irene had not loved their husbands, that was obvious to me even as a child. They might have done to start with, but after so many children their feelings had changed. But they still produced baby after baby. So there was a good chance I could be pregnant.

I couldn't let that happen. What should I do? I was trying to keep calm, but a rage and a feeling of helplessness was building. The rage was against that . . . that monster who had the nerve to call himself a man and my ignorance of what to do next. I knew that some women got rid of their babies. That they either did it themselves with a knitting needle or scalding water – but I had no idea exactly how you did it – or they went to 'secret women'. But I didn't know who these women were and who could I ask without giving it all away?

If I was pregnant, it was so close to my marriage, I may get away with it, but not if the, the . . . thing . . . I couldn't think of Dudley's child as human, so if the thing had red hair, then I was exposed. Tom was not Dudley's real brother. Tom didn't have a trace of red in his hair and no one in my family did either. I screamed suddenly: a piercing expulsion of rage and powerlessness and then I remembered the neighbours and was fearful they would hear. But I couldn't hold it in and turned my face into my pillow and screamed and screamed and screamed. I thumped my fists and feet into the bed until I was hoarse of throat and sore of limbs. I broke into uncontrollable sobs. The drawstrings on my bag of emotions had already broken. I knew I'd have to repair it, and soon.

*

How I got through the next three weeks was a miracle to me – how I kept myself together. Always at the forefront of my mind was the word: pregnant.

I turned away from God after Dudley. It wasn't a conscious thing, it just happened. I went to church many times between 'that time' as I called it, and my wedding, but God didn't speak to me. They were empty visits and I wondered if I would have to endure a lifetime of empty visits. Could I find God again? I had no idea but I knew I couldn't stop going to church and pretending I believed in Him because to stop would entail explanations I didn't want to make.

To cover over my injuries, I told everyone I'd slipped running up the stairs and fell down them, hitting my face. They were all sympathetic and no one queried it. Tom was still the loving, funny and relaxed person I'd fallen in love with. I still loved him, but the physical side of things had become so hard for me. My body hurt all over and I couldn't bear to be touched and hugged by Tom because of the bruises left by Dudley. Tom, bless him, was so sympathetic and gentle with me, I felt awful lying to him, and that made things harder to cope with.

Dudley, thank goodness, had told everyone he'd got drunk and scalded his hand and that the doctor had told him to rest it. He kept a low profile and I didn't see him and for that, I was so very grateful. Maybe I'd hurt him more than I knew.

It had been arranged that after our marriage, Tom and I would go and live with his mother. That was fortunate in one way as my own family wouldn't see me so often and realise something was wrong, and unfortunate in another very important way, as it meant Dudley would have free access to the house, and therefore to me. But it was unavoidable as Tom and I couldn't afford the rent on another house while he was also supporting his mother, and it was usual for a young couple to live with the groom's family when starting out.

I continued to work on my wedding dress. I had been proud of its whiteness but now, it was like a slap in the face.

I tried to cover my feelings but Aunty Annie knew something was wrong.

'What's the matter, Kate bach, are you not feeling well?'

'It's just nerves, Aunty. Nothing to worry about,' and it felt hollow even as I said it.

I was terrified of having Dudley's child. I should have had my monthly by now. I had always been very regular. I couldn't eat. I was too churned up.

Still, my monthly didn't come.

One week before the wedding Aunty said, 'You haven't had your monthly yet, Kate. Are you all right?' She looked at me long and questioningly. 'You haven't been indulging with Tom have you? I wouldn't blame you, he's a lovely boy, but you really should have waited.'

'No, Aunty, I haven't. Really we didn't. I think it must be nerves. I can't think straight. I feel so awful.'

She jumped up. 'A nice hot bath it is for you then. It always does the trick if the monthlies are playing up. I'll get the bath in and put on some water to heat up.' And with that, she was a flurry of activity. She put three pails of water on the stove to heat up and moved the kitchen table aside. She set our small tin bath in the middle of the room, and when the water had boiled she put the pails of hot water and two of cold into the bath. She closed the curtains and locked the door. 'No one can come in and disturb you now. I'll take myself up to bed and read my book. It'll be a real treat for me to do that. You relax in the bath for an hour. I've got another three pails on for you, when they heat up, get out and empty them in the bath. That'll give you lots of hot water to soak in. The hotness of the water will move those monthlies along like nothing else. Enjoy it, my lovely.'

I undressed and stepped into the bath with some trepidation – what if this didn't work? But I let the water soothe me and as soon as I heard the water bubbling on the stove I got out and filled the bath up. I sat there with my knees bent and the water up to my breasts. The metallic smell of the zinc was always unpleasant to me and the roughness of the bath hurt my tender buttocks, but it was still sheer heaven. After a while, my thoughts and worries refused to let me be and the solitude and relaxation unleashed my tears again. I cried until the water went cold.

*

The next morning I woke up with my insides feeling like they were being dragged out of me. Then I realised my monthly had arrived. I was ecstatic. If I hadn't lost my belief in God I would have thanked Him; instead I thanked Aunty Annie, which is probably nearer to the truth.

I met Tom that night and was able to blame my moodiness and distance on my 'women's problems'. The relief that there wasn't a devil inside me gave me hope.

'Oh, Katie, cariad. I was worrying that you'd changed your mind and didn't want to marry me, but it was only women's problems. I'm so relieved. Come and cwtch.'

Only 'women's problems' I wanted to shout. They're not important, are they? What's important is that you get your cwtch and feel better. I gave him his cwtch wondering if Tom really understood women at all.

119

CHAPTER TWELVE

My wedding day arrived as my monthly disappeared. I was disappointed it had finished if I'm honest because it would have been a good excuse not to 'do' anything that night. That special time, that culmination of our love that I had so looked forward to, was now a nightmare. Everything was gone except the feel, smell, anger and poison left by Dudley. And how was I going to prove that I was a virgin? Would Tom hurt me as much as Dudley? I was frightened of myself and my reactions to Tom, and the fear of him suspecting anything. I had to keep him from that – whatever happened.

That morning, when Aunty Annie came up to my bedroom to help me dress, I took a deep breath, then another and another. They steadied me somewhat. After I was dressed, Aunty held the mirror up so that I could see myself in full.

'You look a picture,' she said and I realised I did look beautiful. The length of my dress was just right to show off my white satin shoes and was not only fashionable but elegant too with its straight white satin skirt tucked into a high waist. The lace on my shoes matched the lace hoops around the hem and hips of the dress. The rounded neck was set off by Tom's gift of a deep blue pendant that used to belong to his grandmother, my something blue, and the short sleeves left my arms bare to lead the eye down to my watch, my something old, and my treasured possession which I'd saved hard to buy when I first started work. My something new of course, was my dress which now mocked me.

Edie and I, together with our small posies of flowers, a present from my father, and a dab of lavender water behind our ears, left my home. I, on the arm of my father, with Edie following close behind in a small procession that would take us to the nearby church. I knew my father was uncomfortable in his only suit. The one he called his 'weddings, christenings and funerals torture suit'. He kept pulling at his brilliant white collar which aunty had laundered with ferocity. The three of us walked slowly in the middle of the road, like royalty. The neighbours came out and cheered and clapped, which echoed around the canyon of our street. Some called out, 'Good luck.' 'All happiness.' 'You look beautiful Kate.' With each shout I felt a terrible sadness but smiled and waved.

As I walked down the aisle I didn't see Tom or the congregation, but the image of the double bed Tom and I had bought from Gwilym Evans' Department Store in town. I tried to shake it off, to concentrate on what has happening, but my mind wouldn't let me and even the altar took on the shape of the bed. It was as if I was possessed. I was terrified of tonight. What would I do? What would I tell Tom if he realised? I didn't want him to kill Dudley. An unbecoming sweat broke out on my face and under my arms. My knees started to shake and then I saw Dudley standing there in the front pew. He turned to look at me and lifted his heavily bandaged hand up in mockery. I thought I would faint. The triumphant smirk in his eyes as he looked me up and down and lingered on my breasts and personal bits down below made me shake even more. He raped me all over again with those eyes.

My father held on to me very tight as he felt me wobble. Tom turned when we approached him and his look of love washed over me. I grabbed hold of his arm as a woman falling off a cliff would reach out for a passing branch. I couldn't control the shaking and Tom smiled indulgently and reassuringly at me. Innocent, unknowing Tom . . . and during our vows all I could think of was bloody Dudley and how I hated him.

*

The reception was held at the church hall and everyone else was in good humour so I tried to pull myself together enough to function without drawing undue attention to myself. Aunty and her church ladies had made a good job of decorating the hall. The tables had clean, freshly pressed white tablecloths with a vase of wild flowers on each. The place settings were laid out neatly with shining crockery and sparkling cutlery. The trays of sandwiches had little bits of greenery as decoration. Aunty had made a two-tier wedding cake and her friend, who was a wiz at decorating cakes, had iced it. Two little figures stood on the top which Tom had whittled in elm to look like us.

Aunty Annie and my father came over to Tom and me as we stood in the centre of the room with people coming up and congratulating us.

'It was a good turnout at the church,' Aunty Annie said. 'It was full. It's a pity we couldn't invite everyone to the reception, but well, there you are.'

'We're pushing the boat out to feed the thirty that are here,' my father said. 'Come on now, Annie, we're doing very well under the circumstances.'

She smiled at him and put her hand on his arm. 'I know, Matt. I know. I was just thinking out loud. But you're right we're doing very well under the circumstances.'

I saw Davy over by the door. He looked like a film star in his fashionable suit. He wore a dickey bow for the occasion and I wondered where he'd bought it. Fussy, high fashion clothes like he was wearing weren't available in Ponty.

'Excuse me, everyone,' I said. 'I just want to welcome Davy.'

'So, he came then,' said Aunty in a disbelieving voice. 'Some people have no shame.'

My father laid his hand on Aunty's arm. 'Now, now, Annie love. Let the boy be. Kate's his sister after all. They've been through a lot together. He should be here. You know we discussed it.'

I smiled at my dad and his eyes filled with tears, but he turned away, embarrassed by his emotions.

I went over to speak to Davy. He kissed me on the cheek, and he smelt of good soap and cologne which was unusual for a man who worked in the pits.

'You look beautiful, Kate,' he said as his eyes searched mine. There was a lot of noise in the hall with people laughing and chatting and it was easy for us to talk without being overheard. 'But there's something wrong, isn't there? You can't fool your brother, I know you too well.'

'Please, Davy, if you care for me, leave it. Don't ask me anything . . . just be happy for me on my wedding day.' I went to turn away, but he caught my arm.

'Just tell me one thing. Is it Tom? Is he the problem? Because if he is, I swear I'll sort him out and make him pay if he's making you unhappy.'

'No!' I whispered harshly, surprised he'd think such a thing. More calmly I added, 'No, it's not Tom. Please don't worry. Tom's the best husband a girl could have.'

'Then it's that bloody brother of his,' he hissed. He was still holding on to my arm and he felt me stiffen at the mention of Dudley. 'It is him, isn't it?' I didn't answer. 'I see,' he said. 'I'll kill the bastard if he's done anything to hurt you. I swear I will. He deserves every bad thing that comes his way.' He was getting red in the face.

'Please don't do anything to Dudley. You don't know him like I do. It's not worth it.' He looked like thunder. 'Please, Davy, don't spoil my wedding day. I can cope with Dudley. I know how to.' I hoped he wouldn't see through my lie. 'Leave this to me.' I tried for levity, 'I am your big sister after all.'

'Yes, but I'm all grown up now. It's my turn to protect you. Goodness knows, you protected me enough when we were little. Let me do this for you, Kate?'

'No!' I exploded as I pushed his arm away, I had to discourage him from challenging Dudley, 'I said no, and I mean no.'

'What's going on, Kate?' Aunty asked, as she approached quickly. 'Is Davy bothering you?' Her eyes were cold and her body stiff. I could see she was looking for trouble. But before I could answer her, Davy beat me to it.

'There's nothing wrong. Don't worry, I'm leaving.' And with that, he strode out of the room like an angry bull. I felt relieved that Davy had left, but sad that both he and Aunty still couldn't share the same air without animosity.

I reassured her. 'Everything's fine. Forget it please.'

She smiled lovingly. 'It's your day. I'll do as you ask. Let's go and talk to Tom. There'll be no bad words between you and Tom, I'll warrant.' I managed to return her smile.

Aunty and my father looked so proud and didn't stop grinning all afternoon. Everyone was having a good time, but Tom had sensed something coming from Dudley that was not right. Tom kept looking over at him and Dudley returned his look with smug arrogance.

Tom and I spent the reception, close up, like Siamese twins, avoiding Dudley, but I felt his eyes on me like a plague of spiders crawling over my skin.

The reception passed in a blur of sandwiches, wedding cake, cups of tea, beer, congratulations and speeches. Later in the afternoon, Tom and I went on our honeymoon. My father and Aunty Annie had given us money and told us we must use it to go on honeymoon. It was vital that a newly married couple had a honeymoon away from everyone, they said. It will give you time to get to know one another better.

In a wave of excitement, we'd chosen Barry Island, a seaside holiday town less than two hours away on the train. A real treat under normal circumstances, but now I was dreading it.

The journey was a blur to me. I don't know what I said, or what Tom said to me. I can't remember the scenery or the other travellers, nothing at all until we reached our guest house and it was bedtime. That was something I had to get through somehow and it loomed over me like a big, black storm about to break. I couldn't stop thinking, how was I going to prove to Tom I was a virgin?

Would it hurt as it had with Dudley? What should I tell Tom if it hurt too much? Would I like Tom being intimate with me, or had Dudley taken that joy away?

Tom, bless him, was as gentle as a new-born pup to start with, but kept telling me to relax, which had the opposite effect. 'It's me,' he kept saying, 'me, your new husband, the man who loves you more than life itself. It'll be good, honest it will.'

I felt sorry for him and really tried my best. None of this was his fault. Dear, sweet, Tom. He tried his best too, but I soon realised that he was not good at lovemaking, even though he had had girls before. I wondered what kind of loving they'd done – probably in dark corners somewhere, getting it over as quickly as possible before someone discovered them. That's how it felt as his kisses got rougher and his hands were everywhere, like a starving man searching for food in an unfamiliar dark place. And his hands were miners' hands: rough and hewn, like the coal they extracted.

I wondered what had happened to all that passion and desire I'd felt for Tom in the past, when we were fully clothed and holding back. Now, I felt nothing. No anticipation. No desire. No pleasure. Maybe, if he had taken his time – given us the time – to caress and stroke each other like we did before our wedding: arms, face, neck, shoulder, legs. We'd spend hours when we were alone, just touching each other, sharing the tingling excitement of a gentle hand eager to explore the areas of our bodies that weren't looked upon as sinful. But it was still lovemaking: that build up to a more profound experience that could end in a baby being created. Tom had forgotten this, or thought he didn't need to do this anymore now he had the right to have all of me. He went for the parts of my body he hadn't been allowed to touch before. I couldn't blame him I suppose. He was an uncomplicated soul, but I was still tender after Dudley and could not respond when my body was bombarded by Tom's insistent attention. Pain kills passion. I discovered the truth of that. If only he had taken his time to see how I was feeling, to realise I needed gentle handling. I tried to tell him, but he said, 'Why wait? This is what we've been waiting for. Oh, Kate, you're so beautiful, I want to touch you: possess you. Touch me too, Kate. Touch me here.'

But that's what Dudley had said, 'Touch me, you cunt, or I'll slash your face.' How could I tell Tom? How could I touch him and feel desire? It was all too soon after the rape. That was my only defence. I shut down my emotions again, like I had all

125

through my life. It wasn't my fault and it wasn't Tom's either. We were victims. That bastard Dudley had changed everything.

I didn't sleep all night, while Tom slept like a baby. I spent the night in despair, thinking how I could convince him that he'd taken my virginity. I hadn't come up with any foolproof ideas but in desperation I decided on one of them. If I could only do it well enough. It might just work. But I wasn't an actress and had never been good at lying.

At first light, I got up very quietly. It was vital Tom didn't wake up. I looked at my side of the sheet, and as expected, there was no blood. I crept over to my bag and took out my clean hankie and moved over to the bowl and jug in our room. I dipped my hankie in the jug of water and crept back to the bed and rubbed an area I felt was in about the right position until it was wet. I then hung my hankie over the edge of the bowl and sat in the chair and looked at Tom's calm, sleeping face.

Forgive me, I said to him silently.

After a while, I coughed a few times until he woke up. He looked relaxed as he saw me sitting on the chair, in my dressing gown, smiling at him. A smug look settled over him, 'Kate, my lovely Kate, how are you this morning?' He stretched. 'I feel so good.'

'Me too, Tom,' I said, making a big effort. I mustn't spoil this for him. He'd waited for me. We had a life together now. 'You look so smug,' I said, smiling. 'I don't think I'll ever forget that look.'

'I hope you don't. I feel like the cat that's got the cream.' He let out a soft, 'Meow, purrrr,' as he pretended to wash his mouth with his paw. He touched my heart with his humour. I was determined to give him as good a honeymoon as I could.

It was now or never and with my heart thumping with nerves, I said the words I'd been rehearsing, praying I could do it convincingly. 'I've been up a while,' I said quietly, embarrassed, 'and noticed there was some . . .' I looked down, 'blood on the sheet . . . you know . . . that . . . kind of blood.' I blushed, and he smiled, knowingly, like a man of the world. 'I didn't want

126

the landlady to see it, it would be too embarrassing, and if I'd left it, it would have been hard to remove, so I wiped it off with my hankie and some water.' I nodded towards my drying hankie on the wash bowl.

He pulled the sheet and blankets back and looked down and put his finger over the wetness. He looked smug again and believed every word. Bless him. He reached out to me. 'Another go?' he said still with that smug look playing on his face. But the look of love that shone out of his eyes told me everything I needed to know and, taking off my dressing gown, I climbed back in and cuddled up to him determined to be what Tom wanted – or appear to be. But having to tell that lie to Tom was another band of hatred which was tying itself around me against Dudley.

Tom was insatiable with his lovemaking and during our honeymoon we went to bed early every night and got up as late as possible every morning. We had to leave our Bed and Breakfast place by eleven each morning and we went out to enjoy the thrills of Barry Island. I laughed with him at the fun fair, ate seafood from fairground stalls, held his arm during our walks, splashed about with him in the sea, drank soft drinks in the pubs so that Tom could have a couple of beers. Our landlady provided dinner. She was a good cook and kind with it.

It should have been the happiest time of my life, but the dread of the nights of lovemaking hovered over me. Each night, I felt like a piece of meat being used for my husband's enjoyment. And all I could do was to let it happen – as if I *was* a piece of meat – not a human being, a woman who had known intense passion for the man she was now with. Things were out of my control. And as the week went on, the pain got worse. It was agony sometimes, and a cry would escape from my lips, and Tom seemed to take this as a sign of pleasure and cry out himself.

Towards the end of the week, I couldn't take any more, it had become unbearable. I had to tell him that my down below hurt. But how to tell him? How to convince him? I decided that I had to pull myself together and forget Dudley and what he did to me. This was Tom, my Tom, so I made the excuse that he had been such an ardent, passionate lover, my body was not used to it. I was a virgin after all. My body needed time to adjust.

'Oh,' he said, surprised.

'Well, we have . . . you know . . . done it a lot this week. I'm not complaining, Tom, please don't think that. I'm just sore. It's me, it's my fault, I have a very delicate body.'

'Your body is wonderful,' he said thoughtfully. 'And yes,' he laughed, 'we have done it rather a lot. That's the power of you. I only have to look at you and . . . well . . . you know . . .'

'Yes, sweet Tom. And I'm flattered. But maybe, well, maybe I could touch you? You know, rather than you touch me?'

'You touch me?'

'I'd like that, Tom. I would make love to you, rather than you to me. I'd like to please you.'

He was in deep thought for a while, caressing my face. 'Yes, I see,' he said finally. 'Yes, I do see. If you had touched me as much, then I would be sore too. Oh, darlin' Kate, I've been so selfish. I'm sorry. Yes, let's do that – but there's just one thing.'

He looked at me with a glint in his eye. 'Can we start now?'

I laughed. So relieved. 'You try and stop me,' I said as I ran my hand down his stomach and he shivered.

I was grateful when the honeymoon ended. I knew that once Tom was back at work he would be too tired or too busy to indulge as much as we had. It was my gift to Tom, the non-stop lovemaking. Tom called it 'loving you'. That was sweet of him. It made him vulnerable, like a child asking for something that he shouldn't have. But my struggle against the demons Dudley left behind was overwhelming me. How I hated that man. He took everything away from me, my virginity, my faith, my peace of mind and my relationship with my husband.

Before Dudley, I wanted a good husband and many children, a family life to kill the demons I had left from my years in the care of my aunts. Now, after Dudley, I wanted this more than ever. I saw the arrival of children and a big family around me as my security blanket, my reward for enduring the pain and suffering of my early years. I wanted children I could love and who loved me in return. As far as that was concerned, I still had a fairy-tale story in my mind and I was determined to live it.

CHAPTER THIRTEEN

We arrived back from our honeymoon at Tom's house in time for dinner. It was a turning point that took me from my old life into the new one. His mother had prepared a mutton stew followed by apple tart and custard. It was delicious and I was ravenous, as if I hadn't eaten all week. Tom remarked upon it.

'I've had a very busy week, I'm hungry!' I said quietly, looking into my pudding.

It made him blush and he lowered his head to his dinner and didn't say another word. But really, I was just so pleased that the honeymoon was over and now our love life would be constrained by work demands and the presence of his mother. I relaxed and recovered my appetite.

The house was just the same as every other one on the Graig – small, two up and two down with a narrow passageway joining up the rooms. We lived mostly in the square back room which doubled as the kitchen. We kept the front room for guests and would never have dreamt of living in there ourselves. The gas cooker was in the corner of the back room with a small low cupboard next to it which contained plates and cutlery with a few shelves above it for tins and dried food. The washing bowl was kept on top of the cupboard and the water tap was outside the back door. There were two old brown leather armchairs in the corners, either side of the fireplace, one for Mrs Mallow and the other which Tom and I had to share. This meant, of course, that when Tom was in, he had the armchair and I had to make do with a wooden kitchen chair. I would never have dreamt of sitting in Mrs Mallow's.

*

As Tom went off to work for his first day as a married man he was full of smiles. 'I'm looking forward to my bath tonight. Don't forget your promise to massage me wherever I want,' he whispered as he stood in the doorway. We laughed.

'Well, let's see . . . how about your toes?'

'I can think of a much better place than that.'

'What are you two whispering about?' Mrs Mallow said disapprovingly, as she came down the stairs. I think she was jealous.

'Nothing!' we said in unison like children caught doing something naughty. Tom winked at me and gave me a kiss and kissed his mother on the cheek as he left she looked dour.

Later in the afternoon, I told Mrs Mallow that I would start to cook Tom's rice pudding. Like many a miner, he always had a bowl of rice pudding when he came in from work as he was so hungry he couldn't manage his bath without some nourishment. The pudding was soft and easy to digest so many miners' wives cooked it for their husbands and sons.

'Don't you worry about that, I'll do it,' Mrs Mallow said.

'But I'm his wife now. It's my duty to cook it.'

'Look, Kate, I've been cooking his rice pudding all his life, I'm not going to stop now,' she said, busying herself with bowls and ingredients. 'He'll notice the difference.'

I was incensed but tried not to show it. 'I know mine won't be as good as yours, but Tom is my husband and it's a wife's job.'

She ignored me and just went about making the pudding. I didn't want bad feeling between us, so decided to wait and talk to Tom about it when we were in bed. He'd back me up. I just had to bide my time.

I needed to get away from her. If I went up to our bedroom it would look childish, so the only place was the privy. 'I'm going down the back,' I said politely.

All of us spent a good while in the privy to get some space and read and relax, so she didn't express any surprise when I didn't return for half an hour.

'All right?' she asked as a peace offering.

'Yes, thank you,' I said over politely.

'Get the bath down, would you please,' she asked equally over polite. 'I'll get the water on.'

I had wanted to prepare Tom's bath too. It was my job, but I didn't argue. I would talk to Tom tonight.

When Tom came home, he opened the front door and shouted he was home. I rushed to the door and my love surged as I saw the huge grin on his black-encrusted face peering around the doorway. He stepped just inside and I took his jacket from his outstretched arm and put it onto the newspaper laid on the floor for his dirty clothes.

'I shook it out before I came in,' he said.

I winked as I said, 'Good boy. Let's start our married life as we mean to go on.'

'I'm all for that, and my next trick is . . .' He undid his shirt buttons, slowly, smiling at me all the time.

'What's taking you so long?' Mrs Mallow shouted from the kitchen. 'Your rice pudding's getting cold.'

'Sod the rice pudding,' Tom said quietly to me, still smiling as he started to undo his trouser buttons.

Mrs Mallow appeared at the end of the dark passageway. She was outlined by the light of the room behind her so we couldn't see her face. 'Get undressed quick now. Your bath is ready and I haven't got all day.'

'But, Mam, Kate will help me with my bath now. She's my wife, it's her job,' Tom said confidently.

She walked towards us and crossed her arms over her ample chest like a challenge. 'And who decided that? I wasn't consulted.' She looked from Tom to me and back to Tom. 'Am I to be part of this family or not?'

'Oh, Mam, of course you are, but things have to change now that Kate's here.'

She looked daggers at me. She didn't like any of this. But what did she expect? Things had to change.

She took me by surprise as she said, so sweetly, 'Tom love, like I said, no one asked me and if they had I would have said that I have given you your bath since you were a baby and helped you with your bath since you were a boy collier. Your father would turn in his grave if I gave that duty to another woman. It's my job to scrub your back and rinse you off.'

'But, Mrs Mallow,' I interrupted, 'I helped my mother bath my father and my aunties with their husbands. I want to help Tom too. He's my husband now.'

She bristled. 'That may be so, but he's still my son and that will never change.'

She looked at me as if she thought I'd not be his wife for long. I was starting to feel panicky as I realised this was not a fight for who did Tom's bath but for which woman would be boss in this house. This was one fight I couldn't lose. I looked at Tom pleadingly and his mother gave him a challenging look.

He looked confused and then looked pleadingly at me. He looked at his mother and she smiled. 'Come on, Tom, love. It's only a bath,' she said gently. 'Get those dirty clothes off and come and get clean, dinner is nearly ready.' She walked down the passage, her back straight and her stride full of purpose.

Tom looked at me and shrugged. 'She's right. It's only a bath.'

Tears filled my eyes. 'Tom, please? It's important to me.'

'There's nothing more I can do,' he whispered. 'I don't want a row straight off. She can be very stubborn when she wants. It's not important.'

I watched him take off the rest of his clothes and put them carefully on the newspaper. He smiled at me and either didn't see the tears in my eyes or chose to ignore them. I'd lost round one.

'Get in the bath, Tom bach,' Mrs Mallow said gently and as he settled himself in the hot water she handed him his rice pudding. I watched him scoff it down like a starving dog.

Mrs Mallow turned to me. 'Go get his clothes from the passage, there's a good girl, while I take care of Tom.'

I swallowed down my fury. 'But . . . but,' I was getting tongue-tied, 'I'm Tom's wife so I should be washing him and you should be taking care of his clothes,' I challenged. I couldn't give up without a fight.

She drew herself up to her full height, which was a couple of inches taller than me. 'Look, as I said, I've washed Tom since he was a baby and I've no intention of changing now. Wife or not, I'm mistress in this house. Go and get his clothes and take them out the back.'

My heart was pumping fit to burst. She'd never spoken to me like that before – and in front of Tom too. Anger flew through my body until I started to shake. I wasn't having this.

'Tom?' I said.

He didn't respond.

'Tom, please tell your mother our plans. I'm going to wash you and take care of you when you come home. Cook your rice pudding and everything. We decided.'

He turned his head and looked at me, his eyes pleading. 'I'm sorry,' was all he said.

I felt betrayed. Had I married a man or a mouse? How could anyone change in such a short time? He wanted me to help him wash as much as I did. I was well aware that Tom's reasons were different to mine, he was a man after all, but for me, it was about sharing intimate moments like a husband and wife should, to have silly secrets and behave like juveniles, at least until the novelty wore off. I wanted to be a real wife to him, and to me, real wives took care of their husband's baths. It was a matter of pride. Tom paid the rent and was the man of the house and that made me the woman of the house, not his mother. This was our marriage and I should be the most important woman in his life. I had superseded his mother, or at least, I should have. It was a matter of dividing the roles and the pecking order.

The two of them looked at me, Tom pleadingly and his mother challengingly.

'I see,' I said to Tom, 'so that's the way it is, is it?'

His pleading look didn't change as he looked down into the blackening water, remaining silent.

I had no choice but to collect his filthy clothes and take them out the back. I hid my tears until I was outside and pegged his clothes to the washing line. I was furious as I picked up the clothes' beater and thrashed those clothes so hard, it frightened

134

me. I would speak to Tom when we were alone.

*

As we got into bed, Tom, all nice and clean from his bath and his belly full of dinner, tried to kiss me but I pushed him away.

'Tom,' I said.

'What is it?' he whispered.

'You know what it is,' I whispered back so that Mrs Mallow, in the next bedroom, wouldn't hear. 'Why didn't you stick up for me when your mother took over your bath? You should have done.' Annoyingly, tears rose up.

'I'm very sorry, Kate, my lovely Katie,' he said trying to cuddle me. I pushed him away again.

'You have to answer me. Why? Just tell me why? I don't understand. I'm your wife now. I'm your first priority. Not your mother.'

'But it's not a big thing. We couldn't have done anything anyway. She made it obvious she wasn't going to leave us alone. We'll have our nights together. That will be our time, we don't need bath time. It's not nice anyway, all that filthy water, it's best this way. She'll be happy and we have our nights together.'

He sat up and the moonlight shone through the thin curtains onto his face and muscled body. He looked so handsome.

I sat up too and he looked at me in the moonlight and stroked my cheek. 'Kate, please. I know you're disappointed, but it's only a small thing.'

I tried not to show my anger. 'You might call it small, but it's a battle between us over you. I can see that so clearly . . . and I lost the first round. I wouldn't call that a small thing.'

'Oh, Katie, please understand. It's hard for her to adjust. She's always been in charge, even when my dad was alive, she was the boss. We didn't mind, my dad was happy about it, anything for a peaceful life was his motto.'

'And you're going to be like him? Weak?'

Tom's silence made me realise I'd overstepped the mark. He glared at me. 'Don't you ever talk about my father like that. He was *not* a weak man as you put it. He was brave, braver than

135

you will ever know. He loved my mother, he wanted to please her and if that was how to please her, he was happy. Don't you ever talk about him like that again.'

I took hold of his hand. 'You're right. I'm sorry. I'm very upset, that's all. I never knew your dad, I'm sorry, Tom.'

He smiled and put his arm around my shoulders. 'It's all right. I understand your feelings, but please try to understand my mother's. As time goes by, she'll get used to us as husband and wife, you'll see. She'll settle down. You don't want to make an enemy of her do you? It would make life very difficult for all of us. Have patience. We have to win her around, not go against her.'

'Oh, Tom, I don't know how we do that. If we give way to her she'll be encouraged.'

'Well, lovely girl, I'm caught in the middle of you both. I love you, you know that. But I also love my mother. She saved me, gave me a good life after my father disowned me. I owe her everything. She made so many sacrifices for me. I can't go against her in such a small thing.' He looked at me. 'I just want a peaceful home life. I get enough aggravation at work. I don't need it at home. What do you want, harmony or upset?'

'I want your support,' I answered, frustrated. 'You're my husband now. It should be us against the world.'

'Families should stick together. It's family against the world.'

I could see he didn't understand my point of view, so I snuggled down and turned my back on him. He went to sleep well before me. I lay there and wondered if I'd made a mistake. Did Tom see my acquiescence as acceptance of his mother's dominance over me – I didn't fight for it so it can't be important? But I didn't know what else to do. We were at the beginning of our marriage and I didn't want to cause bad feeling. I was young, inexperienced in such matters, and if I'm honest, I was afraid of his mother. She was so confident and a powerful figure. She had authority and I always respected authority, it was the way I was brought up. I didn't know how to counteract it.

But I did win a considerable victory over her through her own fault. It was at the end of Tom's first week in work as a married man and I was expecting him to give me his wages. He came in as usual and was stripping off in the passageway. Before he took off his trousers, he delved in his pocket and took out his wages. Two ten shilling notes and a few coppers. He hesitated as his mother came down the passageway and then offered it to her. I was furious. She took it without comment and walked back to the kitchen. 'Tom!' I hissed. 'How could you give your wages to your mother? I'm your wife!'

He looked sheepish as he struggled out of his trousers, trying to keep the coal dust from flying everywhere. 'I had too. She'd been taking my wages since I started work and took my father's before. It's what we always do.'

Before I could answer she yelled from the kitchen, 'Come on you two, I haven't got all day. I've got a nice surprise for you, Tom.'

He shrugged his shoulders in that way I was beginning to hate, and walked off to the kitchen. I picked up his dirty clothes and as I approached the kitchen I heard Tom say, 'God, mam, you've lit the fire. It's only August, mun.'

'I know, Tom,' she said as I walked through the kitchen, 'but it's cold and windy today, even though it's August. I thought I'd give you a nice treat. You deserve it.'

I noticed she put the ten shillings notes on the mantelpiece with the coppers next to them.

As I went out the back with Tom's clothes my anger increased as I realised she was toadying up to him. As I put Tom's clothes over the line ready to beat them, the coal dust was blowing up in the wind and into my face and I got overtaken by a bout of sneezing. I opened the back door to get a hankie at the very same time our next door neighbour opened the front door, calling, 'Hello, Mrs Mallow, it's only me, Mrs Jones.' The two doors opening at the same time in that strong wind exacerbated the through draft and blew the two ten shilling notes from the mantelpiece and into the fire. Tom leap out of his bath.

'No, Tom,' his mother shouted, but it was too late, his hands went in the fire and he pulled out the badly burned notes.

Mrs Jones had come in by this time and had seen what had happened. She was carrying a jug of ginger ale she had made and was a gift for Mrs Mallow. Her quick thinking by throwing the contents over Tom's hands saved him from a lot worse than he got and put out the flames on the money. I took what was left of the notes from him as his mother rushed him out the back to the tap and ran his hands under the cold water.

'Get a bowl and fill it with cold water,' she shouted to me. I filled it and shouted that it was ready.

She poked her head around the door. 'That's it, Kate. Put it on the table, far end.' She nodded to the place. She brought him in and sat him on a chair, covering his nakedness with a towel. 'Put your hands in there, Tom, love. Keep them under the water for fifteen minutes. You'll be better then.'

I could see it hurt him but he didn't say anything, Miners never do. They are used to discomfort and injury and their pride makes them shrug off things that would floor a lot of people. So, he just sat there with his hands in the water. Miners' hands are tough, tougher than old boots many say, and that saved Tom from serious burns. He had sore hands for a while, but that was all.

He went down to town the next day to visit the bank. He told them the story and showed them his damaged hands and what was left of the notes. They believed him and gave him two replacement notes. But from that day onwards, he gave his wages to me. Serve his mother right for toadying I thought.

*

Life settled down to a routine. Mrs Mallow and I divided up the jobs around the house to her liking. She cooked, I washed up. She dusted and tidied whilst I swept the floors and beat the rag mats. I hung them on the washing line in the small back garden and beat them with my wooden beater until all the dust flew away. The mats were cathartic in a way as I imagined they were Dudley and every beat I gave was a bull's eye on Dudley's head as I smashed it to smithereens. I knew then that I wanted to kill him: I was capable of killing him. And more dangerously, I didn't care. He was festering inside me.

Mrs Mallow cleaned the kitchen, and I, in my lowly status, the privy. But I didn't mind because it got me out of the house. It was at the end of the garden and I could take my time in cutting up the newspapers we used for toilet paper into neat squares and putting them on the spike that was screwed into the door. On Fridays I scrubbed the wooden toilet seat with carbolic soap and vinegar. It was a large piece of pine, long and wide with a chamfered hole cut into it, made comfy by bottoms on countless visits. I loved that toilet. It was my place of solitude and I was in charge of it. Every day I brushed the pan until it shone. I made sure there was always a candle, some matches and a library book in there. You could sit there and rest your back on the wall in great comfort as you enjoyed your book. We were connected to sewage pipes, thank goodness, but we had no flush, so I made sure the bucket of water used to flush it was always filled up and ready for use. When we were doing our ablutions at the outside tap every morning, we caught the waste water in a bucket. We prided ourselves on keeping clean – we may have been poor, but we didn't smell. We stripped off for a good wash outside and only ever washed indoors in warm water when it was icy. Then, we all had to use the same bowl of water as it was too expensive to heat up that freezing water more than once. Therefore, we all stuck to washing outside until the weather turned us blue.

Dudley came to the house every Sunday for dinner and stayed until the early evening. He never looked happy to be with us and I wondered why he bothered until I realised it was his way of annoying us. None of us wanted him there, but Mrs Mallow said he had a right to come and so he did. I think she felt guilty about him. I remembered her telling me she thought she'd let him down when he was a child and loved Tom more. I suppose this was her way of trying to make it up to him.

I always tried to keep out of his way, keep close to Tom, but he'd take every chance to speak dirty to me if he could get away with it without anyone else overhearing. He'd whisper, 'How's your love life, Kate? I bet that Tom is a softy in bed.

You need a real man. I'm always free whenever you need my services.' And when he was in a bad mood, he'd colour it with crude words that he knew embarrassed me. If I could have stuck a knife in his cold, spiteful heart I would have. If Tom saw Dudley whispering to me, he'd glare and ask later, 'What's he been saying to you? If he upsets you, I'll get him, I swear.'

I would cajole him and say Dudley was just being stupid, trying to work Tom up so that he had an excuse to pick a quarrel. I persuaded Tom he wasn't worth it.

And then, something extraordinary happened.

Mrs Mallow was always over bright during these meals, trying to include Dudley in our chats. One afternoon she said, 'And what have you been doing, Dudley, since I last saw you - anything nice?'

'Well, let me see now. I went to church a few times and helped several old ladies over the road and with their shopping. I gave some money to beggars. I think I might study to become a priest. I can ogle all those lovely young girls who come in to pray, get them alone in the vestry and tell them God wants me to-'

The clatter of Mrs Mallow's chair as she threw it back made me jump as she stormed over to Dudley and slapped him hard across his cheek. 'How dare you,' she said in a low threatening voice I was glad was not directed at me. 'How dare you talk about the Church and to us with such disrespect. You never set foot inside this house again. Get out. Now.'

Shock, and something more flashed into Dudley's eyes. He tried to hide it and it was only fleeting but I saw into his soul during that look. He loves her, I thought. He really, really loves her. He wants her approval. I remembered how upset he became when I threatened to tell his mother about the rape. And then I realised he can't help himself. He can't help the nastiness in him coming out. Tom's right, I thought. He is mad. And then he astounded me.

'I deserved that,' he said softly. He looked up at his mother. 'I really deserved that. I'm sorry, Mam. I don't know what came over me. I'm sorry.' He looked down at his dinner and then up

140

at her again with puppy dog eyes. 'Please forgive me, Mam, I promise to be nice. I don't know what came over me.'

I was shocked to my core. I didn't know he could speak like that. Tom was looking at him with his mouth hanging open.

Mrs Mallow looked at him closely and I could see her anger dissipating.

'Please, Mam,' he said again, still with his puppy eyes pleading.

She looked unsure, but after a while said, 'Well, if you promise. I won't have that kind of talk in this house. You speak respectfully.'

I expected some look of triumph from Dudley, but he smiled at his mother and looked grateful.

Mrs Mallow picked up her chair and sat down to her dinner. She put her hands together and said, 'May the Lord make us truly thankful,' and picked up her knife and fork and started eating. She kept her head down and I risked a look at Dudley. He too, had started to eat again and I caught his eye. I expected to see a look of triumph, but I only saw sadness. Again, it was fleeting before he looked down again. Tom and I exchanged a look of incredulity. What had just happened?

But it didn't last long. Since the rape Dudley had left me alone, and it was blissful. But about three weeks after the row with his mother, he was obviously in a bad mood. He took every opportunity to be particularly obnoxious to me, as if he had something to prove. He knew I'd seen into his soul and he didn't like it one bit. We'd all finished our dinner and I needed to go to the outhouse urgently. I always made a point of staying within touching distance of Tom or Mrs Mallow when Dudley was with us, but sometimes nature gives us no choice. I hurried as quickly as I could but when I came out, Dudley was walking up the garden path towards me. I tried to rush past, but he grabbed hold of my arm.

It was the last straw, I'd had enough. 'If you don't stop pestering me,' I hissed, 'I'm going to tell your mother about the rape. I don't care anymore. You've pushed me too far.'

He paled. 'You dare,' he hissed, 'and I'll make sure you suffer even more.'

'You can't make me suffer anymore than I have. And I've found your weak spot. You love your mother. You want her to love you but you don't know how to make it happen. You're weird. You're not normal. You don't know how to act in a civilised way. There's something cruel and nasty in you. You know it and I know it. Your mother knows it too. She told me.'

He squeezed my arm even harder. 'Let go of me,' I hissed, 'you're hurting me.'

He increased his pressure. 'What did my mother say about me?'

'Leave me alone,' I almost screamed. I tried to keep control through the pain.

'Tell me or I'll make your life unbearable,' he hissed.

His face was inches from mine and I could see no humanity there. I wanted to hurt him as much as he had hurt me. 'Let me go and I'll tell you.' I challenged his look with one of my own. Two can play at this game. I'd discovered his weak spot and would be as hurtful as I knew how to be.

'Tell me and then I'll let you go,' he snarled.

My heart was beating hard and my knees were shaking. 'You squeeze any tighter and I'll scream and then everyone will know everything.' I'd almost reached the point of no return, it was only my love of Tom that stopped me screaming.

His look intensified and then he suddenly let me go. My arm dropped painfully to my side. I pulled myself up to my full height and looked into his eyes. 'Your mother told me,' I said glacially, 'that if she hadn't seen your red hair and screaming, ugly face attached to her cord when you were born, she would not believe you were hers.' Then I added maliciously, 'She said you were born bad and you grew up bad, and she wished you were not her son. That she didn't want you to be hers. That she hated you. That she wished you dead.' She hadn't actually said that in so many words, but hell, he deserved it and I had no qualms in digging in the knife.

Shock was written all over his face. His cold eyes bore into mine in icy disbelief and then turned to hatred. I turned and ran from him as fast as I could. I slowed as I approached the kitchen and Tom opened the door and looked out. 'Oh, there you are. I saw that bastard sneak out and thought I'd better check you were all right.'

'I'm fine, thank you, Tom.' I put my hand on his arm and squeezed it lightly and smiled in an effort to reassure him.

As I stepped inside I said, 'Let me help you with the washing up, Mrs Mallow.' I put on my pinny and picked up the tea towel, busying myself to disguise my shaking hands. After a while, Dudley came back in and closed the door gently. I could see he was furious, but afraid to upset his mother. His face was as white as a new sheet and a huge frown dominated it. His mother's back was to him as she washed up.

'Thanks, Mam,' he said casually, 'must be going. See you next week.'

He glanced at Tom and ignored me as he disappeared through the front door. I felt joy surge through me. I'd found his Achilles' heel and hurt him.

*

Mrs Mallow kept undermining me in all sorts of little ways. We'd got on well enough before the marriage, but now, living together, we rubbed each other up the wrong way. I think she thought things would stay the same but I had my ideas of how Tom and I should live and they were not hers. Tom would tell me what he fancied for his dinner, but Mrs Mallow would say that was not enough for a miner and would prepare him something entirely different. She criticised the way I did the washing, the way I used the iron, I'd not got the best vegetables in the market, I'd let people cheat me, I was a bad shopper. It went on and on. She had her own ways and she wanted me to do the same. She couldn't change – or wouldn't.

I tackled Tom again about it while we were in our bedroom, getting ready for bed. 'She's making my life miserable, Tom. I can't do anything right and she sometimes comes after me and does the job over. She doesn't say anything, but then, she doesn't need to. I can't bear it any more. You have to do something. Help me, Tom. Please help me with this.'

'I can't. You know I can't.'

'I don't know any such thing. I'm your wife. You have to support me.'

He climbed into bed and propped himself up on the pillows. 'Look,' he said as I joined him, 'we've had this conversation before. You know I can't go against her.'

'Why ever not? Why take her side before me, your wife's? I don't understand.'

He ran his hands through his hair and took a deep breath. 'Kate, you know how much I love you. You know that.'

'Well, then, show me. Show me how much you love me. Stick up for me.'

'I can't go against her.'

'You've already said that, and keep your voice down, she can hear you. She's always listening.'

'I think you're being unreasonable. You know my mother's history. You know she took me in when I was a baby. No one else wanted me. She gave me my life, kept me healthy and went without food so that I could eat. She made many sacrifices for me.'

I sighed. 'Many mothers do that. That's their job.'

'She lost her husband and thinks it was her fault. She persuaded him to go to war when he could have stayed here safe in the mines.'

'But he could have died in a pit accident like so many others. And he chose to go and fight. He didn't go just because she pushed him. He had a choice.'

'And then there's Dudley,' he said with emphasis.

'Ah! Dudley! Now maybe we're coming to the point.'

'Look, Kate, she took my side against Dudley many times. She protected me from him. I couldn't have survived without her support. I owe her everything. I love her.'

'More than me: I see.' I was deeply hurt. 'I see how it is. You put your mother above me because you love her more than me.'

'Oh, Kate, I didn't mean it like that. I love you just as much.'

'But not more.'

'This is getting us nowhere. A man loves his mother and his wife, especially a good mother like mine. I think you're being over sensitive. Wives always have to adjust to mothers-in-law. It's the way it is.'

'Yes, and some mothers-in-law take advantage of that.'

'Oh, Kate . . .'

'She doesn't want to give you up. That's what this is all about. She doesn't want you to have a wife, but you're a normal man, you have to have one, she can't change that, so she'll make do as long as she rules. She was all for our marriage before, so maybe she thought she could rule me. Thought I was pliable because I didn't say much and kept to myself. Well, she's got another thing coming. I won't have it, I tell you. I may be pliable on the outside, but inside I'm a fighter. She's just selfish and jealous and can't bear our being happy.'

'You're being unreasonable.'

'Unreasonable! You dare to call *me* unreasonable. How dare you.'

I got down under the blankets and turned my back on him. Dudley and his mother had come between us again and I didn't tell him what I'd been longing to all day. I'd wanted to wait until we were alone. The doctor had confirmed I was pregnant.

CHAPTER FOURTEEN

I took Tom up to the rocking stone a few days later. We sat on it looking out at the town below us, holding hands. 'Do you remember,' he said, 'this is where everything changed for us - this rocking stone.'

I squeezed his hand tighter. 'I always think of it as our place, our special place. It brought us together . . . and now . . . well, I hope it will keep us together.'

He looked at me, quizzically. 'What do you mean? You're scaring me. Keep us together?'

'Yes, my lovely, Tom. Keep us together – and add to our number.'

He jumped off the stone and stood in front of me. 'Y-you mean?'

I was grinning so hard I couldn't speak, so I nodded.

'A baby?' He said in wonder as he looked into my eyes and stroked my hair. 'A real baby?'

I laughed. 'Yes, Tom, a real baby. Our baby.'

Tom's eyes filled with tears. 'God, mun, I'm so proud. Proud of you and yes, I'll say it, proud of me!'

We laughed together and I felt reassured by his obvious love for me.

*

One Sunday a few weeks later, Mrs Mallow and I were in the kitchen getting our things ready for church. We were on the point of leaving when Aunty Annie came crashing through our front door so fast she ended up hitting the staircase before she could stop. We heard the thump and it must have been painful, but she didn't acknowledge it, just shouted, 'Kate, it's

Daddy.' She paused in the open doorway of our kitchen as she took in several lung full's of air and angrily pushed back the hair which had fallen out of her bun onto her face.

'There's been an accident at the pit and he's badly hurt.'

My heart flew into my throat as I gasped. It had come then. The dread every miner's family lives with. Mrs Mallow was the first to react. 'Oh, my God, go quickly, Kate.'

Aunty and I ran for a while, but had to stop before our lungs burst and we developed a half-run, half-walk gait that got us the two miles to the Albion pit. My father always worked on Sundays as that was the only day in the week that the pit was closed. As he was the fireman he had the responsibility of making sure the pit was safe for work the following week and that there was no build up of gas. Make sure the ventilation shafts were working, the pit shafts in good condition, the track and trams serviceable: everything really. It was a very responsible job, but it did mean that he was almost alone underground with only a few men to assist him. Not ideal if something goes wrong.

All sorts of thoughts were going through my mind, most of them denial. It couldn't possibly be true, no, not my dad, he was always so careful, life couldn't be so cruel. I wasn't sure I could cope. No, it would be alright, there was some mistake. A couple of ambulances passed us going in the opposite direction with their bells ringing and we stopped and looked at them as they sped by, but we remained silent. We couldn't even think the unthinkable.

When we got to the entrance of the pit there was a gathering of miners and Aunty shouted out, 'Matt Williams, what's happened to Matt Williams?'

They all turned and looked at us but their eyes slid away quickly. Then the pit manager approached us. 'Mrs Williams, I'm so sorry. Your husband's been involved in an accident underground and has been taken in an ambulance to Cardiff Infirmary.'

I could see Aunty was struggling with her emotions. 'What happened?' I asked. My voice sounded like sandpaper in my dry throat.

The manager looked uncomfortable. He was a tall, thin man, more suited to a vicar than a mine manager. He cleared his throat. 'He was underground doing safety checks with some other men and while they were carrying out these duties, as far as we can gather at this stage, six or seven trams broke loose of their housing and ran into them without warning. Mr Williams was crushed along with a couple of other men. All were seriously injured, but Mr Williams was the worst. I'm so sorry, it was an accident.'

Aunty surprised me by shouting, 'Aye, you look like you're sorry too. How could such a thing happen? Trams don't usually run free unless they weren't secured properly in the first place. Someone should answer for this.'

'Believe me, it was just an accident, Mrs Williams. No one is to blame I'm sure. We'll look into this very thoroughly,' he replied calmly, condescendingly.

This spurred Aunty to shout, indignant, 'Ha! Like you looked into Ben Evans' death last month? Not our fault, just an act of God, you managers said. Act of God my foot. Act of greedy management more like. Your owners want ever more blood out of our men and it's not possible you know. They give you enough already. It's about time you gave something back.'

'Now, now, Mrs Williams, you're upset. That's natural. I'm sure Matt will be very well looked after at the infirmary. We're in touch by telephone; we'll let you know if there's any news.'

I've never seen Aunty give such a withering look of contempt as she turned to walk away. And she shocked me to the core when she turned on her heels and said to him, 'Up yours!'

I'd never heard her say such a thing before. She was always the lady. It knocked the manager too, who paled considerably. Serve him right.

Being a fireman meant my father was an official of the pit, part of management, albeit in a lowly capacity. But unlike most management, he was popular as he always played fair and looked after the men's welfare, both above and below ground. He stuck up for them. He was the only official Tom had time for.

We rushed back to my father's house to get the money for the train to Cardiff. Aunty picked up the tin on the mantelpiece where they kept their money, and looked inside. She knew exactly how much was in there, every wife did, but she made a show of looking. She took out two ten-shilling notes and gave one to me and she took the other. 'That's in case we get separated. You need money in Cardiff. It's not like being in Ponty where people know you.'

I gasped. 'Ten shillings, Aunty? That's too much. We'll never need that much.'

'You never know,' she said as she picked up her coat and handbag. 'It's better to have too much than too little.' I couldn't disagree with that.

'Come on,' she said, 'let's collect your coat and bag and tell Mrs Mallow where we're going.'

*

As we sat on the train, her look of shock and bewilderment touched me to the core. I tried to puff some hope into her. 'He might be all right, Aunty. You know how strong he is. Don't give up hope.' But I knew my words were falling on deaf ears, as she looked at me with hopeless eyes. We both knew what 'seriously injured' meant. It was unlikely he would survive. It was almost more than I could bear. The journey was agony and I hoped against hope. He was a good father and I loved him and I began to regret not seeing him as often as I should have. Since my marriage I hadn't seen much of them as Mrs Mallow had taken against Aunty Annie and there was some animosity there. I think it was because they were both strong women and rubbed each other up the wrong way. So, I went to see them every fourth Sunday to spend the afternoon with them, and sometimes, Tom came too. I loved that, my other new family coming together.

When we got to the hospital we were told that it was all over. He'd died in the ambulance. They wouldn't let us see him, said it was better to see him after the undertakers had done their job.

Aunty said, 'What more can they do to us? Will this misery never end?'

I'd never heard her speak so before and didn't know what to say, so I said nothing. I desperately wanted to cling to her, like I had when I was a child. But I could see that she was only just holding on to her composure so I did no such thing. Our stiff upper lips clashed like gladiators and kept us apart.

When we got back, to my surprise, Mrs Mallow was waiting on Ponty station for us. When she heard the news, she hugged me. This was the first time we had been so intimate with each other. I smelt the lavender she kept in her wardrobe on her clothes and carbolic soap. Our brief hug was followed by her strong hands gripping my shoulders as she gave them a little pat and nodded her head.

Then she put her arms around Aunty and hugged her close. I'd never seen her do such a thing before and was deeply moved. Aunty burst into sobs and clung to Mrs Mallow like a distraught child to its mother. I was envious. I wished I'd had the courage to do that to Aunty.

I hated the Albion Pit. It had ended the life of my grandfather in the pit explosion and now it had got my father.

*

The day of his funeral was warm and fine. I walked with Tom and Mrs Mallow in our black funeral clothes as we made our way through the streets and down the steps at the end of Graig Street. When we got to the bottom we continued descending as we went carefully down the steep, damp steps of the gully between the houses and the chapel. This was a short cut to Rickards Street where my father lived and we walked along it in silence. But as we rounded a corner we stopped in mid-stride as we saw what lay ahead. It took my breath away and Mrs Mallow gasped. In the distance there must have been more than a hundred miners gathered around my father's house, all dressed in their funereal black. Black suits, ties, waistcoats, bowler hats and shoes with the only relief being their sparkling white shirts. Every miner had funeral clothes, no matter how poor.

My father was a man of principle and mining was his life. He had often fought with management against cutting corners to speed up extraction. He couldn't be bought and was respected and admired by both sides. I knew many a miner who'd come through the ranks like my father and been promoted to an official, who let this new power go to his head. Shouting at men from across the street, 'Make sure you're not late again, Jones. You'll be in trouble if you are.' Shouting out this kind of thing, and worse, when the poor man was walking with his mates, or devastatingly, with his family. It was disgraceful. But my father concentrated on building up a man's self-worth and confidence. Making him feel he mattered and letting him know that he would fight for his welfare. Men were rarely late for him. And now they were showing their respect.

A haze of smoke hovered above them like a cloud, as, almost to a man, they smoked roll-your-own-cigarettes, or puffed on pipes, and waited silently. With them, at least another one hundred people had gathered, making sure they kept separate from the miners. He belonged to many societies and organisations around the town and I realised just how popular my father had been. You could have heard a pin drop.

Tom let out a long breath, 'I'll be,' he said. I could see he looked as proud as I felt. The men all took their hats off as we passed them, saying nothing, but they didn't need to.

As Tom and Mrs Mallow went into the house, I saw Davy standing alone and apart from the others and went up to him. 'Come into the house with us, Davy love. He was your father too.'

'No, I won't thanks.' He looked upset. 'I want to be here, but alone. I can't come in with Aunty being there.' I kissed him on the cheek and hugged him for the first time in years. That set him off and he started to cry. He was always an emotional boy, took things too hard I always thought. 'I loved him,' he said. 'I'm sorry I was such a disappointment to him.'

'Oh, Davy, you weren't, I know you weren't. You mustn't

think like that.'

'I wasn't worthy of him, I know that. He hated everything about me.'

'No, he didn't. He loved you. I know how upset he was when you left home.'

'But he only came to see me once after that,' he said, wiping his eyes with the back of his hand and sniffing. 'If I bumped into him at the pit, he'd say, "Hello, how are you then?" And he'd walk on.' He took out his hankie and blew his nose. 'I didn't want . . . oh, God, what a mess it all is, Kate. I was a disappointment to him and I couldn't make it better.' He blew his nose again. 'My family is with Mrs Richards now. But I want to say goodbye properly, so I'll just follow on at the back. Don't worry about me. I'm fine. Please just go in and forget about me.'

I hesitated.

'Please go in, it's the way I want it to be.'

'Oh, Davy bach how I wish our mother hadn't died. It would have all been so different then.'

'I know,' he said, putting his arm around my shoulder, 'and I also know how hard you had it with our relations when we were little. You had it harder than me. I remember, Kate.' He smiled and kissed me on the cheek. 'I remember what went on and I'm so sorry.'

I squeezed his hand and a look of love passed between us that had been lost somewhere along the line. I'll treasure that look.

'I'm sorry too, Davy, you know that.' I hesitated, unsure if this was the right time to tell him.

'What? What is it?'

I smiled. 'You always knew when I needed to say something . . . well, I'm not sure this is the best time to say this, but sometimes good news goes with the bad.'

I hesitated again and his eyes were very soft as he looked into mine.

'Well, I'm expecting,' I blurted out.

His face lit up with a huge smile. 'That's marvellous, yes,

marvellous news. I'm so happy for you and Tom. Dad would have been proud. Yes, so proud of a grandchild. I'm glad you told me, Kate. It makes a difference to my feelings about today. His grandchild will follow his hearse. If he's looking down on us now, I'm sure he's smiling.' He kissed me again on the cheek and we hugged and clung to each other like we did when we were little.

And then the hearse arrived and we parted. 'I have to go now,' I said wiping my tears. He nodded and I kissed him again and rushed into the house to tell Aunty that Dad was here.

I found her among a bevy of distant relations and close friends. I held her coat out for her. 'He'd be proud at the turnout,' I said. She took my arm as we made our way to the front door, where she stopped me by putting her hand on mine.

'How are you, Katie love? You sure you're up to all this in your condition?'

'I'm fine, Aunty. Don't worry about me. I'll tell you if I'm not.'

She nodded and I opened the front door and she stepped outside.

'My God,' she said, stopping suddenly. I'd assumed she knew of all the people gathered outside. 'My God,' she repeated. 'Oh, Matt, Matt.' She buried her face in her hankie and sobbed. I gently led her to the official car we had hired for our immediate family.

The hearse was parked directly outside the house and my father's coffin was covered with so many wreaths it was difficult to see it. I knew people had gone without to buy these wreaths and it touched me deeply.

The miners had lined up in front of the hearse, two abreast, like soldiers, with their straight backs, jackets done up, bowler hats squarely on their heads, and their black shoes shone like mirrors glistening in the sunlight. They stood higgledy-piggledy, mates with mates, tall and short all mixed up together. I realised just how respected my father was for miners don't turn out in such numbers, and on parade, for just anyone.

When we were ready, the miners started marching slowly in front of the hearse. I'll never forget their backs, for that was all I could see, walking ahead like ramrods. The hearse, all black and gleaming like polished coal, followed them, with our car behind and the rest of the mourners walking behind us.

It must have been a sight to behold as the long procession made its way down Rickards Street into Wood Road and followed it down to the Catholic church, then round and up into Cemetery Road. The car windows were open a little and all I could hear was the tramp of feet on the road. A discordant, reassuring, incredible noise that sent goose-pimples throughout my body and filled me up with such emotion I don't know how I didn't burst. Aunty spent the journey grimly looking ahead with a body so tense I wonder she didn't break. She held my hand so hard, it hurt for days afterwards.

It took us about half an hour to get to the cemetery, and in all that way, no one spoke a word that I could hear. As we passed people in the street they stopped and stared, men took off their hats and Catholics crossed themselves.

Ponty hadn't seen a funeral like this, for one man, in a long time. I was deeply touched and it sent shivers of pride and excitement through me that I belonged to such a society: one that can put on such a show for one of their members. Not someone important – just my father, a man respected.

*

It was a few weeks later that the backlash came. It was all about Aunty. She got her statutory compensation for my father's death and made the decision to move back to Tonypandy, which she did quickly and without fuss.

Tom was furious, 'She's buggered off and left you then,' he said spitefully, 'fine stepmother she is'. Actually, Aunty had confided in me but asked me not to tell anyone. She said she'd had a good marriage and that my father was a fine man. She didn't regret anything. But that life was now past. Davy was lost to her and I belonged to another family, one where she wasn't welcome. She said she'd been a valley girl before her marriage and was always uncomfortable in the largeness of Ponty. She wanted to return to the valleys where she had some relations and the smaller town life felt more comfortable to her. We both agreed that this was the best course of action for her. She'd offered me half of the compensation, but I'd refused it, knowing that she needed it more than me. I had Tom to look after me, she had no one now. Only my father's compensation and her widow's pension to last the rest of her life. She knew she'd never marry again she said. I wished her luck and promised to visit whenever possible.

'She should have given you something, a few pounds from his compensation, after all, he was your father,' Tom said.

I didn't tell him I had refused her offer on the compensation money. He would never have forgiven me for not taking it so I held my tongue. I owed her so much – everything really. I needed to give her something back for my own satisfaction. That was more important than the money to me.

I thought of my parents being united again in death. They'd been apart for so long but I know he never forgot my mother. I could see it in his face. He'd kept the two pictures of Italy, the ones my mother loved so much and had them on his bedroom wall, as my mother did. Aunty Annie knew of their history and gave them to me. I put them on my bedroom wall, opposite my side of the bed. I don't think Tom even noticed.

CHAPTER FIFTEEN

It was when I was seven months pregnant, that our lives changed forever. Dudley had been even more obnoxious to me and he'd started to "bump into" me several times a week. Every day I had to go into town to shop, down the Graig Hill, finding its steepness more difficult with each passing month. I often had to stop to recover my breath. Dudley would suddenly appear from around a corner or an alleyway and say things like, 'Why, Kate, darlin', nice to see you. How's the little baby? Are you going to call him Dudley? We had such a good fuck, Kate. What will Uncle Tom say when he sees the baby's red hair? I'm sure it's mine.'

'Bugger off, Dudley,' I'd hiss and was angry with him again for forcing me to use the words of the gutter for it was the only language he took notice of.

He'd often walk next to me and whisper things like, 'Fuck me, Katie. No one will know. You're already pregnant. I'm yearning for you, my dick's hard even thinking about it. Come on, Kate, let's do it again.'

It was like a Chinese torture with his non-stop barrage of abusive language and suggestion. I was stuck between Tom and Dudley like a butterfly caught in a net. The more I struggled the deeper I was caught up. It was a living nightmare that made me angry and upset until, finally, Tom noticed.

It was a cold spring and I was uncomfortable with the baby who kicked forcefully inside me. I'd panic and think, it couldn't be Dudley's, could it? Then I'd tell myself not to be silly, I'd had my monthly before the wedding.

Tom and I were sat in the kitchen drinking tea, him in his armchair and me on an uncomfortable kitchen chair, having yet another row. Our relationship had deteriorated over the past few months. I felt powerless and trapped in Dudley's family, unable to avoid him, and by Mrs Mallow always being there. I was not adjusting to my new life well.

'Keep your voice down Tom,' I pleaded. Your mother will hear us, she's only upstairs.'

'No, she's not. She went out to her church meeting when you were out the back, but quite frankly, I'm fed up of always having to talk in whispers. This is my house, I'm the man here and I'll talk as loud as I like. And I'll love my wife as loudly as I like too.'

I kept hold of my mounting irritation. The baby kicked hard and I put my hand over my stomach. 'Then we won't love each other ever again, because I can't bear your mother listening in from the other side of the wall. It's embarrassing and I can't face her next morning. She looks at me sideways in that way of hers. She doesn't like it, she's jealous. She resents me being with you. She wants you for herself.'

'For God's sake, you're being silly.'

'I'm not,' I snapped. 'She undermines me every way she can and I don't know what to do about it.' I so wanted Tom to understand how I felt. 'Help me, please. I'm so unhappy.' I despised the pleading in my voice.

He turned on me. 'What do you mean unhappy? Are you sorry you married me? Is that it? Is that what this is all about? Why, Kate? Why?' He stared into space with a big frown on his face. 'We were so happy before we married and now it's all changed, you've changed. You're not the girl I married. Is it me? Don't you love me anymore?'

I was shocked by his words. Did he really feel like that? 'Oh, Tom, of course I love you. This is difficult for me to say . . . but . . . I can't get close to you. You work so hard and when you come home you go out drinking with your mates, or mope and argue with me. You always take your mother's side in everything. I feel like an intruder who's coming between you.'

'Don't be ridiculous. It's all in your mind.'

'It's not, please believe me. She's trying to take me over, and

157

I don't know how to stop her without a big quarrel, and where would that leave us? I don't want to lose you, but I feel like I am. I'm losing you to your mother and you don't mind. You never stick up for me and always take her part.'

Tom stiffened as he clutched the arms of his chair and his knuckles turned white. 'How dare you talk about my mother like that. She's been very good me – and to you. You sound ungrateful and I don't like that. It's not nice.'

'Of course I'm grateful to her, but she's always here. She does your bath and washes your back. She knows I don't like it, don't like her seeing you naked and that's why she does it. It's power over me.'

'Now you're being stupid. We're a mining family. Women always help their husbands and sons to take their bath. It's just practical. You don't expect us to come home from the pit, exhausted and get out the bath, boil the water, fill it and lounge and relax with soap suds and perfume like Lady Muck do you? We need to get in and out as fast as possible, get our dinners and some kip and get on with the little time we have above ground.'

I was getting more upset; he was deliberately misunderstanding and patronising me. I tried again but it came out all wrong. I was shouting when I didn't want to shout. I knew I was losing control but couldn't stop. 'She wants to keep you to herself and shut me out – and she's succeeding. She hardly ever goes out, I can't be alone. If I decide to go for a walk she comes too, "To keep you company," she always says. She's wearing me down, even more than Dudley is.'

My breath caught as I realised what I'd said. I looked at the floor, wishing I could bite back those words. Tom was silent and I dared not look at him. He was motionless and I could feel the intensity of his stare.

To my horror, I began to shake. Gently at first, but soon my hands and legs shook uncontrollably. I started to cry, big gulping sobs that took me by surprise. I was out of control. All the trauma, fear and dread of the last year overcame me as my world collapsed.

158

I don't know how long I sat and sobbed but it seemed eternal. I felt ashamed that I couldn't control myself. It had never happened to me before. I felt like another person, someone I didn't know.

I was very aware of Tom. He hadn't moved at all. Finally, as I started to calm, he said in an ice-cold voice, 'What's going on between you and Dudley?'

I gasped, I couldn't help it.

'I know there's been something. I told myself that there was nothing to it. That you wouldn't do that to me, but now I wonder. Tell me Kate. TELL ME!'

'Nothing!' I yelled. 'Nothing has been going on.'

He shot out of his chair. 'Don't lie to me,' he said as he paced up and down. 'I know when you're lying. There's been something. I can feel it in my bones. That bastard would do anything to get back at me, even steal my own wife if he could. Is that what's been happening? Is he stealing you away from me? Because if he is I'll kill him.' He stood over me, threateningly.

My head was spinning, my body shaking. I'd lost the ability to think straight.

'No, Tom, please. It's not like that. I would never let Dudley near me if I had the choice.'

A silence hung.

'What do you mean . . . if you had the choice?' His voice was icy. 'Tell me before I knock it out of you.' He had never spoken to me like that before and I was scared. I tried to gather my wits. I couldn't let him discover the rape.

'I swear to you, nothing has been going on. It's just Dudley being Dudley. He just speaks dirty to me whenever he has the chance and it upsets me.'

That silence again.

'What do you mean, whenever he has the chance?' His voice was rising in anger. 'When does he have the chance? Do you give him the chance?'

'No. No. No. Never!' My brain was spinning.

'Well, there must be times when he gets the chance otherwise

159

he can't say those things to you.' His aggression made me scream my innocence as he probed with his words. Determined to get whatever it was out of me.

Without warning, he changed tack and went down on his knees in front of me and put his arms around me saying whatever had happened was not my fault. Whatever it was, he didn't blame me.

His sudden change of tactics fooled me into relaxing and I felt my old Tom was back, the way he was before our marriage when I could say anything to him.

'You don't know Dudley as well as I do,' he said.' 'You don't realise what he's capable of.'

The words came out unbidden, before I realised I'd uttered them.

'I do know.'

'What do you know, Kate? What do you know about Dudley?' He kept his voice soft and caring. 'Tell me. It's all right, cariad. Nothing can harm you. You're my wife. But I must know, I must put my mind at rest. Please tell me, it would be better to tell me because it can't be any worse than what I'm imagining. Please tell me.'

His caring and sympathy went straight to my core. The strain of everything overcame me and, without warning, the words burst out: uncontrollable, unstoppable.

'He raped me!' I whispered.

'He what?' Tom said, equally quietly.

I couldn't look at him. I had no way out of this but the truth. 'He raped me. Three weeks before our marriage he came into my house when I was alone and raped me. He said he told you that he would f-f . . .' I forced out the word, 'fuck me before you did. He was going to ruin me for my husband. That's what he told me and that's what he did.'

I glanced at Tom then, and saw his disbelieving look turn into deep anger. I could see his mind working its way through the events in the lead up to our marriage. Small sparks of memory developing into an understanding. His face turned dark. He finally realised I was telling the truth. The facts fitted.

He stood up slowly, and walked away from me. He turned and stared at me with such a look I felt the devil had surfaced.

'Is the baby Dudley's?' He asked in a quiet, cold voice.

I gasped. 'No, thank God. It's your baby Tom. I had my monthly after the rape and before our wedding. There's no way it can be Dudley's.'

He didn't know whether to believe me or not. I could see his chest heaving. I tried to pacify him. 'Please believe me, it's your baby. It's yours, I promise you.'

'Did he hurt you?' He asked it so quietly, I hardly heard him. I looked down at the floor and couldn't stop the tears flowing as my sobs came back. I was broken. My spirit crushed. I realised then that I was just an ordinary woman who'd tried to be strong and not let things cower her but there is only so much one person can take. I think I could have kept control of myself if Tom had ranted and raved at that moment: shouted and been abusive. I could have used that as my crutch to prop me up and continue in my world of living apart from everyone else. Of not letting them see my weaknesses, of pretending that I was happy and contented. Suddenly, all that broke like a mirror crashing to the floor and my real image, behind the mirror, was laid bare for all to see. Especially to Tom, for he looked at me then with new eyes. The love he had for me had been stripped away. His eyes were cold and rage was developing in them.

But he kept his voice low and quiet. 'I want you to tell me all about it, Kate. How did it happen? What did he do to you? I must know for my own sanity. Tell me everything. Don't leave anything out. I need to know. Please do this for me.'

'I can't,' I pleaded. 'Please don't make me live it again. I've tried so hard to bury it. I couldn't bear to live it again.'

'Kate, for God's sake, it can't be as bad as the terrible thoughts I'm thinking. Please tell me.' He walked up and down the kitchen like a caged tiger. Finally, he looked out of the window with his back to me. 'You didn't . . . you didn't . . . *like* it did you?'

His words hung in the air, spiteful and barbed.

How could he think such a thing? Does he not know me

at all? Is there so little understanding between us? I knew that comment was the end of us. I couldn't forgive him thinking of me like that. He had no real understanding of who or what I was. He saw only his image of me.

'How dare you say that to me,' I screeched. How could you think such a thing, let alone say it?'

He turned around fast and faced me. 'You haven't denied it,' he accused.

In a fury, I flung myself at him and hit him on the chest with my fists, screaming, 'No. No. No. I did not enjoy it. It was hell. I've lived in hell ever since.'

Tom held me at arm's length, looking at me intently. I pleaded with my eyes. I had to make him understand.

'He ruined my life,' I sobbed. 'He ruined me for you. He took away everything I had to give you. My virginity and the tenderness I felt for you. It was all taken away before I had the chance to give myself to you. I couldn't do that afterwards, Tom. I curled my emotions into a tight ball protected from everything. I can't uncurl those emotions because I think I would kill Dudley if I did. I want to kill him. And that frightens me. Sometimes I wish I had never met you because then I would not know Dudley. He would not have come into my life and ruined it.'

Tom pushed me away and started to pace again. 'That bastard has ruined everyone's life. I swear to you, I'll find him and kill him.'

'Tom, please no. Don't do it. He's not worth it. I can't lose you, you're my husband and we're about to have a child. Think of the child. Oh, please, think of the child.'

He pushed me to one side and I fell awkwardly against the kitchen chair trying to protect the baby. By the time I righted myself the front door had slammed and I could hear Tom running down the street.

I sat on the chair and sobbed. My struggle for happiness had come to this. Our marriage was ruined, we couldn't mend this breach. I felt desperately sorry for Tom, for the baby to come, and for me. So I curled my ball of emotions even tighter, pushing it into the back corner of my inner-most feelings. I needed to keep control because I knew one thing: I couldn't let Tom find Dudley.

CHAPTER SIXTEEN

I threw my coat on and rushed out into the early evening air, as best my huge belly would allow. It was cold and fresh and the air smelt sweet and I thought how strange was that sweetness in the midst of my anguish. I searched for a couple of hours and forced myself into each pub I passed – just in case Tom was there. I frantically hoped he would be, as it would mean that he wasn't looking for Dudley. But it was a fool's errand and I finally went home and started to prepare some supper for Tom and his mother, thinking that something ordinary and mundane would settle my nerves. I was surprised that Mrs Mallow wasn't home yet, but glad too.

She came home later in a quiet mood, saying she'd had a difficult meeting at church and had a headache. She wanted to go to bed without any food. That suited me fine. I waited up for Tom, hoping and hoping that he hadn't found Dudley. It was the only thing left for me to do. Impotency hung from me and sapped my strength.

He finally came home at midnight, brought home by two of his pals, drunk out of his mind: legless. They got him up the stairs and put him to bed, where he snored all night stinking of beer and cigarettes and I remembered my wedding vows, 'For better or worse', so I climbed into bed next to him and tried to sleep. It was a fruitless task as all I did was worry that he had found Dudley and done something terrible to him.

The next morning, I got up and left Tom still snoring. I went downstairs and made a pot of tea. As usual, Mrs Mallow's inner compass worked its magic and she came down two minutes after the tea was made. She looked pale and drawn and I said, 'Are you all right? You don't look well?'

'No, I'm not feeling very well. I think I'm starting a cold or something. But I'll be all right soon, don't worry about me, it's not serious. Let's have a nice cup of tea, that'll put me to rights.' We sat in silence, which was unusual for her, and then she disappeared to the privy.

Tom got up then, coming downstairs with his braces down and his shirt buttoned up all wrong. I jumped on his dishevelled state as an excuse to fuss over him and try to get some sort of rapport going between us after our terrible row. He pushed me away as I tried to fix his shirt buttons and said he had a bastard of a hangover. I poured him some tea as he sat with his head in his hands over the kitchen table. I plucked up the courage to ask, 'Did you find Dudley?' There was no answer, so I asked again, and again.

'I can't remember,' he finally snapped.

'Are you sure?'

'Damn you,' he yelled. 'I told you I can't remember, now leave it, woman. Leave me alone.'

I busied myself by making breakfast, stale bread with a hunk of cheese was all I found in the cupboard, so I made toast with a bit of cheese on the top, and called to Mrs Mallow to come for her breakfast. She appeared shortly afterwards and sat down opposite him. Tom didn't eat a thing and was like a bear with a sore head.

'Where did you go last night?' his mother asked him, none too gently.

He glared at her. 'I told Kate and I'm telling you too, I don't remember last night. I went into the pub and drank my miseries away. Now leave me alone.' I'd never heard Tom speak to his mother in such a dismissive way before.

It was cold and I shivered in my thick dress and cardigan, my feet as cold as the ice that was around Tom's heart. I tried to touch his hand but he pulled it away as soon as he saw what I was about to do. He could remember our quarrel then. I wondered again if he'd found Dudley. He didn't have any new injuries on him that I could see, but then, he was a miner, and miners were always sporting cuts and bruises. I felt so alone, sitting there between those two people who were now my family but were strangers.

Mrs Mallow decided to go back to bed and I was left alone with Tom, who said he was going out and would not be back until the end of his shift tomorrow morning. I didn't try to stop him.

I had to find out about Dudley, so I decided to go to his lodgings and ask if he was there. He wasn't, and that made me worry more. Had Tom found him? And done something awful to him? Did I have a murderer for a husband?

The next few days were a torture and there was no sign of Dudley. Soon, it was Sunday, the day when Dudley came for dinner. I helped Mrs Mallow with the preparations, and she said she'd got some parsnips from town, especially for Dudley as it was his favourite vegetable. I hated them, but I didn't say anything as the wonderful aroma of the meat in the oven and the roast potatoes cooking alongside filled the kitchen. We had meat of some sort on a Sunday. It was always the cheaper cuts and not too much of it as it had to last us for the next few days in various kinds of dishes. It was our best meal of the week and we all looked forward to it.

On Sunday mornings it was my job to scrub the table and kitchen chairs with carbolic soap. Scrub out the grime of a week of coal dust so that they were nice and clean for the Sunday tablecloth and our best clothes. The specialness of Sundays encouraged us all to keep to our best behaviour and added an extra dimension to our special meal.

We waited an hour for Dudley and Mrs Mallow kept our dinner warm on the gas stove. She sat in her armchair and kept looking at the clock on the mantelpiece, uttering every so often, 'Where is he? He never misses his Sunday dinner. There must be something wrong. Why isn't he here?'

'For goodness sake, Mam, leave it,' Tom snapped. He'd been dozing in his armchair but had woken up in a temper. 'Why are you so concerned about him? We're better off without him. Let's start our dinner, I'm starving.'

'No, let's give him a little more time. I know he'll be here. He must have been delayed.'

'Yes, in the pub,' Tom snapped again, getting up and sitting at the table. 'Come on, let's eat.'

'But I've got parsnips, he loves parsnips,' Mrs Mallow said.

'Look, that's enough. We've waited long enough, parsnips or no bloody parsnips.'

We ate our dinner in silence. It was only just warm and dried up and none of us enjoyed it.

'I wonder what happened to Dudley,' Mrs Mallow said as she and I washed up. 'It's not like him.'

I wondered why she was so concerned about him and then realised that she might be thinking the same way as I was. Tom. Had he done something to Dudley?

I tried to hide my concerns so suggested we go to his lodgings to see if he was ill or something, hoping against hope that he would now be there. I'd prefer an ill but alive Dudley to a dead one who my husband may have killed.

'Good idea,' she said. 'I've never known him to miss his Sunday dinner.'

'Shut up about that bastard,' Tom shouted from his armchair.

His mother retaliated. 'Don't use that kind of language on a Sunday, young man. We have standards here and I'll not allow it.'

Tom looked thunderous, but didn't say anymore.

As Mrs Mallow and I approached Dudley's lodgings, we could see his landlady on the doorstep, talking to her neighbour.

'Hello, Mrs Toms,' said Mrs Mallow, 'is Dudley in?'

'No, Mrs Mallow. I haven't seen him for a few days. Sometimes, he stays over with one of his mates but not usually for so long. But I wouldn't worry too much,' she said, laughing, 'he'll turn up, bad pennies always do.'

'Yes, well, you're probably right,' Mrs Mallow said. 'When you see him, please send him up to us so we know he's all right, although why we should worry about him, I don't know. He can take care of himself.' And with that, we made our way back home in silence, lost in our own thoughts.

The night Tom found out about the rape was the last anyone

saw Dudley. Everyone was talking about his disappearance so it was easy to ascertain he'd been drinking in The Clarence pub until about nine 'o clock, saying he was going to The Bunch of Grapes as he'd arranged to meet someone there. He was drunk leaving The Clarence and had bought a half bottle of whiskey to take with him. He never arrived at the Bunch of Grapes. People assumed he'd got himself into trouble again and had decided to make a quick exit. He'd threatened to, 'Get out of this God forsaken hole' many times. Others said someone's husband had found him and beaten him and thrown him in the river. Everyone was glad really, and no one wanted to look for him, especially me, who was convinced that Tom was that husband.

I don't know if it was the ordeal over Dudley, but my baby was three weeks late. Tom came in from work at the end of the third week while I was sitting at the kitchen table with a plate of haddock in front of me. It was my favourite and Mrs Mallow had saved up for it and given it to me as a special treat. She thought I would have a bad time of it soon and needed all my strength. It was sweet of her but I did wonder if she was more concerned for the baby than me. But it did neither of us any good as when Tom came in and smelt the haddock, looked at my plate and then at his mother's and his own plate, which held a hunk of bread and some jam he said in a spiteful voice, 'Oh, it's all right for some, they get haddock for their tea, us working men have to make do with bread and jam.'

I saw red at his selfishness and picked up my plate, haddock and all, and threw it into the grate, shouting, 'I don't want it, go to hell.' With that, I stormed upstairs as quickly as I could and lay on the bed, and within an hour I went into labour as my first baby tried to get born. I was too small for the baby, or he was too big for me, either way, both of us got into a lot of trouble.

Mrs Mallow was my midwife. I didn't want her sharing this intimate moment and putting myself in her power, but I had no choice. A proper midwife was for people with money to spare. We didn't have that luxury. She roped in the next door neighbour to help. Between them, they had ten children, so were qualified by experience alone.

I was in agony and in labour for two days. The baby just wouldn't come. I kept looking at my mother's pictures of Italy on the wall opposite the bed and praying to them to help me. As if they could! I was that desperate.

I was only just conscious and dimly aware of Mrs Mallow saying, 'The baby's in the breech position.' Then the neighbour examined me and agreed. 'We need a midwife,' she said.

Mrs. Mallow told me later that when she told Tom we needed a midwife he insisted on fetching the doctor. 'I don't want my wife and baby to die and hang the cost,' he'd said, running out of the house.

It touched my heart and I couldn't help hoping that the love we once shared was still there, deep down. But even that thought was drowned by the ever worsening pain and the doctor arrived just as I thought I was going to die. I'd settled my own mind to it and I didn't care. I was in agony and just wanted it to end. Two days of it had left me weak and defeated. What did it matter about Dudley? What did it matter about Tom and his dark thoughts? Or even his love – if it *was* still there, that is. I decided then that if I got through this alive I would never let anyone get close to me again. I'd always keep a distance. It was the only way I could cope.

I don't know what the doctor did in my semi-conscious state, but Mrs Mallow told me the baby was pulled out with forceps. I remember the relief as the baby left my body and the doctor saying in a gruff voice, 'Get rid of it. He's dead.'

I lifted my head and just caught sight of Mrs Mallow taking the baby to the dressing table where a drawer was awaiting the birth. I vaguely remember her fiddling over the baby, moving very swiftly and she told me afterwards that she was cleaning out his mouth and nose as fast as she could. She held him upside-down and slapped him several times but the baby stayed silent. She fiddled some more, I couldn't see what she was doing and I wanted to shout to her, 'It might be Dudley's, let it die.' But I couldn't. Poor little thing, it wasn't his fault. Finally, a weak cry came from the baby and the doctor looked over and said, 'It's alive! My God, I thought there was no hope for it.' He went over then and attended to the baby and I passed out. When I came round, the baby was in his drawer, all washed and smelling sweet, looking puckered and pink. Mrs Mallow put him to my breast and he sucked like his life depended on it, which it did of course. As he suckled, I looked at his hair. It was pitch black, just like Tom's, with a little curl on the ends. The relief was so overwhelming, I started to sob. Damn me and my emotions, and in front of Mrs Mallow too. But I couldn't stop and that started the baby off. Mrs Mallow patted me on the shoulder and said, 'There, there. It takes some women that way, don't worry, you'll be alright.' She meant well, and I pulled myself together, thinking it's not Dudley's, it's not Dudley's. I realised then that I hadn't quite believed that it wasn't his. But it wasn't and I was overjoyed.

I named him James, Jim, and to hell with Tom if he didn't like it. He wanted to name a boy Tom, but I wasn't having that. A baby deserves its own identity, not his father's. So Jim it would be. I'd read a book where the hero was called Jim and I'd loved him. To my surprise, Tom didn't demur. When he saw the baby and his black hair he knew, as I did, that it wasn't Dudley's. And love shone out of Tom's eyes once more.

I felt it was my fault the baby had such an unhappy womb to be created in. No wonder he kicked about so much and was reluctant to come into the world. But his sunny nature belied his pre-birth experiences, and although he was not my brightest child, in every other way he was perfect. He wasn't Dudley's. He was mine and Tom's first child.

Even so, my relationship with Tom remained strained and difficult. We lived separate lives and only came together in bed. That was the trouble for Tom still wanted his 'loving' as he continued to call it although loving was the last thing it was. He treated it as if it was a bodily function, like emptying his bowels: a little distasteful but necessary and once attended to dismissed as of no consequence as he rolled over and fell instantly asleep.

There were consequences of course. Over five years, I had four healthy children and three miscarriages. Being pregnant virtually non-stop Mrs Mallow took over, which was part of the problem. She took charge of every baby as soon as it was born and I was lying in. I was malnourished and my milk was too weak for the poor things so she decided to feed them on watered down evaporated milk. It was sweet and sticky and gave those poor babies such upset tummies they became even more malnourished than if I'd been feeding them. In the end, she had to admit that she'd been wrong and she started cooking oats, rice or barley and vegetables and mashing it to a pulp. She'd often chew on a piece of apple and give it to the baby rather than swallow it herself. I hated that, but if I'm honest, she probably saved their lives as I couldn't have cared for them as well as she did because I was constantly pregnant. The fact that none of them died, while around us so many children did, I put down to Mrs Mallow.

We'd had three boys, who I loved dearly, but I so longed for a daughter. My fourth child nearly killed me. I lost consciousness as the baby slid out. The next thing I knew, Mrs Mallow was calling me from afar and then her voice got nearer and nearer as I regained consciousness. She was sat on the wooden chair at the side of the bed gently rocking the baby who was wrapped in a warm, soft blanket. The one we always kept for the babies. 'Your baby is waiting for you,' she said as she got up and put him into my arms. I'd been so weak during the pregnancy I worried about the baby's growth and was surprised to see he was full size. His black, curly hair was just like Tom's. His nose and chin were pure Tom too. I opened his blanket up, needing to make sure he had everything he should have. He had two arms and legs and the right amount of fingers and toes, but then I gasped. I looked up at Mrs Mallow and she nodded and smiled. It was what he didn't have that made me the happiest woman in the world. He wasn't a boy after all – and she was the most beautiful baby girl I'd ever seen – perfect in every way. At last I had a daughter! I looked up at Mrs Mallow again and blinked back the tears that welled up at the same time my smile almost split my face in two. She was looking equally ecstatic as she leaned closer and cooed over her. I vowed then that I wasn't going to lose her to Mrs Mallow, like the boys. My resolve to stay apart from emotions and love melted away as I looked down on my sleeping baby girl. For her, I'd make an exception. I was going to keep her close.

Mrs Mallow had arranged with a neighbour who had given birth a few weeks ago and had plenty of milk, that, if my milk proved to be too thin for the baby then she would help out and feed her as much as she could. But I was determined to keep her mine. So, with nervous fingers, I undid the top of my nightdress and gave my small breast to my Meggie. I'd always known I'd name a daughter Megan. Meggie, Little Meggie. I put her to my breast and she took to it instantly, sucking hard for all she was worth. 'I've got some milk,' I shouted out in excitement. 'I've got some milk.'

Mrs Mallow bent over us and smiled a loving smile. She had wanted a granddaughter too, I could see. I'd have to be very careful to keep Meggie mine.

'We won't need the wet nurse now,' I said. 'I can feed her.'

'Well, we'll see how we go. Your milk may be too weak for her.'

I determined there and then to get back on my feet as soon as possible and sod the laying in. It was old fashioned anyway. I'd heard many a mother say they didn't want to do it anymore. I'd be one of them. I also knew that Little Meggie would have to be our last child. I'd looked at other mothers and realised that it was those very babies that were the cause of many of their problems. Young women with so many kids looked haggard and twice their age. Lots of them died young, worn out with the whip of pregnancy and progeny. I had to do something or end up like them. Tom and I were too fertile. He used to say he had only to take his trousers down and I was pregnant. Well, one can't change nature but you can change relationships.

It was a few months after Meggie was born and one night as I got into bed with Tom he reached out for the first time since the birth to pull me into another loveless embrace. I knew where this was leading so took a deep breath. 'Don't you think it's time we put this kind of thing behind us? It will only result in another child and we can't feed the ones we've got properly. I can't have another child, Tom,' I pleaded. 'I just can't. It will kill me. I'm too weak.'

He paused and then let me go, rolled over and went to sleep. And that was that for the rest of our marriage. We never talked of it of course, and I don't know why he capitulated so easily. I convinced myself that he did it for me. That he did still have some feelings for me, somewhere deep down. It was his way of saying so.

CHAPTER SEVENTEEN

Little Meggie was a year old and doing well even if she was on the small size. One warm day, when the sky was blue and clear and the wind was but a gentle caress, I took Meggie to the rocking stone. We sat there, me with my legs dangling, and Meggie sitting on my lap waving her arms around and laughing as we looked out over the town. I kissed the top of her thick hair and thought how much like Tom she looked. She was beautiful. I told her our story, Tom and mine's. Of how this rocking stone was our special place. Of how it was witness to our hopes and ambitions, our love and desire and wished her as much happiness as Tom and I had during that precious time of innocence and love. And that, for her, it would not go wrong as it had for us. My hopes were in Little Meggie. If she could find the happiness I so craved, then everything would be worthwhile.

I told her about our town and its history – how a remote farming community of immense beauty could turn into an industrial scar on the landscape. How people desperate for work, desperate to feed their families, desperate for a life, moved here from all over. And how the rich, selfish people turned those desperate and honourable folk into pawns for making money, and how that affected men like her daddy. I wanted her to know it all, so told her now just in case I lost my nerve when she was older and able to understand.

And then, of course, he entered my mind – as he always did when I was happy and contented. Dudley! He flew around like a hornet in my mind. Stinging me and reminding me to expect him to reappear any time. Biting at my memories of the rape and bringing them to life again. But I did not tell Meggie any of this. This was not her problem and I would never discuss it with her. But the fear of him reappearing never left me.

But eventually, people stopped talking about him. Pleased, I believe, like us, to forget about him. To push him out and excrete him like a poison from the body. And I for one was grateful for their silence. Whenever he flashed into my mind I pushed him out instantly. I couldn't afford to let him take over my thoughts. Mrs Mallow and Tom probably had those moments too, but if they did, they kept it to themselves.

Tom worked all the hours he could, bless him. That was the one thing he did for us. He worked hard. But it soured him. He was being worn out by the work and the attitude of the pit owners and their officials.

After the war ended and the prosperity of the valleys plummeted, it became clear our coal was getting more difficult to extract and coal was cheaper to buy in other countries and import to Britain. Also, oil was taking over from coal, especially on ships and our coal was especially suited to ships. Miners were laid off by the hundreds of thousands and there was a lot of bad feeling between the owners and the men. In 1925 the owners tried to force the miners to take a cut in wages and to work an hour extra a day, but opposition was so strong, a Royal Commission was appointed to look into it. It concluded that the industry was in dire need of modernising and that some parts of the country, including South Wales, should accept the cuts. The owners took advantage and insisted on large cuts whilst the miners and the union fought on for a fair wage for a fair day's work.

And then, on the last day of April in 1926 – a date I will never forget – the miners who refused the cuts were locked out. Literally, locked out. The mines were closed to them and they were refused work.

Tom was one of these. He took it bad and would sit in his chair looking defeated. He'd rage at me regularly, the same thing over and over as if he had a groove in his head he couldn't get out of. He didn't stop for breath, just stared straight ahead, his hand clutching the arms of his chair until they turned white while it all spewed out of him in a desperate utterance. I despaired for his sanity.

'It's the fault of those bastard owners. They've done this to us, mun. They cut our wages to slave labour rates and compromised on safety to get the coal out faster. But we miners wouldn't have it – life-threatening conditions for a few shillings. What did they want from us: our lives? There were already accidents galore and I'll tell you another thing, they weren't accidents. Murder I say it was: murder by another name but murder just the same. The dirty tricks they pulled, compromising on safety while covering it up. Forcing men to use less and less props to hold up the tops as they dug. Telling lies when the roof collapsed, saying it was the dead men's fault, accusing them of trying to cut corners to make more money. Bastards!'

Telling the officials to close their eyes to gas underground and making them say there were plentiful roof props when it was the opposite. All to get more coal out as fast as possible. Bastards!'

His eyes were bright and staring, unseeing. He was in his own world: a man's world. One I couldn't enter; or he wouldn't let me enter. I'd learned to let him get on with it, to get it out of his system.

'Over the years we had nothing but conflict when we should have been working together. We should have been modernising but that cost money and God forbid if you took any profit from their pockets. Call themselves bosses? They couldn't boss a dandelion and make it grow. And now look where we are – other countries producing coal so cheap they can transport it around the world and still sell it cheaper than we can extract it for. It's a tragedy, that's what it is.'

He paused for breath; still staring ahead as sweat appeared on his brow. 'And that farce of a general strike! Solidarity they called it. Betrayal I call it. That bastard government called it revolution and brought out the army and sent a warship to Newcastle. Can you believe that? It's not revolution, mun. It's fighting for your right to live a decent life as a decent human being. Not to be exploited because you're poor. Poor parents have poor children, rich parents have rich children. It's quite simple and not our fault. We all do our best with what we're given. And don't talk to me of that bastard, Baldwin! And that bastard union turncoat – Thomas! I can barely say his name – betrayed us all he did. Called off the strike and left the miners high and dry. Why?' He thumped the arm of the chair with his fist. 'That's what I want to know. The lily-livered, quivering coward. We didn't want revolution, we wanted fair play.'

He went silent for a few seconds, wiping the sweat away. 'And look at me. What a poor specimen of a man. I've no money for baccie or beer. I'm fed up of bread and water to fill up my belly. My family is starving, and I can't help them. I'm powerless. Do you hear me? Powerless!'

Then he'd sit for hours, not saying a word. It was awful to watch and my heart went out to him. But I couldn't help him because Mrs Mallow always pushed in to take his hand and talk to him. He never responded, but talk away she did. She did it so that I couldn't. She took every opportunity to put her grains of sand into our relationship. Tom raved about the bosses and I wanted to rave about her, but of course, I kept silent. It would only have made everything worse.

I started to realise something then. Years ago, before Tom and I married, Mrs Mallow told me that Tom always ignored Dudley as much as he could. That Tom's nature was like his real mother's, kind and gentle. Now I understood she meant that Tom was weak and didn't like conflict. It was then I started to understand Tom more, but it didn't really help any.

Tom and the other miners had a one-track mind in my opinion because while they were fighting for their lives so were their women. More women died than miners but they were overlooked. No one fought for our rights. I only had to look around my area and see the wives dying. The hard work, the constant children and sacrificing their food for their families finally wore them away with depressing regularity. I thought I would be one too, but for some reason I didn't die. I always put it down to my Boadicea spirit. Oh yes, she was still with me, keeping my spirits up and driving me on.

We had no other industry in our valleys, everything depended on the pits. If the miners didn't work, everything else dried up too. Every other business depended on the miners getting their wages. It was a time of survival: nothing more and nothing less.

Over the next four years we learned how to eat even less, stretch out our paltry dole money so that we could all eat. Mrs Mallow had her widows' pension, of course, and she always spent it on us and the church. She'd put half aside for the church and half for us and she wouldn't be moved on this. 'The church is the backbone of our society,' she said. 'If that goes, we go too.'

She had been a cook in her youth and she'd brought up four children on a miner's wage, so she knew how to make things last, but even she had to invent new ways of stretching things. We never ate any fruit without it being in a pie with pastry thick enough to fill us up. The fruit would be bulked out with stale breadcrumbs. We bought mouldy lentils and dried beans cheaper, 'a bit of mould nor dirt never hurt anyone', was Mrs Mallow's mantra. Every Saturday morning, she'd go down to Lipton's store on the Tumble with a bowl. She'd buy as many cracked eggs as she could for six-pence. Sometimes we got more than other times as it depended on how many eggs had been damaged. Every delivery, the assistants would check all the eggs and take out any damaged ones which they'd crack open into a huge bowl and crush the shells into a box. The raw eggs they sold by the ladleful and the shells they sold to gardeners for improving the soil and keeping off slugs and snails. Nothing was wasted.

We lived on gristle and fat which Mrs Mallow put in the meat grinder with the bit of meat we could afford, and we didn't dare spit out a bit of gristle without having Mrs Mallow giving us what for. 'That animal died for you,' she'd say, 'so eat its lovely meat and it's horrible gristle, it all goes to make the animal. No gristle, no animal, so eat it up. Acknowledge the sacrifice that animal made for you.' It always made me think when she said that to the kids. I hadn't thought about animals like that before. She had a tender heart sometimes and I could almost be fond of her.

Jimmy was five and about to start school. We had a special relationship Jimmy and I. He was a mammy's boy and I loved him just as much as I did my little Meggie. The other two boys, Sam and Frank, were typical boys who love rough and tumble. Tom would play with them and take them up the mountain from time to time when he was feeling up to it. I used to teach them to read and encourage them to act out the stories of King Arthur and they'd fight over who'd be the dragon. We had great fun, especially when we all visited Edie.

I'd take the kids over to her house once a week. She had four of her own too and they were of similar ages. We'd let them run riot in the kitchen as we drank tea and chatted. Little Meggie was starting to take notice and wanting to join in with the boys. It was comical to watch her. She was rejected of course as she was still too little – and a girl – so Edie and I would find baby things to do with her.

'I know,' Edie said one day, 'let's make balls out of newspaper and she can throw them up in the air. Come on, boys, who can make the best ball of all – the roundest and firmest. Betcha I can,' she'd yell as she made a dive for the pile of old newspapers in the corner.

'You'd better make sure you have enough paper left for the toilet,' I laughed as they all dived in. The boys followed Edie's example and rolled up the paper layer after layer trying to make the best one.

'You know, Kate,' she said leaving the boys to it, 'my big lug surprises me sometimes. He's only gone and joined a brass band. He's got enough wind for a trumpet that's for sure the way he shouts around the house, but to make that same breath into something beautiful, well, we'll see.' She laughed her infectious laugh and as always, it set me off.

'You're lucky, it gets him out of the house, but Tom won't join anything. He just sits around the house and mopes or goes to the pub with his mates. He tells me he makes a glass of beer last all night. But, well, I'm not so sure. He comes home a bit tight sometimes.'

'Oh, Kate, let the man be. He's a different sort to my big lug, he's simple, but Tom thinks more, that's his trouble. If he finds someone to buy him a drink, so what? He leaves you alone, doesn't he?'

I nodded. 'Yes, thank goodness. I can't afford any more kids.'

'I know what you mean.' She laughed again and winked.

'What?' I said, laughing.

'Devious means, that's what we women need to keep the baby at bay.'

'Oh, you and your devious ways,' I joked. I looked at the boys who were still intent on making the perfect paper ball. 'Be careful what you say in front of the boys, they're starting to pick up on things.' I laughed again. 'I don't want them telling the things you tell me to Tom or even worse, to Mrs Mallow.'

Edie exploded with glee. 'Oh, my God, Kate, can you imagine Mrs—'

'Stop it, Edie,' I said trying to control myself.

The boys looked up wondering what we were getting hysterical about.

We all loved our afternoons with Edie. She helped me cope and kept me sane. The simplest things in life can make all the difference.

*

And then, as if we didn't have enough to put up with, the depression hit us. And for South Wales it was catastrophic. Tom's small unemployment benefit had long run out and he was now 'on the parish'. It was means tested and so humiliating. It was the thing that broke Tom of his last vestiges of respect. The way they treated those men was shameful. Being 'on the parish' seemed to be a code word for the officials at the Labour Exchange to be superior, impatient and downright disrespectful. There was no privacy and everyone could hear what everyone else said, every plea, every cry of despair.

It crushed Tom. 'It's the lack of respect, mun,' he'd say. 'Why should I be treated worse than a dog? What did I do wrong? What did any of us do wrong? Nothing I tell you. Nothing, except to try and live a decent life and look after our families. Is that wrong?'

It was the beginning of the thirties and the newspapers said Wales was among the most depressed countries in the world. I could believe that because we didn't know a miner who was still in work. We had to rent a cheaper house, although there were not many cheaper than the one we had, but one came up at the end of Graig Street. It was the last house in the street and abutted the mountain. It was an unusual house because although it looked like a terraced house it was semi-detached. This was because of the lie of the land and these two houses had been squashed tightly on a knoll sitting above the street by several feet. As the knoll was narrow and long, the two houses were double fronted and only one room deep. So we had two small rooms side by side downstairs and two side by side upstairs divided up by the steepest staircase I'd ever seen. When someone stood at the top anyone standing at the bottom, looking up, could only see the person's feet up to their knees, and the reverse looking down. Mrs Mallow refused to go up them.

Also, they had something no one else on the Graig had. Both houses had a long front garden. I loved that. But in reality, it was only mountain scrub and you couldn't grow anything as it was too stony. They were there because it was the only way to reach the houses from the street so the builders made a feature of them. From the street you opened the gate – yes each house had a gate! – and mounted five steep steps which led to a rising pathway through the centre of the garden, and then up six extra high steps which defeated many a small child or old person. Access would be a problem so that's why the two houses were cheaper. Also, the mountain impinged very close to them at the rear. It was held back only by a high stone wall which had been turned black by the wetness seeping down from the mountain. The side wall of our house abutted the mountain and people walked up and down the pathway there

181

where the tufty grass and gritty stones rubbed against the wall. The house was part of the street, but apart from it too and I thought of that bit of the mountain surrounding us as being mine. It was an untidy mountain, windblown and uncared for, like a tramp with his trousers tied up with string and holes in his clothes, needing his hair brushed and a shave as it undulated in a scruffy overcoat. But I loved it. And, best of all, from our front garden, whenever I looked up, I could see the rocking stone where Tom and I had lain and first declared our love for each other. Our innocence lay there. A memory embedded in the rock.

Now, living in sight of it, I resolved to visit it whenever I needed to get away, to get some time for myself, for however short a time I could spare. It had been mine and Tom's special place and I was going to keep that magic close.

Mrs Mallow had taken the left-hand downstairs room as her bedroom and said, 'I'll share this room with Meggie. It will enable you and Tom to sleep well. I'm so old now, I don't need to sleep,' she smiled. But I wasn't having that. She wasn't going to steal Meggie, my Meggie, away from me. I put my foot down and stormed upstairs with her cot and nearly fell down those damned stairs and broke my neck. But I had succeeded in making my point and Meggie slept with Tom and me. The boys shared the other upstairs room.

The remaining downstairs room was where we lived, cooked and ate. And small as it was, it had, unfortunately, three doors and a window in it. The first door opened onto the tiny area between the front door and the stairs. The window overlooked the front garden. The back door was opposite the window and the third door led to the cupboard under the stairs.

We had gas lighting in all the rooms, one light hanging from the middle of each ceiling. We never put the lights on until it was too dark to see, then we would put it on as low as our income.

But that cupboard under the stairs was a great advantage for a kitchen of sorts had been set up in it. A gas cooker had been fitted there, hard up in the corner with a window to the side of it which let in a little light. A deep porcelain sink with a cupboard under it was next to the cooker. The sink was connected to the drains, but had no tap; that was outside in the back yard attached to the stone wall which held back the mountain. There were a few narrow shelves above the sink and a few shelves under the declining roof of the staircase; under these we kept a vegetable rack. We called it the cwtch. And from that cwtch, the smell of cooking would fill the little house: bread, pies and cakes baking, vegetables simmering, bones boiling for soup. Those smells filled us up via our noses and thoughts first and then through our stomachs when we ate them, so we got two meals out of each one. I often wondered if that was the secret of surviving poverty.

In late August, we'd all go up the mountain to pick whimberries. We'd make a little bag out of newspaper and climbed to the best spots and if the berries had survived the wind and rain on their low-lying plants and the weather had been kind, then we got sweet black berries, if not, then they were too tart to eat comfortably. The trouble was so many people were starving they'd go out in July to pick them red, or even green. Then there were no ripe berries for anyone. But I loved a good whimberry and apple tart.

Mrs Mallow was an astute shopper who could always beat down a price. Ponty held a large, twice-weekly market that served the whole of the valleys on Wednesdays and Saturdays, and on Saturday nights, around seven o' clock, just before the market closed up for its well-earned sleep, she would take her four baskets and walk down the hill to Market Square. There, she would barter with the stallholders for the bruised and damaged fruit and vegetables; for the unsold meat or scrag ends that wouldn't keep until Monday. She even rummaged through the food thrown away as pig food. Tom went with her to help her carry her baskets.

I'd stay at home with the kids and I always looked forward to this special, alone time together. I'd clear the kitchen table and we'd sit around it and play and chat. Meggie always wanted to draw.

'Mam, mam,' she'd say, trying to get my attention and showing me her book. 'Look I drew a daffodil in school and coloured it in.'

'That's a funny daffodil,' Sam would say. 'I can draw a better one.' So we'd all draw daffodils, and so on.

'Come on now,' I'd say, 'whose reading what in school?' And they'd all rush to show me their latest book. Their school was a good one and I was pleased at the way the children were taught and I'd instilled a love of reading in all of them. Tom and I were raising children who would not be miners. I made sure of that.

We had guessing games of what Mrs Mallow would bring home this week. 'What's in season?' I'd ask them as they all rushed to name fruit and vegetables.

'I hate squashy plums,' Meggie would say in her loud, sweet voice. She'd learned to speak up and hold her own with her exuberant brothers.

'Well, bully for you, 'cos I love 'em,' Jimmy would say, laughing. 'All the more for me,' he'd sing out.

'I like strawberries,' Frank would shout out. 'I want strawberries, strawberries, strawberries.'

'Peaches, peaches, peaches,' Sam would join in.

'Apples, apples, apples,' said Frank.

'No! Pears, pears, PEARS,' Meggie would shout out laughing. 'Your turn, Mam.'

'Well,' I'd drag out the word and look at them all one by one, building tension. They'd jump up and down in excitement. 'Whimberries, whimberries, WHIMBERRIES,' I'd shout, jumping up and down. We'd all join in, jumping around shouting out whimberries like mad things.

Simple things brought us together. We became our own little family on these Saturday nights – mother and children – just us. It was blissful.

When Mrs Mallow and Tom got home, we'd lay newspaper over the table and she'd lay out all her purchases. 'Those pigs eat well,' she'd sometimes say as a preamble. 'Nothing wrong with squashed anything, it all gets worse than that when it goes in your mouth.' I knew then she'd found some things in the pig food box. We got those for next to nothing.

She'd put the most damaged fruit and vegetables on one end and grade everything until the best stuff was at the opposite end. If she'd been extra successful in her bargaining, and had a bit of money left over, she'd buy something perfect as a special treat for the kids. Well, we all need to feel special sometimes and get a treat.

We'd all gather around to inspect her wares. The kids were in a heightened state of excitement and this was the highlight of the week for us all. Sometimes there were lots of potatoes, other times, carrots, onions, cabbages or rotting apples were the main thing. Soft fruit in summer were a godsend, squidgy strawberries, squashed and runny peaches, flattened plums. Whatever it was, we would all get to work and pick out the best. Mrs Mallow was the chief giver-outer and controller and she was conscientiously fair in who got what. She made sure we had enough for our main meals for the week and the rest we could gorge ourselves on. The worst were put aside for cooking, and the vaguely edible were eaten there and then, rotten bits and all. The kids were allowed to stay up for this treat and we all enjoyed it more than anything else.

Sam was the worst. 'Look at this squidgy plum' he'd say with relish to Meggie. 'I'm going to suck out all the bad bits, mm, delicious, then, I'm going to save the best bit for later.' He'd put it on the table in front of him until he had a little pile.

'You be careful, young Sam, you'll spend all day tomorrow out the back you keep eating those plums like that,' Mrs Mallow would say.

Funnily enough, he never did get an upset tummy; made of iron that boy.

The meat she'd managed to get meant that we always had a roast dinner for Sunday and the rest was rationed out for the week in pies and soup. When the food ran out, we ate bread and jam. Mrs Mallow was a prolific jam and chutney maker. Then, the next Saturday, we'd start all over again.

The depression bit deeper and droves of people started to leave the valleys. All those people who had come to find work here a generation or so before, were now either returning to their roots or looking for work in the Midlands where new industries were starting up. But my family never once talked of leaving Ponty. It was our home. We couldn't envisage living anywhere else.

It was during this time that Mrs Mallow opened up a bit to me. She had never told me anything about herself, it just wasn't her way. I have to admit that I sometimes wondered if she had anything to hide – so secretive was she about her past. 'The past is past,' she always said. 'What's the use of raking up old things?' But one day, as we were sitting in the kitchen drinking a cup of tea and I was enjoying a rest in Tom's armchair while he was out, she took me by surprise.

'I've had a letter from Polly, my sister in Lyme,' she said.

'Oh!' I looked up sharply. 'I didn't know you had a sister.'

'Yes,' she replied quietly and after a pause, 'and a brother.'

'Oh,' I said again, lost for words. This was the first I'd heard of any of her family and I wasn't sure how to react.

'She wants to come and visit me. Says her husband has died and she's lonely.' She looked into the middle distance. 'We're the only ones left, you see.'

'And she lives in Lyme you say. Where is Lyme?'

'It's in Dorset. Lyme Regis.'

'Oh, I see, yes, I've heard of it. Posh place I think.' I could have bitten my tongue off.

'Yes, well you see, Polly married well. Her husband was a professional man, a solicitor.'

'I see,' I said, my mind working overtime. Why had Mrs Mallow ended up in Ponty, married to a miner, when her sister obviously came from a good-enough family to be able to marry a solicitor? I was burning with curiosity. But I dare not say anything more as her face was sour.

'She's coming tomorrow,' she said in a resigned voice.

'Tomorrow!'

'That's typical of her. No consideration for others. Do as she pleases. She knew I'd put her off, so she's let me know with no time to say no.' She sat there staring into space for a good ten minutes. I kept silent.

'Well, there's nothing we can do. She'll either turn up or not. She says she'll be here in the morning about eleven. She must be staying overnight somewhere as it's too far to be here by such an early hour.'

Well, this was a turn up. I was intrigued. I tried to hide my excitement and hoped she didn't send me on some kind of errand and I missed the mysterious sister.

I needn't have worried. Mrs Mallow stayed silent for most of the rest of the day and left me alone. It was blissful.

CHAPTER EIGHTEEN

The next morning, with the kids in school, Mrs Mallow, Tom and I waited in silence. At eleven on the dot, there was a loud knock at our front door.

'That's her,' Mrs Mallow said, 'always punctual and strident.' She went to answer the door and Tom and I looked at each other curiously. We had no idea what to expect as a small, elegant and expensively dressed woman came in looking like she'd stepped out of a picture frame. She wrinkled her nose in distaste as she looked around. Her gaze stopped on Tom, sitting in his armchair in his best suit and tie and his hair all wet down. I too was in my Sunday best, but we looked ragged and poor against her.

Mrs Mallow came in behind her and said, 'Polly, let me introduce my son, Tom and his wife, Kate.'

I jumped up from my kitchen chair and urged Tom up from his armchair. I indicated the armchair to Polly. 'How nice to meet you,' I said in an unnatural voice, trying to be posh. 'Would you like to sit down?'

She looked at the chair disdainfully, not bothering to hide her feelings. I didn't like her at all.

'Here, take my chair.' Mrs Mallow indicated her own armchair and Polly deigned to sit down.

'I'll make us some tea,' I said rushing into the cwtch. We drank our tea in strained silence until, surprise, surprise, Tom came to the rescue. She seemed to like him, or at least be willing to share some conversation with him and they spoke about the state of the mining industry and the depression.

She turned to Mrs Mallow. 'It reminds me of when we were young, Adele, and the pit in our village closed or as good as –

so many people out of work.'

I remembered that Mrs Mallow came from Somerset so I jumped in, curiosity getting the better of me. 'Where was that? In Somerset?'

She looked at me in a superior way. 'Yes, that's right, dear. We lived in a village called Nailsea. Our father was a miner. I've managed to better myself,' she preened.

Then, to our amazement, she said to Tom and me, 'Would you be so generous as to leave Adele and me alone for a while. We have a lot to talk about.'

It was the first time I'd seen Mrs Mallow struggle for words. Tom jumped up and took my arm. 'We'll take a walk,' he said as he led me out.

'Well, what do you think of that!' I said as we got outside. 'What a horrible woman. No wonder your mother wanted nothing to do with her.'

'It's strange,' Tom said, 'but she's never mentioned having a family. She told me they were all dead.'

'Well, I bet she wishes they were.'

We hung around for a while, but it was cold. 'Well, I'm not staying outside too long,' Tom said, shivering. 'It's my home she's in – cheeky so and so.'

We went back a little later and opened the front door very quietly having decided we would try and eavesdrop a little before knocking on the kitchen door. We crept in and both put an ear to the door.

'But, Adele, surely you can't stay here. Not now I've come with this offer for you. You can live in comfort with me in Lyme. I have plenty of room and money. You can't possibly want to stay in this God-forsaken hole of a house in this equally God-forsaken hole of a place.'

'How dare you!' Mrs Mallow spat. 'How dare you come here with your superior ways, throwing about your posh house and your lots of money. You have no idea of family or love or commitment.'

'How dare you, Adele,' Polly answered condescendingly, 'to talk of family love or commitment when you left us all in

Nailsea to come and . . . if I remember correctly, "To keep my independence and find my own way in the world." And you ended up here in this dead-end grimy place. I've never seen such poverty in my life. Look at you. You're starving! You're so thin and gaunt looking and you live in this dreadful little house and it's freezing in here. There's no comfort. And what's your son doing here at this time of day? He should be at work and earning money and keeping you in food. I'm sure you kept him in food when he was growing up.'

Tom flinched and I put my hand on his arm and shook my head. I wanted to listen to more. Their voices were so loud we had no trouble in following their every word.

'How dare you talk about my son in such a way,' Mrs Mallow said in her threatening tone of voice that always sent shivers of apprehension up my spine. 'There was never a better son than Tom and I don't care what you say. He looks after me fine. It's not his fault if there's no work for the men here. Most of the men in this area are out of work and have been for a long time. But we're family. We look after our own. And yes, I go without food so that my grandchildren can eat, but so does Tom and his wife. Yes, we're starving, cold, scrabbling away for rotten food like animals. But that's my life, the life I created here from nothing. I found love here, Polly. I don't think you know what that means. You and your stuffy husband in your comfortable over-heated house with food on the table and in the cupboards and money in the bank. What do you know about my life and how I want to live it?'

'But, Adele, you'll die if you stay here. You're old, you need your comfort. I can give you that. Please. I'm family too. Wouldn't it be nice to spend our last years together, supporting each other?'

'Oh, yes, like you supported me when I had my battles with father. The way you all wanted me to marry that awful man with his pot belly.'

'That pot belly got there because he could afford a pot belly, you seem to forget. He could have given you all you ever wanted: a nice house, education for your children, status, money.'

'And it all comes down to money with you, doesn't it?' The sarcasm in her voice made me shiver. 'Any man is acceptable if he has money, even ugly ones with pot bellies. I never met your husband. Was he ugly with a pot belly?'

I heard the triumph in her voice and said to myself, good for you.

'How dare you! You know nothing of Gerald.'

'And how dare you come down here after all these years and try and pry me away from my family just because you are lonely. It's just like you. You were always the selfish one. Our family was never any good that's why I wanted to leave. Oh, yes, I know we had money once but you seem to have forgotten that we were evicted from our lovely house and life in Bath and dragged to Nailsea. He'd bankrupted himself – we had nothing left. He was lucky to get work in the mine, his drinking was so bad. We ended up a miner's daughter and don't you forget it. We paid the price for his stupidity. He was violent and nasty and he wanted me to marry a man like him, one of his cronies, just because the man had money. And he thought I'd accept because I was big and plain and no catch. He didn't offer you to him and that says it all. You were pretty and delicate and could do much better for yourself. But I wasn't having it, not at all. I came here and I fell in love with a miner, a good man and he loved me. Loved me, Polly. Regardless of anything, he loved me. I'll never regret it. Not once, never!

'And another thing,' she went on in her threatening tone, 'this place is not awful. It's full of caring people who look after each other and there's love here, so much love. Yes, the men have had a hard time, but I'm proud of living here, of being one of them. They're proud too, but not too proud to help anyone out. This is a place of struggle and strife but also of courage and pride. Things you wouldn't know about, wouldn't understand with your money and comfort. I want you out, now, and I never want to see or hear from you again.'

Tom and I looked at each other in amazement, and a surge of pride for Mrs Mallow swelled up inside me. 'We'd better go in. We don't want to get caught,' he whispered.

I nodded as I opened and closed the front door noisily as if we had just arrived, and knocked on the kitchen door. It was thrown open by Mrs Mallow who had her arm on her sister's in none too friendly a fashion.

'Goodbye, Polly,' she said coldly. 'Please don't bother to contact me again. We're better off apart.' She moved aside so that Tom and I could come in and her sister gave us a look of contempt. I knew then that Mrs Mallow had made the right decision for her, even though I would have loved to have seen the back of her, it was not to be and I had to accept my fate.

Mrs Mallow and I continued our lives as if nothing had happened and I dared not ask her anything about it and she said not a word. Not even to Tom. And, of course, Tom being Tom did not ask her. But I did begin to understand her a little more. She must have been brought up in luxury and they lost it all because of her father. She had a chip on her shoulder about it I think. She must have had dreams of a good future and she ended up with a miner, and a dead one at that. And the son she loved was not hers. And the son that was hers was rotten. That's a terrible burden. And her good son ended up marrying me, a woman of such dreams that fell by the wayside, the same as hers had. What kind of woman would I have been without Mrs Mallow in my life? What kind of woman would I have been if I had had the support of a caring, understanding husband? What kind of woman would I have been if my mother hadn't died at such a young age? What kind, what kind, what kind? I could go on forever, and where would it get me? Just the same place as I am now, so I threw those thoughts away, they would do me no good and I'd end up like Mrs Mallow: bitter and angry. I must stay nice and kind and caring for my children.

Meggie was my joy. We were so close and I made sure Mrs Mallow couldn't influence her too much. I had to be careful, I didn't want to alienate the two of them from each other, but Mrs Mallow and I came to an unspoken agreement about Meggie. She knew how I felt about her and understood it I think. I had to have something for myself: something to keep me alive and give me hope. We can't live without hope. Meggie was my hope for the future. I couldn't rely on Tom. He'd never supported me. He'd let his mother take over the upbringing of the boys, and in a way, if I look at it from her point of view, she did what she thought was right. I was weak physically as each pregnancy took any strength I had. I suppose she kept me alive by taking over the boys: alive to breed again. Our futures were in our children – boys especially. Well, whatever, I didn't know how to stop her. My Tom, the one I married, got lost in the realities of life. Mrs Mallow was right, he was a weak man who would do anything for a peaceful life.

*

Our children grew up 'on the parish', but they were not alone as everyone we knew was in the same boat. The men created all sorts of things to keep themselves entertained. Marching bands, cricket matches, walks over the mountain, cards games played for matchsticks, teaching the kids football, all sorts of things to try and keep up moral. But Tom was not interested in any of them. He just sat and moped and I despaired for him. He had the melancholy that was obvious to me but he wouldn't talk about it, got nasty if I mentioned it. There was no treatment anyway, not for a miner, and even if there had been he had too much pride to seek it.

I took in sewing to give us a little extra. As everyone was in the same financial situation I agreed with my customers that if they supplied the material then I would make whatever it was they wanted and they would pay me what they could afford, either in money or other necessary things like food. There was no other choice. It was that or nothing and I never reckoned my time was worth much. I cut up worn out clothes and made patchwork dresses and shirts from the salvageable pieces. Often, people came with old clothes of dead grandparents and I made modern clothing from them. Nothing was wasted.

I took a chance and bought a Singer treadle sewing machine on the never-never. It was a big machine that you worked with your feet so that your hands were free to control the work.

This meant I could sew anything from delicate baby clothes to curtains. It was a heavy piece of furniture in its own right. Made of thick, polished oak, it had a flat top which, when you pulled it up, rolled over and rested horizontally on a pull-out arm giving you a work surface for the material you were working on. Underneath that top was the machine itself which you pulled up and clicked into place. It was ingenious and I loved that machine. The design, the usefulness, the way it could earn you a living and be an elegant piece of furniture too. I was in seventh heaven.

I had nowhere to put it except under the window of our kitchen. It took up valuable space but at least I got the light. So I sewed while the kids played on the floor behind me, Mrs Mallow cooked and Tom sulked, when he was there that is. He only seemed to be around when it was dinner time. What he did for the rest of his time, I really don't know – and had learned not to ask him. My sewing made the difference between our children having enough in their bellies or very little. It was a hard time all right, especially when the spies from the council called unexpectedly. Word got round that 'the socials' were in our street and we all hid any work we were doing on the sly. What did they expect from us? We were starving. We couldn't afford to be honourable. Honourable people died because if we were found to be doing any paid work our benefit was cut. And it was a mean benefit to start with.

*

Then, to my horror, I found out what Tom had been doing with some of his time. All I'd known was that he was out. That's all he would ever say. 'Where are you going, Tom?' I'd ask, as he left the table after his dinner and put his jacket on.

'Out,' was all he ever replied. I did know that he always came back smelling of beer and I often wondered how he could eke out his money so far, but didn't give it too much thought. If he could get more money for himself to spend on beer, then let him be was my philosophy. That was until one day, a neighbour told me that he was surprised to see Tom down the

Greyhound pub. 'What do you mean, surprised?' I asked him.

'Well, he was taking orders at the tables and getting beer in for the men, waiting on them, you know, with a tray. Then every so often, someone would say, "Have a half on me, Tom." And Tom's face would light up and he'd say, "Thanks, I will." A couple of the lads who were desperate would do this kind of thing, but I never thought I would see Tom doing it. I always thought it was just the alcoholics who did that.'

I tried not to show my despair. 'I think he likes the company and he's a good husband, he gives all his money to me.' That was true. Whatever the situation with our marriage, Tom always looked after us and gave me all his pay packet or dole money. He would ask for a shilling for himself, 'If we can afford it, Kate, make sure you have enough for the kiddies.' Often, he didn't get his shilling, but he rarely complained. He was good like that. I had no idea that he was practically begging for beer in the pub. I felt a soaring pride in Tom's selflessness, but at the same time, humiliation that my husband was doing such a thing: that we were reduced to this.

I had to do something about it. I had to help him keep his pride. So I decided to say nothing but to do something constructive. We 'd grown apart but he was still my husband and I didn't want his mother to know about it, so I made even more economies, went without more myself, to give Tom two shillings a week. His eyes lit up when I told him. He was like a little boy in some ways. Taking what was doled out to him and not questioning where it came from. 'Oh, thanks. Thanks a lot,' he said as he spat on the coins and put them in his pocket.

When he came home that night after everyone else had gone to bed, he was stinking of beer and drunk as a skunk. He'd spent it all – in one night. I was furious, but with an effort I kept hold of my temper. I could use this to my advantage if I played my cards right. No one had mentioned Dudley for years, for which I was grateful, but sometimes, usually at inopportune moments, he'd come flooding back into my mind and upsetting me all over again. I was still raw if I gave myself the time to think about it. Consequently, I pushed him out of my mind as soon as he entered it but the thought that Tom might have killed him was like a persistent worm wiggling around my mind, and now, Tom was so drunk and we were alone. I might just be able to catch him out as he sat in his armchair by the cold fire and started singing and giggling.

'Tom, just sit there tidy now and drink this nice cup of tea, there's a good 'un.' He took the cup and drank deeply. I brought my kitchen chair up to his armchair and sat facing him. 'Do you remember when we got married and how happy we were on our honeymoon?' (I'd always kept up the illusion that I was happy on our honeymoon.) 'How we laughed and played in the sand and sea, you built me sandcastles, do you remember?'

'Yesh, and you buried me in the shand,' Tom slurred and swayed.

I laughed, 'Well, you encouraged me I seem to remember.'

'Never!' Tom tried to look me straight in the eye, but he couldn't focus properly. This is my moment I thought.

I made my voice soft and sweet. 'Can you cast your mind back to just after that time? Can you remember? Tell me what happened to Dudley?' He looked at me puzzled for a moment. And then swayed again, still trying to focus on me. I was unsure whether he'd understood my question. 'You met Dudley didn't you? Something happened between you because we never saw Dudley again. What happened? It's all so long ago, you can tell me now. I won't hold it against you, never that, in fact I'd be grateful to you. My life has been so much easier without him.'

By now he had focused on me and was looking at me with a cold and ferocious stare. I don't think I had ever seen such a look on his face before. 'Damn you,' he shouted. 'Damn you to hell.'

He swiped his arm sideways, deliberately smashing his cup and saucer into the grate and got up with a struggle, swaying dangerously. 'I've told you before, I don't remember, can't you just leave it at that? If you ask me again, I swear I'll swipe you and not the tea cup.' He staggered towards the stairs and shouted, 'Just leave me alone, woman, give a man some peace.'

The next day, we didn't speak of it. As usual, burying unsavoury things into our inner beings, to fester there and turn bad inside. I never stopped wondering what had happened to Dudley. Had Tom killed him? If so, how had he got rid of the body? Or did Dudley leave the country as he threatened all those years ago? No, I didn't believe that, he would have come back by now, he was that sort, he couldn't resist stirring up trouble, he would have come back all right.

So, nothing else was said except that I told Tom his money had to last him all week and if he came in drunk again I would stop the money altogether. I never saw him drunk after that, and I think he frightened himself into temperance, afraid of what he might say under such a barrel load of beer. However, I knew Tom had a secret from the very fact that he never got drunk again, although he still drank; but it was never enough to make him senseless.

But there was another side to Tom.

'Here you are, Sam,' he said one day, giving him the train engine he'd been whittling for days.

'Oh, thanks, Dad, that's smashing,' he said as he took the engine and showed it to Frank in great excitement. Tom had made Frank a bus a few days before and Sam had been waiting for his toy.

'Me, me too, Dad,' Meggie shouted.

'You next, Meggie, love. What would you like?'

'A shop,' she said instantly.

'A shop?' Tom echoed. 'A real shop, with a counter and tins and eggs and things?'

'Yes,' Meggie shouted out, getting very excited.

'Oh, Tom, don't promise what you can't deliver,' I said gently. 'Be careful you don't cause her disappointment.'

'Don't worry,' he said with a smile, 'I'll start on it straight away. She won't be disappointed.' He picked up a piece of the scrap wood he always kept by his chair. 'Now this,' he said bending towards Meggie, 'is a counter I think. What do you think, Meggie? Can you see a counter in this piece of wood?'

'Yes,' Meggie shouted, 'a counter, a counter. I want a counter.'

Tom winked at me and made me laugh.

'Oh, go on, make your counter then.'

'A nice cup of tea will make this counter an even better one I think.' He winked again.

'Oh, you and your tea,' I said going off to the cwtch. 'Tea all round, everyone?'

'Yes,' they all shouted, including Tom.

Those simple things made our life happy.

In the end, Tom made a complete shop for Meggie. The building he made out of cardboard he got from boxes from our local shop and he covered it with newspaper.

'Lovely decoration,' Tom told Meggie. 'Look, old Mr Jenkins has died and Johnny Jones has won his swimming gala, and a lost horse has been found.'

'Yes,' Meggie jumped up and down in excitement. 'My shop is a newspaper shop.'

We all laughed.

The counter fitted perfectly and Tom glued paper shelves to the walls with little drawings of tins and eggs and flour sacks and sweets placed on them. Mrs Mallow and I pretended to be customers and even the boys joined in. Meggie was a proper little shopkeeper and made sure we all paid for everything. Tom had made cardboard money. If I had any spare cloth over from my sewing, I would make a toy for them. Our children were happy in their simple ways. We made the best we could out of our circumstances and I did all I could to disguise my feeling about Mrs Mallow. The children loved her, she was strict with them, but fair and they respected that.

Besides us, Mrs Mallow's life was her church. I went with her every Sunday, but I'd still not recovered the faith I had before Dudley took it from me. I'd tried hard, I wanted to believe, but just couldn't. And I had to disguise the fact that I couldn't believe as it would have involved too many explanations I didn't want to give.

The saving grace of going to church was Edie. We met up every Sunday morning for service and left our husbands to look after the kids. They couldn't argue with their wives going to church. Edie and I would sit apart from Mrs Mallow, she didn't welcome us into her little circle and we most definitely didn't want to be in it. Edie was a believer, even if it was a disparaging one. We had great fun as Edie sang out the hymns at the top of her voice, which wasn't melodic, and I sang alongside, far more demure. All the old dears would give her bad looks as she belted out those hymns. And then she'd disarm them later by offering to help.

'Can I do anything for you, Mrs Jenkins?' she'd ask, full of concern as Mrs Jenkins struggled with her arthritic limbs to get up from the pews.

'How about you, Mrs Thomas, do you need a steadying hand?' As Mrs Thomas limped down the aisle with her stick.

'Mr Rudd. Take my arm, please do. You're poor leg is bad today I can see.'

And she meant it too. She hated to see suffering, but always made a joke of things. I understood Edie and saw beneath her light exterior into her caring soul.

'Why do you stay friends with that . . . that person!' Mrs Mallow said. 'She's a disgrace.'

'She's my friend, and I like her. She has a kind heart.'

'That's as maybe, but she's disrespectful.'

'Oh, she's just full of fun. She does no harm. Don't be so hard on her, Mrs Mallow.'

'Well, she's not my idea of a church goer. She's far too . . .' she hesitated, unsure what it was that Edie was, 'well, disrespectful, like I said,' she bristled.

Edie was a bone of contention with Mrs Mallow, and I loved Edie all the more for it.

The church was my life too. It was free and that was a huge consideration. My friends were also there, and my social life was built around it. We went on trips to the seaside with our families once a year, had tea parties for the kids, reading groups for the more backward children, all sorts of things that gave me enjoyment.

*

Whatever happens in life, it goes on regardless. At fourteen, Jimmy left school. Of course, he couldn't find work. The next year, Frank joined him on the dole and then Sam the following year. They were good boys, steady and ambitious and it broke my heart to see them unable to work. But I, and if I'm honest, both Tom and Mrs Mallow in their own ways, had instilled in them the desire to work and improve themselves. We encouraged them to go to the market every week, looking for casual work humping boxes around, maybe working on a stall if they were short staffed. It taught them a bit about life even if it wasn't the bit I wanted for them.

Then, it was Meggie's turn to leave school. She'd proved to be good at sewing like me, and she helped me in my sewing business, starting with hems and cuffs and buttons. Meggie made my life worth living. Oh, I know I shouldn't say that, I had three lovely sons, but it was Meggie who lighted up my day, who gave me the impetus to carry on struggling.

Nothing lasts forever, people always say, and they had said it for years in the valleys but nothing changed. Then, in 1937 something miraculous happened. And it changed all our lives totally.

Out of the blue, well, for me anyway, the powers that be had got together and decided to build an industrial estate to create jobs for the valleys. By some fluke of good fortune, they chose Treforest to build it. Treforest was so close to Ponty, it was almost in Ponty. At first, it was just a few factories which opened up and started recruiting. There was almost pandemonium at the Labour Exchange but it soon became clear that only young men were wanted. They could be trained far more easily than hardened, belligerent miners. Therefore, Jimmy, Frank and Sam found themselves the proud owners of jobs. Menial jobs, but none the less, jobs with prospects for improvement. For the first time in years, we had steady incomes coming into the house.

All except for Tom: he wasn't given a job and my heart went out to him. But what could I do, except say, 'Don't give up, Tom. Please don't give up.'

He took my hand. 'No, you're right, I must start to hope now. Things are changing, that's clear. I won't give up.' His eyes shone and I could see the hope behind them. I so dreaded him being disappointed again. But he still had the power to surprise me. Shortly after this, one market day, just before the boys were to start their new jobs, he went out early in the morning and came back around mid-day. Wrapped up in proper little bags were three ties. He gave one to each of the boys and told them they were to wear them to their new jobs. 'Nice, good ties for nice, good jobs,' he said. 'It's important to look nice.'

We all wiped a tear away as the boys unwrapped them. They were tasteful and of good quality: a dark green one for Jimmy, a dark blue one for Frank and a maroon one for Sam. They put them on and we all cheered. They looked a picture and so proud that their dad had bought them. It was the first time he'd ever done such a thing and it touched us all deeply. Goodness knows where he got the money from. None of us asked but I suspected he gave up his beer money.

Then a few months later, Tom got a job. Just like that. It came up at the Labour Exchange and he applied, like he'd done hundreds of times before, and they gave him the job. He was to be the new odd-job man at a works in Nantgarw. It was a bit further away than the new estate, but Tom didn't mind. It was a job.

I laughed when he told me. 'You! An odd-job man! You're useless at odd jobs.'

He laughed too. 'Can't deny it, but it's mostly cleaning, sweeping up, bit of painting. Nothing complicated. I'll manage. Oh, Kate, it's a job! A job! Someone's given me a job after eleven years on the dole. I can't believe it.'

He was so happy and proud of that job. His pride had been returned to him. He had money for the pub and could talk about his job to his mates. I think he embellished it a bit, but why not.

And he kept that job. I'd been afraid they would sack him once they realised how useless he was at odd jobs, but he must have done something right. There's a lot a wife doesn't know about her husband and vice versa. Maybe that's just as well.

But unemployment had taken its toll on Tom. He looked a lot older than his late thirties. He was as thin as a stick and his lovely thick, black curly hair had thinned out and was turning grey. He had the look of a defeated man about him. But after getting his job he got his sparkle back and his face lit up and he smiled again. It was wonderful to see. Everything had taken its toll on me too. Thin like Tom, although I could accept that, but it was my hair, my pride and joy that made me cry. It was cut by Mrs Mallow, 'practically short', as she'd say, and washed in carbolic soap. Whenever we had some spare cash, I'd buy some vinegar and pour it over my freshly washed wet hair to try and give it shine. Some hope! But most other women had the same problem and I didn't look in the mirror much.

*

Finally, the depression ended. We were all employed and beginning to realise that we could enjoy life again, that someone or something wasn't going to snatch it all away from us. And then, like some bad joke, war was declared. We were at war with Germany. I couldn't believe it. I was dazed for days. Mrs Mallow was particularly badly hit. 'Not again,' she shouted when she heard. 'We've only just finished fighting the war to end all wars. My husband died for us to have our freedom and now we are at war *again*.' It was pitiful to see. I wondered how much more we all could take.

And there was another thing to think about – Dudley! As soon as I'd heard the news, he'd jumped into my mind. He loved the army and war. If he was ever going to return it would be now. Images popped into my mind unbidden: him, in uniform, walking around a corner and bumping into me, accidentally on purpose, as he used to do. He'd start messing with me again, making my life impossible – or worse. I couldn't see any reason why the passing of the years would have made him a better person.

I had to talk to myself seriously. 'Look, Kate,' I'd say out loud when no one was around, 'he's too old to be in another war.' But then I'd think he'd manage to wheedle himself in somehow: he was good at that. I was terrified he would appear again but as time went on there was no sign of him and for that, I was eternally thankful.

Then, to my amazement, it became clear that the war was bringing us lots of benefits. Emergency factories were built on the trading estate bringing work for thousands and thousands of people. They were government or military factories making munitions, machinery and goodness knows what else that were needed to help us win the war. Also, as resources grew scarce and utility became the watchword, my sewing business prospered. With the men off fighting in the war, women were employed in the factories. For many of them, it was the first time they'd had a job and a wage of their own and many were determined to spend some of it on themselves. The clothes shops were full of utility drabness for we were not encouraged to waste anything or buy anything that cost a lot to produce, either in materials or labour. So, women came to me with their new-found wages and I made pretty dresses and coats and anything else that was needed. Things they couldn't buy in the shops. There was a good business going on at the market with stalls selling pretty material at quite high prices, but nobody complained or asked where it had come from. Everyone was just happy to have fashionable patterns to buy with their new wages and they brought them to me as my reputation and reliability for good work grew. Meggie helped me a great deal, especially as her sewing skills increased. I was totally and utterly spoilt with four wage packets coming into the house, which meant I could choose the kind of sewing I wanted to do. I thought I'd died and gone to heaven.

CHAPTER NINETEEN

As the war went on, Jimmy joined up and then Frank and Sam did too. I was terrified for their safety, but it was something they all felt they had to do, so I didn't discourage them. Meggie decided to join the land army when she was eighteen. Poor Meggie, she wasn't keen on the hard, physical farm work, but she kept her humour and I was pleased she was out in the world making new friends. When she came home on weekends she was a picture of health and I could see the budding of the young woman she would become. I was proud of my Meggie. She was beautiful, well, I would say that wouldn't I, but it was true. She had a nice nature to go with her looks and reminded me of my mother.

'I'm proud of our children,' I said to Tom one night as we were getting into bed.

'Me too. I don't think I have the words to say just how proud I am.'

We smiled at each other and to my consternation, a few tears welled up.

'There, there,' he said. He put his arm around my shoulders as I snuffled into my hankie. I was the first time we'd had contact like that for years.

'Proud,' he said again. 'We did good. We brought up our children well, despite everything. And do you know what, Kate?'

I shook my head as I blew my nose.

He pulled me a little closer. 'Not one of our children has gone down the mines. We did it, Kate. We promised each other before we were wed that none of our children would be miners and none of them are. You know, I'm proud of us too.

Very proud.'

'Me too,' I said through tears. 'Oh, me too, Tom. So proud.'

*

Mrs Mallow and I were alone in the house as she dozed in her armchair in front of the fire. She did a lot of that these days as the war dragged on. The coal was damp and not giving out any heat. The smell from it caught in my throat. I hated that. It reminded me of my mother when she told me about the Albion pit disaster and of how, afterwards, she could never stomach the smell of damp coal burning.

I went out to the coal house and brought in a bucket full of coal and laid it in out in the hearth to try and get it to dry out so that we wouldn't have damp coal the next day. It happened like that sometimes. The coal came from the coalman damp or wet and in the cold weather it took an age to dry out.

I was a bit bad tempered about it and went into the cwtch to make a pot of tea hoping it would warm us up. I heard Mrs Mallow get up and groan, but then she often did as her back gave her gip. As I was putting the tea in the pot I heard a loud thud that echoed around the room. I turned quickly, spilling the tea as I looked back into the living room. Mrs Mallow was lying in a heap on the floor. I stood frozen for a moment, not sure of the reality of what I was seeing, then pulled myself together. Slowly, I went to her expecting the worst and, I'm ashamed to say, I hoped it had come at last. That I would be free of her.

I bent over her, and gently pushed her onto her back. Her eyes shot open and I jumped in shock. Her look was confused at first and then became focused as she stared up at me. I felt sorry for her then and took her hand in mine. 'Stay calm, now,' I said. 'I'll get the doctor.'

She could hardly breathe but found the strength to squeeze my hand. I was amazed at the strength of her grip. And then she just ceased to be. Still. No movement. Eyes staring. Mouth slack. Her last thoughts unsaid. She had gone into that other world she so fervently believed in: the world of her God. I kneeled back and looked down upon her and to my surprise, instead of feeling the relief I thought I'd feel at her death, I just felt empty. I saw a lonely, rather pathetic figure. A woman I'd lived in the same house with all these years, yet who was a stranger. What had she been thinking before death claimed her? I closed my eyes and concentrated on the now and not the past. She was dead. My nemesis was dead.

I stood up and looked out of the window over our scrub of a front garden trying to adjust to this new dimension. I turned around and looked at her again and went over and checked for a pulse. I had to make sure. There was nothing. No sign of life. I closed her eyes for her and went back to the window.

I felt a calm take me over, a settlement of emotions that I could now put to rest. I felt relieved and liberated. For the first time in my adult life, I felt at peace, my own person. I'd waited a long time for this moment. I don't know how long I stood there, getting used to it. A pleasure started to creep up from my feet until it filled my whole body, and then the guilt set in. I let it linger for a while and then pushed it out. I needn't feel guilty. I'd done my best. Other people influence your life and whatever had happened between her, Tom and me, it was all of us that had contributed to the outcome.

Mrs Mallow had put on weight over the years and was much too heavy for me to lift, so I went unhurriedly into Mr and Mrs Farmer's next door. Mr Farmer and one of his sons came and lifted Mrs Mallow to her bed. We sent for the doctor to get the death certificate. He came straight away and declared her dead of a heart attack.

'One life has ended, doctor,' I said, 'but there will be another who was born at the very moment she died who will take her place on this earth. Life is a wondrous thing.'

'Yes, the circle of life and death, Mrs Mallow. I see it every day,' he said wearily.

'Like a rondo,' I answered rather wistfully, and he nodded and looked at me strangely. Maybe he thought, how does a woman like me know a word like that? But I knew many things I kept to myself. Things I'd learned through books, vocabulary

I practised in my head but dared not use in daily life for it would have ostracised me. I had enough sense to know that people didn't like know it alls, especially in a woman.

When the doctor had gone, Mrs Farmer called round. 'Yoo-hoo,' she said, knocking and coming in. 'Would you like some help laying her out, Mrs Mallow?'

She saw the relief in my eyes. For years, I'd been dreading having to lay her out when she died. I had not seen any part of Mrs Mallow's body except her hands, face and lower legs, in all the time we'd lived together. She had seen all of me in minute intimate detail, but had kept herself private. I didn't want to be intimate with her, even – especially – in death.

Mrs Farmer was a sensitive woman and understood this without me having to say anything. 'You sit there, Mrs Mallow,' she said. 'I'll go and get Mrs Thorpe to help me. We can take care of everything. Just prepare me a bowl of hot water and some towels and rags. We'll make her beautiful for her Maker.'

I cried then, because of Mrs Farmer's kindness and understanding and not because of Mrs Mallow. I'm not sure if she understood this or not. Either way, I was so, so grateful to her.

When Tom came home and heard the news he just nodded. 'Been expected for some time now,' he said as he sat down in his armchair and looked over at her empty chair. He stared into the space around it for a while and then got up.

'I'd better see her. I'd like to be alone.'

'Of course,' I replied. 'I won't disturb you. She's been laid out. Mrs Farmer and Mrs Thorpe did it.'

'Oh,' he said looking at me, questioningly. But he just nodded and went into his mother. He stayed in there for over an hour and the tea I'd made went cold. But I knew he'd deal with her death in his own way. He had loved her and needed this time alone.

He came out with his head bent over like an old man. 'Do you want some tea, Tom?'

He shook his head. 'I'm going for a walk up the mountain. I don't want any dinner.' His eyes filled up with tears and he couldn't say any more. He glanced at me as he picked up his jacket and I saw something in that look. What was it – pain? Yes, but something more. Regret? Yes, that's what I saw: regret and apology. It was only a glance but I'll never forget that look. Oh, Tom. If only!

I went out into our front garden at dusk, worried about him, and looked up at the rocking stone. Tom was sat there, motionless. There was nothing I could do to help him, so I went back indoors and didn't see him until midnight and he came home smelling of beer, but not drunk. He went straight up to bed and never was another word said between us about our life with his mother.

Tom was heartbroken, but I was free.

Mrs Mallow had been paying into the Prudential towards her funeral costs for years. The woman from the Pru, Miss Ridge, came every Saturday afternoon and took Mrs Mallow's pennies from her and marked her book. 'You don't need to worry about my funeral,' Mrs Mallow would say intermittently. 'I can afford a decent send off.'

It was important to her, so we got the best funeral her money would allow and added a bit more in from our own pockets. She'd had no luxury in her life, so we gave her a luxurious coffin. It had white satin lining and was highly polished elm wood with brass handles. Dressed in her Sunday best, she looked the epitome of a woman of substance. It would have pleased her. And Tom insisted on hiring a car to take the family to the church, even though it was only a couple of minutes walk away. 'She'd be tickled pink, mun,' he said. 'I owe it to her. A good send off.'

Mrs Mallow lay on her bed in her coffin for over a week while we sorted out her funeral. Tom went in every evening and spent time alone with her, but I stayed away from that room. I couldn't sleep either during that time. I felt her presence more as a dead body than I had in life. She still dominated me and the funeral couldn't come quickly enough for me.

I found relaxation sitting on the Rocking Stone, letting my mind go blank and breathing deeply. I went there every day

Mrs Mallow was awaiting her funeral and I felt re-energised and relaxed each time. I had no idea how long I sat there. Sometimes, someone would walk by and stop for a chat about nothing in particular. I enjoyed that, anything to stop me thinking about Mrs Mallow's remains.

When the day of the funeral finally arrived the undertakers carried her coffin down our steep steps. I was afraid they'd drop her but after a few dangerous wobbles they got her down to the hearse in one piece.

Tom and I and the kids climbed into the shiny, black limousine and followed the hearse the few hundred yards it took to the church. Some of her cronies walked behind us. The church was packed as she was well liked and it goes to show how someone can be one person outside the home and quite another one inside it.

The service was a simple one and we said prayers and sang a few hymns. The vicar said nice things about her and then it was time to go to the cemetery. Women were not allowed to attend the actual burial and I was pleased about that. Tom and I had put on some sandwiches and tea for anyone who wanted to come back to our house and all her lady friends from church came and we chatted about everything and anything except her, as if it was unseemly to do so while she was being put in her grave. When the men came back we tucked into the food and tea and finally, it was over. When I waved off the stragglers and closed the front door, I finally felt well and truly liberated.

I don't know what I expected, but I felt her passing would change something between Tom and me but our lives went on as usual. We remained separate and only came together for meals and to sleep. I did try to get closer to him, but he had a steel cover over him that I couldn't penetrate, or he didn't want me to. But my life became my own and I started to find myself again: the young woman who had fallen in love with a handsome young man, both of us innocents in different ways. The woman who was me before I got caught between Mrs Mallow's dominance and Tom's weakness: before I was ground down by poverty and events. The young woman who had been full of hope and ambitions gradually resurfaced again.

Mrs Mallow's bedroom was now free, so I did something for myself. Something I had always wanted. Without consultation with anyone, I sold all Mrs Mallow's furniture and turned her bedroom into my room – a room for me. As it was on the ground floor it was originally meant to have been a room for living in, and now it was.

On the never-never I bought a patterned carpet of dark blue and brown that almost touched the walls, a three-piece suite of brown leatherette which was all the fashion. I bought an oak table and matching chairs, something I'd always hankered after, and finally, the best of all, two large, highly polished oak bookcases, which I would enjoy filling up with my own books, not the library's, but my own. I'd never been able to keep a book before as they always had to be returned to the library and used by others. But now I had my own room, my own furniture and a place for my own books. It was heaven and I couldn't stop smiling.

By this time I'd given up my sewing business, my eyesight was not so good, and even with glasses, I had trouble seeing the intricate work. But I couldn't get rid of the machine. It had meant so much to me over the years; helped us to survive the bad times. So I put its top down and used it as a small table. I polished the wood every week and kept a pretty vase on it which I filled with flowers. It looked lovely.

*

The war eventually ended. All the boys had married as soldiers, like so many others, afraid, although they didn't say so, of being killed. They were demobbed one by one and all came to live in lodgings nearby with their wives. I was glad of that. They stayed close. They all got jobs again in the factories on the estate and soon we had grandchildren. We were so proud.

So it was only Meggie, my lovely Meggie, who came home to live with us again. But she too, met a decent young man who worked in an office as an accounts clerk and was training to be an accountant. She'd done so well for herself marrying a white-collar worker. When her daughter, Sarah, was born, I was the proudest grandmother ever.

The new families started to come to tea with me every Saturday afternoon. It became the highlight of my week. Tom too, liked their visits and made sure he was home. We'd have sing-songs and the little ones would stand on the table and sing nursery rhymes. Tom would play games with them and his eyes glinted with pleasure as he made up new ones. One game they all loved was, 'earning a sixpence', as Tom called it.

'Now, then, girls first,' he'd say every week. 'Undo my laces and take off my shoes and put my slippers on for me, there's good 'uns.' Our two little grand-daughters would squeal in pleasure as they rushed to his armchair. They competed with each other every week to see who could do it the quickest. We all joined in with the excitement, grownups cheering on the girls. Simple, good fun that brought us together. While the girls were trying to get Tom's shoes off, he would pretend to sleep and the girls would try to wake him by shouting, 'Wake up Grandsha.' They'd shake him and then he'd pretend to snore. We'd all start shouting at him then. 'Wake up, Grandsha, wake up, wake up.' Sometimes, we couldn't shout for laughing, as Tom made silly faces. They were innocent joys. We didn't need money to have a good time.

Then, Tom would open an eye and look down and smile. 'Oh, finished already?' he'd say as he brought out of his pocket two sixpences. They were always very shiny sixpences and I suspected he polished them up beforehand. There were still vestiges of my old Tom there and I used to struggle with the feeling of what it could have been like without his mother. Then I'd shake myself back to reality. No good dwelling in what ifs. Concentrate on what we had now.

*

By the 1960's when our grandchildren were getting excited by The Beatles and The Mersey Sound, Tom and I retired and received our pension. It wasn't much, but then, we didn't need much. We'd spent our lives without and it was now ingrained in us. Economy was our watchword. We helped out our children when necessary, buying presents for the kids and I was able to save enough to go on holiday twice a year. I'd go with Edie and Mrs Farmer from next door and the women from my church. We'd join bus trips to seaside resorts like Ilfracombe, Western-Super-Mare and the like, or go to London for a long weekend and see a West End show. It was fun and I enjoyed them. On one particular trip, I was going to Torquay for ten days.

'Well, enjoy yourself,' Tom said as he sat in his armchair and watched me putting on my summer coat. Then, he said something extraordinary. 'Tell you what, I'll paper this room for you. When you get back, it'll be all nice and fresh with new wallpaper and paint.'

I was so shocked, I had to sit down and make a conscious effort to shut my mouth. This was unheard of. He never did jobs around the house.

'I don't believe it. Did you *really* say you would redecorate our living room?'

'Yes, that's what I said. I don't know why you're so surprised, I've decorated it before.'

'Yes, you did – once! But that was so long ago and I've got so fed up of asking you over the years that I'd given up.' I looked at him hard and he wasn't laughing. He must be serious then. 'Well, well, I never thought I'd see the day. You volunteering to decorate. What's the matter? Why this sudden interest in decorating?'

'I just feel like it, that's all. Even I can see it needs doing and I'll be able to do it in my own time without you nagging me. I'll enjoy it.' He scratched his head and looked at me as if he was puzzled by my reaction. 'I can make as much mess as I like. Tell me what kind of paper you'd like and I'll look for it this afternoon,' he said with such finality and confidence, as if it was something he did every day. I was even more shocked. Was this my Tom?

'Well, I'll be,' was all the response I could manage.

'Well, that's nice, I don't think. I thought you wanted this room redecorated, you're always on about it.' Tom put on one of his sulks. It was rather attractive in its way and before we were married, he could always get around me with such a sulk. It made me laugh. But I hadn't seen one for years. I didn't know he could still do it.

But there was no time to dwell as Edie was knocking on our door and walking in saying, 'Ready, Kate? Ready for an exciting ten days in the flesh pot of the West Country. Song, sea, sand and men; but don't tell my old lug, whatever you do.' She laughed her infectious laugh.

'Oh, Edie,' I said, laughing too, 'don't say things like that or Tom will believe you and you know we all behave like church women with the vicar looking on.'

I took a sneaky look at Tom, worried he might believe her, but he was smiling. I know he looked forward to these times he had alone. He never wanted a holiday. I like my home, he'd say.

'Well, don't go back on your word now will you? I'd be disappointed if I come back and find it all the same.'

'Don't worry, it will be all new. Go and enjoy yourself and don't think of home.'

I joined Edie at the front door and turned round to Tom. 'Make it roses, Tom. Nice pink roses. I love roses.' And with that I shut the front door and went to Torquay.

*

When I got back, I opened the front door with trepidation. I don't know why, but something was shivering down my back. What had he been up to? I walked into the living room; there was no one there. I called out, but the house was empty. I looked around the room. Sure enough, the window frame was painted a nice, bright white and looked a picture and the doors and skirting boards the same. And the walls were covered in a soft cream paper, with a profusion of pink roses with long green stems: gorgeous, but for the fact that they were all upside-down.

I sat on a kitchen chair, still with my summer coat on, and didn't know whether to laugh or cry. After all these years I still

213

hadn't got what I wanted. Why did I bother? I made some tea, changed from my travelling clothes into something more comfortable, all the while trying to get used to upside-down roses.

When Tom finally got home, smelling of beer, but sober, I tackled him about it.

'No,' he said, 'they're fine. They're roses, aren't they? Pretty roses. No, they're not upside-down.'

'Get yourself some new glasses. They are definitely upside-down.' But Tom couldn't see it at all, and I wondered whether he did need new glasses.

'Well, upside-down or not, I'm not doing it again. It nearly killed me. I'm too old for decorating. Either you put up with upside-down roses or pay a decorator to come in and re-do it. I'm washing my hands of it.'

And put up with them I did: for years. It was easier and after all, it was just Tom and me, and we weren't going to entertain royalty, but it did rankle.

We still didn't speak to each other very much, apart from necessary things like, 'Want a cup of tea?' 'Here's your dinner.' 'Mind your feet,' from me, while Tom's vocabulary didn't usually exceed, 'Going out now.' 'Off to bed.' 'I'm hungry.' Not a lot to show for fifty years of marriage.

CHAPTER TWENTY

Tom and I were entering our seventh decade. My life was full of my children and grand-children. They all visited regularly and included Tom and me in all family celebrations and outings. Since his mother's death, Tom had got to know his children more, especially the boys, and they used to go to the pub together. Life was sweet and we'd reached a point of satisfaction in our lives. Our years of struggle were over. We never spoke of them to anyone, not even to each other.

Then I got a letter. I rarely got letters, except from Aunty Annie and I knew her handwriting, and this wasn't hers. Other letters I dreaded as they usually brought bad news. I didn't quite know what to make of the one that arrived on my doormat because the envelope was addressed to me, in red pen. Did I owe any money? Not to my knowledge unless Tom had got himself into trouble. I put it on the mantelpiece and looked at it for a while, until I chided my stupidity and grabbed it and tore it open.

Dear Mrs Mallow

Please forgive me writing to you like this, but I'm very worried about Davy. As you know, since my mother's death some years ago, Davy continued to live with me and my family. He's an uncle to us all, and we all love him as if he was our own blood. Over the past two weeks, he has taken to his bed and won't leave it. He refuses all food and cries all the time. I don't know what to do. I think he's dying. He won't see a doctor, says he's in no pain, but I don't know. Please help me Mrs Mallow. Please come to visit him. Anytime will do, there is always someone in.

Yours sincerely
Margaret Mace (Mrs)

I went that afternoon and as she led me up to his bedroom, I felt apprehensive and nervous. I hadn't seen him for years as he preferred it that way so I didn't push myself on him. We occasionally bumped into each other in town, but we only stopped to say some pleasantries and then he always hurried away, as if, I always felt, he was afraid I was going to pry into his business.

He was in bed in his pyjamas, lying on his back looking up at the ceiling. He didn't acknowledge me. The air was stale and sour. I quickly took in the neatness of the room, the high polish finish on the wardrobe and chest of drawers. The little table under the window had a pristine white tablecloth over it with a vase of flowers. Davy always liked things nice.

'Hello, Davy,' I said. 'How are you?'

No answer.

'Mrs Mace is very worried about you. She asked me to come and see you.'

'Bugger off.'

'That's not a nice way to talk to your sister. I'm only trying to help you.' His eyes never left the ceiling.

'I don't need any help.'

'No, I can see that. You haven't got up for two weeks, refuse to eat and cry all the time. No, of course you don't need any help.'

'Bugger off.'

I lost my temper then. 'Don't speak to me like that. I won't have it. I'm your sister. Now if you don't care about yourself, Mrs Mace does and it's very unfair on her for you to be like this. She deserves better than that. She's your family and continued to look after you after her mother died, and she looks after you very well from what I can see. This is totally selfish of you. Think of her. Talk to me for her. Haven't you got any gratitude in you?'

And with that, he broke into giant sobs that went on for over half an hour. He couldn't control himself. I could see why Mrs Mace was worried.

I didn't know what to do and he wouldn't accept any comfort.

'Davy love,' I said in the end, 'I'm going to leave you now and come back tomorrow morning. Then we are going to have a chat together, just us two.'

Next morning, I was feeling nervous as I approached the house. They still lived in the same one her mother had lived in when she took in Davy as her surrogate son fifty or so years ago. The front of it hadn't changed, but inside, everything was different. Davy was different. I didn't know how to talk to him. I didn't think I was the best person to talk to him. I was his sister, but only that. We'd hardly had contact from the time he left home and he felt like a stranger. I remembered when I broke down in front of Tom, and how it felt, the powerlessness, the hopeless feeling, the loss of control, the shame, and I wondered if he was feeling the same.

I knocked on the door and Mrs Mace answered. 'How is he?' I asked.

'Just the same, I'm sorry to say. He cried all night after you left yesterday. I don't know what to do. I'd appreciate your advice, Mrs Mallow. Please see him and then come down for a cup of tea, and let's talk about what we should do.'

That was the last thing I wanted. I had no idea what to do about him, but I said, 'Yes, I'll do that Mrs Mace.' I went up the stairs – slowly, gathering my thoughts. I knocked on the door, but there was no answer. 'Davy, Davy, it's me, Kate. Can I come in?' Nothing. Mrs Mace called up, 'Go on in, he often doesn't speak.' Reluctantly, I turned the knob and my hand was shaking as I pushed open the door. Davy was lying in his bed, just the same as yesterday, but I sensed a difference. Something had changed.

'Hello, Davy, it's me again. How are you today?'

I was expecting another profanity to come my way, but to my surprise, he said, 'I can't talk about it, it's too hard.' His voice was so low that I had difficulty in hearing him. I leaned closer. I caught, 'I can't stop crying,' before a bevy of sobs stopped his words. 'I've written it all down here,' he said between sobs as he fumbled under his pillow and pulled out a letter. 'This is for you, Kate, just for you. Please don't show it to anyone else.'

It was written on slightly creased blue notepaper, and even had an envelope, addressed to me.

He held out the envelope, desperately trying to control his sobbing and I could see his pain clearly etched out on his face. Surprised and intrigued as to what he felt he had to write down, I took it from him without a word and walked over to the window and stood with my back to him. My hands were shaking as I took out the notepaper and put the envelope down on the small table in front of me.

The letter was written in Davy's usual small, neat handwriting. That was one thing that never changed with him, he was always so neat. But in a way, I wished his writing was so bad that I couldn't read it, because I found the contents distressing.

Dear Kate,

This is just for you. Please do not tell anyone else what is in this letter. I don't want the whole world to know my secrets, especially my family here. They've been so good to me I don't want to upset them. So before you read on, please tell me that you will give me your solemn oath not to tell anyone what is in this letter.

I turned to him.

'You promise, Kate?' he whispered.

I got drawn into his gaze and knew I had to answer. 'Yes. Yes, Davy love, I promise.' I turned my back to him again and continued reading.

I'm sorry, but I am too upset to speak of these things, I can't stop crying every time I think of it.

I'm just going to have to tell you this straight, get it out as quickly as I can. I'll try and put it so that you can understand. Or maybe, you never will.

You know why I left home and my love for Rhys all those years ago. You also know that I have never married. There is a reason for that. I couldn't love a woman. It just wasn't in me. I could only love men. I buried it deep within myself for years, until when I was forty, I met a man and we fell in love. Unfortunately, he was married with children. He was a doctor, so we always had to be doubly careful. He was the same age as me and we met once a month for nearly thirty years.

218

We'd catch the train somewhere, Cardiff or Swansea or wherever we were not known. We'd book into a hotel separately and in advance, but one of us would book a double room and when we arrived, say his wife had been taken ill and was not joining him. We would then secretly share the double room for the weekend. We always went to the very best hotels, he always told me nothing but the best was good enough for me. We were so happy together. Thirty years is a long time and I lived for those monthly meetings.

We last met two weeks ago and he told me that his wife had become very suspicious and thought he had a mistress. When he was a working doctor, he told her he volunteered his skills one weekend a month at a charity in Swansea. But now he's retired and he's losing his sight. She knew he couldn't practise any more but he still went on his weekend away with me every month. He made up excuses but she didn't believe him.

He told me that we had to stop our relationship. He couldn't bear the shame if he was found out and he would lose all his status in his community. He lives up the valleys and is well known and respected, and as you know, they're very straight-laced up there. He was broken hearted, but he had to do it. He couldn't destroy his family and his reputation. He had a responsibility to them. He had no choice.

That's it, Kate, that's all there is to it. And look at me. I can't do anything but cry. We love each other, very much. I know he loves me more than his wife. She was just a cover to hide his true feelings. In fact, he doesn't love her – you know, like that – at all, but he was so afraid of his feelings that he tried to smother it for years. Until he met me. Me too, I'd smothered it since Rhys died, until I met him. But it was more difficult for him. He loved his children and his job, and I understood that. I had nothing to lose. Look at me, I'm just a little man with a little life and I had a little job. I have no status in the community. No one cares about me except for my family here and, well, maybe you, Kate. But it was so different for him. I understood all that. I was just so grateful that he felt such love for me. It made my life worthwhile.

I don't blame him, but I'm shocked that I've fallen so totally to pieces. I can't stop it. I've tried, believe me I've tried. I knew this was coming one day, and I thought I was prepared, but can you prepare yourself for a broken heart?

I don't know what to do. I don't want to see a doctor because he might *get the secret out of me. Give me drugs or something that would make me talk. I can't talk about it. I have to keep supporting him. I'd die if anyone found out about us and he blamed me. It would destroy him – and me.*

Re-reading this, it all seems so pathetic really, two grown men acting like teenage lovers, but that's how we were for all those years.

I want to die, that's all I can think of. I can't stand this pain much longer. I know he will never come back. Our time together is finished, but it doesn't make it any easier. He was my life. Without him, I have none.

The letter ended there. He hadn't signed it. I was so absorbed in the letter, I didn't realise I was crying. I took out my hankie and dabbed my eyes and blew my nose.

I turned and looked at him. He was staring up at the ceiling again. 'Poor, poor Davy,' was all I could manage.

'Do you hate me?'

'No, of course not. You're my brother, I could never hate you. But it's a shock. I never thought . . . oh, I don't know, I suppose I never thought of you loving someone . . . like this. I thought it was all over after Rhys.'

'And I never thought I'd love someone as much again. I know it's disgusting. Two men like that. Most people would hate me for it, I know that. But I couldn't stop it. It was just natural to us.'

He rose from his bed and in one sweeping movement took the letter from me and threw it in the grate. He took some matches from the mantelpiece and set fire to it. He wasn't satisfied until it was totally destroyed. Then he got back into bed.

My legs started to shake so I sat down on the wooden chair next to the bed and tried to gather my thoughts.

'I don't know what to say. It's been a shock. I just never thought . . . but thank you for telling me. It must have been a hard thing to do.'

'It was, but you're still my sister and under the circumstances I felt you should know my situation, because of – well . . .'

'I won't tell anyone, don't worry. I promise.'

'I've been thinking of our childhood and how badly treated

you were, I didn't want to treat you badly too. I want you to understand . . . if you can, that is.'

'I'm trying to, Davy. It's difficult to understand your feelings for another man but I can appreciate the feelings of love and the hurt of love when it's taken from you.' My eyes closed involuntarily and I breathed deeply as thoughts about my own life, my own disappointments, surfaced. Eventually, I said, 'Love is love I suppose, wherever you find it . . . and however you lose it.' We were silent for a while and then he put his hand over mine.

'Thank you, Kate. Thank you for trying to understand.'

I took hold of his hand and squeezed it gently.

'My life has been so different to yours, Davy. We share the same parents, but that's all that binds us really. Isn't it funny how we could be so different? Same parents, same upbringing, but so different.'

He sniffed. 'I suppose so, but as long as you still think of me as your brother and not as some monster you read about in the cheap Sunday newspapers. I wanted you to know that it wasn't like that. It was beautiful. That much love shared between two people is the most beautiful thing. It makes living worthwhile. There was nothing ugly about it as some people will tell you. We were two human beings in love, how can that be wrong?'

My heart went out to him as I squeezed his hand again. 'It's all right, Davy, love. I don't think you're a monster, far from it. You're Davy, my little brother and always will be. You worry too much about what people will think. If it was right for you – then who am I to say anything different?'

He swallowed hard. 'Thank you,' he said, as his tears welled up. He breathed deeply. 'Whatever you do, don't send for the doctor, I don't want one. I don't need one. I'm better off alone.' The sobs started again. He'd done so well. Between sobs, he asked me to go and not to come back. 'I'm sorry, I don't mean to be ungrateful, but really, I can cope better alone. Don't worry about me.'

I left him reluctantly. There was nothing else I could do. I was shaking with the shock of it but controlled myself long enough to tell Mrs Mace I didn't think anything should be done. He didn't want a doctor and he didn't want to see me again either. 'He wants it this way, Mrs Mace. I don't see any use in going against his wishes. It's his life and his decision. I'm sorry. I know it's harder for you because you have to look after him. But I'm worried if a doctor is called he may take him into a mental hospital. That would definitely kill Davy.'

She looked shocked. 'I never thought of that, Mrs Mallow. Oh, my word, no, that will not do. I'd never do that to Uncle Davy.'

I put my hand over hers. 'Will you be alright?'

She smiled a wan smile. 'I suppose so. Thank you for coming. You've helped me see the way forward. I didn't know what to do for the best, but now I do. I'll give him his privacy and do my best for him. I'll not call the doctor. Not unless Davy says he wants to.'

'Good luck, Mrs Mace, summon me again if you need to, but he did say he didn't want to see me again. But I'll help you if I can.' With that, I left the distraught woman.

A few days later, he disappeared from the house. Mrs Mace came to see if I'd seen him, but I hadn't. She said that he was wearing his best suit, but hadn't taken his overcoat. 'It's cold, Mrs Mallow, freezing, and we've been all over the mountain and down to the river and any other place he used to like to walk, but there's no sign of him. He's been gone nearly two days.' She broke down and cried and I tried to comfort her.

'Have you told the police?'

'No! No, I haven't. I thought about it, but then remembered what you said about taking him away to a mental hospital. I couldn't do that to him. So, no, it's just been the family looking. Oh, God help me. Did I do wrong? Should I have called the police?'

'No, not at all. You did the right thing. Davy would not want any fuss made, you know that as well as I do.'

'Yes, you're right. Sorry, I'm not thinking straight. Davy was such a private man. He hated causing a fuss.'

'You go home now and take a rest. I'll go out myself with

my sons and we'll search for him too. You're exhausted. I can see that, so you would slow things down. Leave it to me now. I'll look for him.'

But I didn't contact my sons, I went out alone. I had a pretty good idea of where he might be. I remembered the spot on the mountain he particularly loved as he'd taken me there, all those years ago, when he told me about Rhys's death.

As I walked up the mountain behind Mrs Mace's house, a strange feeling of peace took hold of me. It was as if I was outside my body and looking down at myself as I approached the summit and the spot I was looking for. His body was lying in the dip, on its back and his eyes were closed. He'd placed his hands over his chest as he waited to die. He hadn't eaten for two weeks so his body was weak and I hoped it had not taken him too long. His face was peaceful and I was happy for him. He was out of his misery.

I kneeled down beside him and bent over and kissed his cold cheek, remembering as I did so the time Aunty Gladys had made Davy and me kiss our mother's cheek just after she'd died. This time, though, there was no terror, only love. 'I loved you, Davy,' I said out loud. 'I loved you more than you knew. I so wished it could all have been different.' I felt a calmness come over me which I fancied came from him. He had found peace and I felt happy for him. I didn't cry. I took strength from him. Davy would not want emotions. For me to remember him with love was enough.

I didn't know the name of the man Davy had loved and who had loved him in return, so I couldn't tell him of Davy's death. I wondered if he'd ever know and felt powerless and so sad.

A week later the post mortem said 'Died from exposure and dehydration'. That was all: so stark and to the point. The life of a human being expressed in five words.

I had no doubt it was suicide, although the coroner didn't say so. And I was glad. Davy would not have wanted that and I, of course, didn't say anything.

I knew now why he didn't want me to visit him again. He knew this is what he was going to do and didn't want me to get caught up in the aftermath.

I missed him more than I could have imagined. We hadn't had much contact with each other once we'd grown up, but I realised he had always been part of me. Part of our childhood and the events that shaped us. We didn't need to see each other often, our bond was always there.

His funeral was a quiet affair, just his adopted family, me and Tom. Some years ago, he'd expressed a desire to be cremated rather than buried, Mrs Mace said. And he wanted his ashes scattered on the mountain he loved so much. About a week later, his adopted family and I went up behind their house and we took turns in scattering his ashes into the wind. It was a breezy day and they scattered around a large area. He would have loved that.

*

Tom came home from the pub as he did every evening and sat in his armchair.

'You know, it's been a year since Davy died,' he said, his speech a little slurred and I wondered if he'd had one too many. 'A year today in fact.'

'Yes, I know. I'm surprised you remembered,' I said gently, putting his tea on the arm of his chair, as I always did.

'I liked Davy,' he said and then he looked up at me and smiled, which was so unusual it took me aback for a moment for it was a smile of pure love. After I recovered from my shock, I felt my old love for him seeping up and found myself returning his look of love thinking, is it still there then – deep inside us? Seconds later, he slumped in the chair.

'Tom,' I shouted. 'Tom!' I shook him, but he just sat there, unable to move or speak. I felt a panic rise up which was unlike me, but this was Tom. My Tom. I shook him again, but it was no use. 'I'll get Mr Farmer, Tom, don't worry, you'll be all right.'

I ran next door and Mrs Farmer phoned for the doctor as Mr Farmer ran back with me. 'It looks like a stroke, Mrs Mallow,' he said. 'My father died of one, I know the signs.'

'Oh, my God,' I said, looking down at Tom, unsure what to

do.

The doctor arrived quickly and confirmed it was a stroke. 'We can send him to hospital, Mrs Mallow,' the doctor said, 'or you can look after him yourself here. There is nothing the hospital can do for him that you cannot. I'm so sorry. I'm afraid it's serious. He doesn't have long.'

I looked at him stupidly, couldn't take it in. Mrs Farmer came in then. 'I've phoned your children, Mrs Mallow, they are on their way.' All I could do was look at her.

'She's in shock,' I heard the doctor say as if from a long way away. 'Make her some sweet tea please, Mrs Farmer.'

He led me to a chair and I sat down hard. Tom? Not long? I didn't know what to do, surprised at my feebleness. I was all a blur until my sons arrived.

'We'll put him upstairs,' I heard Jim say. 'We'll look after him, doctor.'

Somehow, I don't quite know how, they got Tom upstairs to our bedroom. He'd put on a lot of weight in the past few years. Tom and I had shared the same house and family for fifty years and as estranged as we were, we still shared the same bed. It was habit I suppose. I liked to have him near me, it felt reassuring. I don't know why he continued to share with me. I liked to think that he felt the same about me, but I didn't dare ask him in case he decided to decamp into the spare bedroom. I didn't want to be left alone. And now, Tom lay in our bed like a beached whale and I knew he would soon leave me. I couldn't understand my reaction. I thought all my love for him had died, but here it was surging up inside me.

The children stayed with me that night as we sat by his bedside. Megan made tea, but I couldn't drink anything. I dozed off remembering my love for Tom and our youth. Then someone was shaking me awake and I noticed it was morning.

'Mam,' Megan said softly, 'Mam, he going. Hold his hand, he'd like that. Don't let him die alone.' I did as I was bid, and for the first time in what seemed a lifetime, I held his hand. Surprisingly, it felt soft, but very cold. His eyes had been shut, but at the touch of my hand in his, he opened them and looked at me and I saw love shine out of them again. It took me by surprise but then I realised I was returning his look of love. It felt so good. We were together again at the end.

He struggled to say something but it came out like a groan. He took another ragged breath and I put my ear near his mouth. I just made out, 'Now, you can take off the wallpaper.' I looked at him as if he had spoken to me in a foreign tongue. 'Take it off, Kate. Take the wallpaper off.' He closed his eyes then and stopped breathing: a slow closing of his eyes and an intake of breath that never came out.

I kissed the back of his hand and the love I had for him surged up from somewhere down in my boots. The power of it took me by surprise. I think he felt that same love for me reasserting itself on his deathbed. That look of love he gave me was from our past, was between just the two of us. As it had been all those years ago, before life got to us and made us into the people we became, not the people we once were.

He died surrounded by his children and they all surprised me by giving him a kiss on the cheek.

'We'll take care of everything, Mam,' Jimmy said. 'Do you want to be alone with him?'

I nodded. When they all left, for some strange reason, I took his hand and squeezed it. As if he would answer me. But there was no life there and now it was too late. Oh, Tom. What happened to us?

I went slowly downstairs and said, 'I'm just going out for a bit. I'd like to be alone for a while, if you don't mind.'

'Of course not, Mam,' Meggie said. 'Don't worry about anything.'

I went up to the rocking stone of course. Where else would I go? My thoughts jumped about and made me feel dizzy so I made a big effort to get them under some control. I'd never thought of a life without Tom. He was a good man who had turned from a simple loving one, full of optimism and hope for the future, into someone who had turned in on himself and had let life grind him down. There were many men like Tom in Ponty. I could see it in their faces, in their lost, soulless eyes. Years on the dole, without hope, does terrible things to a proud man. I grieved for the man that Tom had been. I grieved for myself and what might have been. For the loss of my independence, confidence and powerlessness over my body.

That bastard, Dudley.

I wanted to kill him, to torture him as he had me. The rape was only an afternoon of fun for him, but it was a lifetime of tormented memories for me. The memory of rape never goes away, it just hibernates and comes out to bite you when you least expect it. Over and over the pain comes afresh.

If only Tom and I could have believed in each other. If we could have talked and not let wedges of doubt and suspicion separate us. If only Tom could have overcome his fear of upsetting his mother. But he couldn't and I didn't want to be bitter.

And what was all that about taking the wallpaper off? Had he gone mad? Had the stroke affected his reason? I couldn't understand it. Maybe he was feeling guilty at making me keep it and it was praying on his mind in his last moments. But I looked on the upside-down roses as a gift of love from Tom. He has done his best, tried to make amends, but it had just gone wrong. So much of our life had gone wrong. So I decided to keep that damned wallpaper in memory of Tom. He meant well.

Tom's funeral went by in a blur and I don't remember anything except crying throughout it, especially when his coffin was taken away for burial. The pain was hard to bear. And then, afterwards, as the days turned into months and I was alone for the first time in my life, I couldn't believe how much pain his death caused me. I spent a lot of time up on our rocking stone, thinking, remembering.

As time went by, the children asked me if I'd like to move into a house with all mod cons. 'You've paid rent on this house for years,' they said. 'It's sub-standard now. You could have your own big kitchen and indoor bathroom with bath and shower and toilet and everything. We'll all chip in and buy you a nice terraced house wherever you want to go.' I was touched to the core, and greatly relieved if I'm honest as it got harder every year to cope with the basic conditions in the house, and the steps and stairs.

I made sure they were not stretching their finances too far and then gladly accepted. 'But I'm not leaving the Graig,' I said. 'This is where I belong.'

They found me a nice modernised terraced house with three bedrooms, one that had been turned into a bathroom and the two rooms downstairs had been knocked into one long room with an enormous (well, enormous to me) kitchen leading off from it. It was like living in a palace and only a couple of streets away from Graig Street. I was as happy as a cat with a saucer of cream. My granddaughter, Sarah and her fiancé, Mark, were looking for a house of their own and she said they would try and buy my old house and modernise it and put on an extension at the back. It took a while to arrange but they were able to buy it very cheaply; well, who would want to live there in those conditions?

CHAPTER TWENTY ONE

I wake up with a start, cold and stiff as I realise with shock that it's morning. Yesterday's newspaper is still on my lap. I read the headline once again.

PONTYPRIDD CHRONICLE

23 August, 1973

BODY FOUND IN WELL

A skeleton was found this week at the bottom of a disused well on The Graig, Pontypridd. With the remains was a Miners' Federation Card dated 1920 in the name of Dudley J. Mallow. Anyone who has information about this person is requested to contact the police.

I'm still in shock. When the newspaper came through my letter box yesterday, I sat down in my armchair with a cup of tea to read it as I did every week, looked forward to it in fact. But after seeing that headline, I felt as if as electric shock had found its way into my funny bone. Dudley Mallow! Dudley?

Fear had gripped me then and I started to shake uncontrollably. That coil of hatred I had for him wound itself around my body again, just as it had all those years ago. I'd never wanted to hear his name again, never thought I would.

229

I'm the only person left alive in our family who knew him and I didn't want to be the person to bring him back to life. But I had no choice, the memories ran through me like a floodgate opening. They ran wild and free, my whole life bumping and tumbling before me.

What I've remembered and what I've forgotten I suppose says a lot about me. And where has it got me? I still don't know if it was Tom who murdered Dudley – because murder it had to be. You don't fall down a well and then get up and put the cover back on. And the cover must have been replaced all those years ago otherwise he would have been found straight away. Nearly forty years he's been down there. Well, serves him right!

If Tom had been the murderer I would have embraced him, kissed him and said thank you. Thank you for giving me back my life.

Is there anywhere else I could have looked for the answer? Have I forgotten something? But that's my life as I've remembered it. Memory is selective and thank goodness for it otherwise we'd go mad. I'm satisfied with what I've remembered and I have to accept the fact that I didn't know what happened then and I don't know now.

I feel drained but unexpectedly elated. My life has had its problems, but so have many others. It could have been worse. My children have been an absolute joy to me, they've made everything worthwhile. I'm surrounded by my family and they all care for and look after me. What more could I ask? The past is the past and will have to stay there.

I doze in my chair until the doorbell wakes me. It's my granddaughter, Sarah. She has a key, but always rings the bell to let me know she's here. Afraid of my poor old heart giving out in fright, I suppose.

'Hello, Nana.' She's bright and breezy as usual, but then looks at me closely. She sits on the footstool in front of me. 'You look tired, Nan, and pale. You sure you're all right?'

'Yes, love, I'm fine. Don't fuss.' I smile at her but it doesn't quite come off.

'There is something, isn't there? I know you, Nan.' She takes my hand. 'Oh, you're cold.' She jumps up, 'I'll go get you your little blanket.' Before I can stop her she goes into my bedroom. When she comes out, holding the blanket she looks worried as she sits back down on the footstool. 'You haven't been to bed, have you?'

'Yes, I have,' I lie, 'I made my bed early this morning.'

'You never make it early, you know you like it to air. Come on now, tell me. What's wrong?'

'Nothing,' I say too quickly.

She picks up the newspaper to put the blanket around my legs. As she puts it back on my lap she reads the headline.

She looks at me for a moment. BODY FOUND IN WELL seems to jump out and mock me.

'I saw that headline yesterday in the shop, but I didn't buy the paper.' She hesitates. 'It . . . it isn't anything to do with this is it?' Her voice has risen and she looks worried.

I don't say anything. Her probing is unnerving me. I don't quite know how to react. I don't want to lie to her. I've never lied to her. We trust each other and I don't want to break that trust.

She takes my hand and looks at me, full of concern. 'This is serious. I can see it in your face. It is about that body, isn't it?'

She looks down at the article and reads it. As she gets to the end, she raises her head slowly and says, 'Mallow? Dudley Mallow? Is he a relation of ours? I've never heard of him.'

She's really worried and I wouldn't have that for the world. I have to say something, but not all. I don't have to tell her all.

'I'm sorry, love, you're right. I didn't want to worry you, but I have been sitting up all night thinking about the past. And you're right again, I did know him. He was your grandfather's brother, although not a real brother as your grandfather was adopted by the parents of Dudley Mallow.'

'Adopted? I didn't know. Wow! Who were his real parents?'

'I don't know, they died and that's why he was adopted as a baby.'

'What sort of a man was this Dudley? Were you worried

231

when he disappeared?'

Again, I couldn't lie to her. 'No. Everyone was glad he disappeared. He was not a nice man. No one liked him.'

'No one? Surely someone liked him? Was he married?'

'No, love, he wasn't, and he was a bad lot, please believe me. When he went missing everyone thought either someone's husband had done him in – he was like that you see – or he'd left the area because he'd done something terrible . . . you know, had the law on him or something. To be truthful, I was glad and so were many other people. But no one had any idea he ended up in a well. Dead. Well, you wouldn't, would you?'

'I see,' she said, all serious. 'It's fascinating, but if you don't know what happened to him, well, you don't know and that's that.'

'The only way I'd know was if I had put him in the well myself and I can assure you on every oath there is that I didn't. This is just as much a surprise to me as to everyone else.'

'Oh, Nan, I didn't mean you'd had anything to do with it. Of course I didn't mean that. That's ridiculous.'

'Well, then, let's just leave it there, shall we? I can't tell you any more than that. I just couldn't stop the memories coming last night and I forgot to go to bed. That's all, the time went so fast. It was morning before I knew it.'

I leaned forward and kissed her on the cheek. She gave me a hug and laughed.

'Well,' I said, desperate to change the subject, 'what are you doing today?'

'I'm on my way to your old house to start on the redecorations. The extension is finally finished and the builders have gone. All we have to do is to redecorate and I'm going to start it today, it's my day off. Mark will join me this evening to give me a hand. We want to get it done before the wedding. I can't wait to live there. It must be so full of all sorts of lovely memories for you. We had such good times there when I was little.'

I blanch a bit but hide it. 'Yes, love, full of them. But you must make your own memories. I got very fond of that house and I look forward to seeing it all fresh and modern. It will be a modern house for a modern couple, just as it should be.'

When she leaves, I realise that I'm going to be asked a lot of questions. I steel myself and decide to tell everyone just what I've told Sarah. Hopefully, the fuss will soon die down.

*

A few days later, Sarah visits me again. 'Hello, Nana, how are you? Are you feeling better?' She's as bouncy as ever and there is a hint of excitement in her eyes.

'Fine dear, I've recovered perfectly. Now, tell me, have you finished your decorating?'

She sits on my footstool in front of me. 'Oh, I wish I had, but no, we'll be at it for another couple of weeks yet. But . . .' she stops dramatically, her eyes showing that excitement, and she gives me a look I can't quite fathom. 'You'll never guess what I found.'

'You're right,' I say, intrigued. 'You'd better tell me. Should I be worried?' I say laughing.

'Well,' she drags the word out, playing with me. I sit patiently waiting for her, raising my eyebrow in question.

'Well,' she repeats, 'you know the upside-down roses Grandsha put up?' She looks at me, raising her own eyebrow.

'Of course. I'm not senile yet you know.' I laugh again, wondering what on earth she's getting to.

'Well,' that long drawn out word again, 'as I was stripping it everything came off easily except the bit behind the kitchen cabinet. It was really difficult to get off and I thought Grandsha must have used some extra paste there. Anyway, when I finally managed to strip it off, there was something written on the wall in paint.' Her eyes are sparkling.

'Something written on the wall?' I repeat stupidly. She's still looking at me with that excitement. 'Well?' I draw out the word as she had done, worried now.

'It said, and I quote, "There is a letter under the loose floorboard beneath our bed. Please read it. It will explain everything. Tom."'

My breath shudders and my heart beats faster. This has to be about Dudley. Would I find out at last? My heart feels as if it will give out as I try to calm myself. That would be an irony if I died with the solution to the mystery unopened in my hands.

Sarah rises up and puts her arm around my shoulders. 'Are you all right, Nan? Nan, speak to me. Oh, what shall I do?' I realise she's really worried about me and that I should do something to reassure her.

'I'm all right, love, don't worry.' I hadn't realised my face had shown so much of my feelings. 'It's just a pain.' I grab my side for emphasis. 'It's the price you pay for getting older. I'm fine.' I hesitate. 'And . . . did you . . . look under the floorboards?'

'It took me a while because, of course, your bed is no longer there, but I remembered its rough location and I found it. It's sealed and addressed to you, so I haven't opened it although I'm agog to know what it says. But I'll go and make some tea to give you some privacy.'

She hands me the envelope and a tingle shoots up my arm as if it's red hot or supernatural. The envelope is yellowing and looks fragile. I'll have to be careful not to tear the letter. Tom obviously didn't use very good quality paper for such a dramatic thing as this. I look at the envelope for a long time. I don't want Sarah here when I read the letter. I need to be alone.

When she comes out of the kitchen she puts the tray on the table. I get up and walk towards the sideboard and open a drawer, 'If you don't mind, love, I'd like to be alone when I read this. Another hour or so won't matter. I'll put it away 'till later.'

'Of course, Nan. I can't say I'm not intrigued because that would be an understatement, but this is between you and Grandsha. If you want to tell me about it later I'll be very happy, but if not, then I understand. He may have left you a love letter, wouldn't that be something.' She laughs, full of innocent joy. She has no idea what this letter is about. And why should she? What do we know of the lives of others and their innermost feelings?

I realise I'm scowling so I think of something nice. Of my mother and the scant memories I have of her. Of the love that shone out of her eyes all those years ago when she lay dying. No one will ever know of that look of love. It was between us and I wonder how many other looks of love have gone unrecorded in the world. Acts of violence or horror always get remembered, but the one thing that the world is built on, that it cannot live without – love – is the thing that is most often lost.

Finally, Sarah goes home.

Now the time is here I'm reluctant: afraid. I go over to the sideboard and take out the letter. My hand is shaking. I can't stop thinking that after all these years, the answer is here, in my hand and that makes me shake even more.

I sit down in my armchair and adjust my glasses trying to keep control of myself. My heart is beating so hard I feel ill as I look at Tom's untidy scribble on the envelope. *To be opened only after my death and only by my wife, Katherine Anne Mallow.* The ink is so faded that I can only just make out the writing. Wouldn't it be cruel if the ink inside has faded too, so much so that I can't read anything? Pull yourself together, woman. Stop this and open the damned thing.

I pick up my letter opener and carefully slit the envelope open and with my hands shaking even more, take a deep breath and gently pull out the letter. There are several sheets and the paper is pale blue, thin but in good condition and the ink is fine. It hasn't faded. Thank goodness. Tom's writing was never good and was always hard to read, but I can see the writing here is quite clear. He obviously took a lot of trouble. His spelling was always atrocious, so I make a mental note to ignore all his mistakes as I start to read.

Dear Kate

This is a hard letter for me to write. Well – you know me I never was one for writing. But I need to tell you things I think you need to know. Maybe I'm a coward telling you like this and I wouldn't blame you if you thought so. I tried to tell you many times but it just would not come out. Every time I tried it just went all wrong. But how could anyone tell someone this?

And if you are reading this letter I will be dead – like I said I'm a coward.

There are two things I have to tell you. One is nice (I hope) and the other is awful. The first is that I love you. Yes I do mean love and not loved. I have not said this to you since the early days of our marriage. I love you Kate. I loved you when we got married and that love did not change. It just got lost somewhere. I tried to tell you many times but I got a lump in my throat each time and it would not come out. Then I was afraid to tell you in case you laughed at me suddenly saying it after all that time. We seemed to be enemies for so long. It was simpler to ignore it. And once I did I could not go back. I tried to prove it to you in other ways but it always went wrong. I do not know why. I am sorry.

You were a good wife to me Kate and I thank you for that. I know you were disappointed in me but I did my best really I did. I know I was never good enough for you and you deserved better than I could ever be. I did my best as a husband and I hope you can forgive me if I did not live up to your expectations. I was at a loss of what else to do. You were always far above me. I never forgot that.

And now for the awful thing I have to tell you.

I promised my mother that I would never tell you or anybody else and I have not. You know I could never go against her even for you. I am sorry and I feel so guilty. You deserve to know the truth. But how could I tell you???

For years after she died I tried to tell you but it just would not come out. I always felt her watching me, even after her death. Then I realised she said nothing about writing it down. I could tell you and not betray my mother. You see, I am a coward. I've twisted things in my mind so that I don't feel guilty about betraying her.

I had the idea of changing the wallpaper and putting it on upside-down and the message on the wall and the letter and everything. I knew you would be angry when you saw the wallpaper and would want to take it down but I knew I could persuade you to keep it. I also knew you would take it off after I died and find my message and the letter. See I do know you better than you think. (And I know I will die first – I want to die first – you see how much of a coward I am.)

This is what my mother told me.

It happened that awful night you told me Dudley had raped you. She had gone to her church meeting but had come home early. When she opened the front door she could hear us rowing and she listened. She heard it all. She was so angry with Dudley she went to find him. But she could not find him and was making her way home when she saw him at the bottom of his street lying on a piece of waste ground – dead drunk and singing. He swore at her and staggered up the street. She followed him not sure what to do as she didn't want to cause a row in the street but when he got to his lodgings he was so drunk he walked straight on and up onto the mountain. She followed him and laid into him then. Told him she knew about the rape and that he was never to see or speak to her or anyone in our family again. She told him to leave Ponty forever. That he was evil.

He laughed she said. Just laughed and swore and said how much he hated us all. And then he stumbled. There was just enough moonlight for her to see he had stumbled over the old well. It had been sealed down for years, but for some reason, kids probably, the top had been pulled off and cast aside. Dudley was laid across the well on his back and struggling to get up. God help her Kate – she pushed him in.

She said she would never forget the thud of his body hitting the bottom. The well was dried up of course had been for years and she told me the devil took hold of her and she put the lid back on so he would not be discovered.

She told me this some months after it happened. She told me because she could not live with the guilt. There was so much talk of what had happened to him she could not get away from the memory of what she had done. She needed to get some forgiveness but she could not tell the vicar. She could not trust him to keep it to himself. So she told me. She said she knew she could trust me and if she did not get this off her chest she would burst. She was in a terrible state. They will hang me if they find out Tom. For my sake keep this to yourself she said.

I was so worried someone might find him I went up and looked at the well one dark evening. I could see the cover had originally been secured with a metal bar across it and the ends had been screwed into the walls of the well. The original screws were missing, rusted away I assumed. My mother had replaced the cover and just put the bar back over the top and no one had noticed it was not screwed down anymore.

I went back the next night with some tools and screwed the damn thing down. I did it to protect her. I could not let her hang. I knew if his body

237

had been discovered she would have confessed, she was on the verge of confessing all anyway. And what would that have done to our family? I had to protect you and the children. It would have destroyed us – and all for that worthless bastard. It was down to me to keep this disaster from affecting our family more than it already had. I had no choice.

But I felt you should know for your own peace of mind. But she absolutely refused to let me tell you. She did not trust you to keep her secret. I am so sorry. I tried to persuade her but she refused and she swore me to secrecy. What could I do?

That is it Kate. That is all of it. I hope you can see now why I could never tell you. She got very jealous of you and did not like us being together – you know – like that. Unfair I know. In some strange way I think she blamed you for the rape. For being too pretty and too innocent about Dudley. Blamed you for making her kill her son. I realise that was nonsense. It was no one's fault but his. I suppose she could not live with the guilt and needed a scapegoat. Unfortunately, you were it. I am so sorry. So very sorry.

I gave her my solemn promise not to tell anyone, but I felt I owed you a duty to let you know that it was not me. I know you suspected me but I really did get blind drunk that night and had no memory of it. I had told you the truth.

I saw a poem recently – yes I know do not die of shock – me reading a poem. But it was in the paper and I liked it. Part of it said

Let love flow like a high river, not a struggling stream: proud and determined.

In death I want to be that river. Proud and determined to tell you the feelings I could not tell you in life.

With all my love forever.

Tom

I can't breathe and clasp my chest. I think I am having a heart attack. The shaking increases and tears come, unstoppable, like my thoughts. I'd spent the best part of my life with Tom and Mrs Mallow and I now realise I'd never known them.

I can't take it in.

And then anger bubbles up inside me and I feel like I'll explode.

'Nooo,' I scream at the top of my voice.

Both knew what had happened to that bastard and they didn't tell me I had nothing to fear from him anymore. They let me live in terror of him suddenly turning up from behind some grotty corner or other.

How could they have done that to me?

So much for Tom's love.

I let my tears flow. I don't want to keep anything inside any more. It needs to come out. I need to grieve for my lost life, for my what ifs.

Time ceases to exist as I try to process this . . . this, betrayal, this cruelty. Did they think so little of me? The sacrifices I made for them both, and this is how they repaid me. It's unbelievable.

I go to bed and cry. I don't sleep and the next morning, I feel drained of all emotion and this makes me calmer. I make myself a pot of tea and sit in my armchair. As I drink the tea I start to analyse it all.

Mrs Mallow had lived with that secret all those years. Lived with the risk of being found out and hanged, or at the very least, put in jail for the rest of her life. That must have been torture for her. I start to look at it more positively because even though I didn't know he was dead, she saved me from a life lived with that bastard always hovering, and God knows what else he might have done. No, she did me a favour. And if I'm honest, I cannot say if the roles were reversed and I had killed him that I would want her to know about it. That I would trust her not to hold it over my head like a threat, imagined or otherwise, with always the risk that she may tell.

And Tom?

What do I feel about him?

How would I feel if he had done the same for me as he had for his mother? Truth is, I would be immensely grateful. Tom wasn't a coward, he's been too hard on himself. He was just a man caught up in circumstances he couldn't control and he didn't know what to do about it. He was weak, yes, but a coward, no. No man who can go underground year after year hewing out that damned coal is a coward. He was just a man unable to express his feelings, who bottled them up, and I could sympathise with that. I started to wonder whether it was living half your life underground and in our narrow valleys made men more insular: unable to respond to emotions. You have to control your emotions underground and it becomes a habit.

I could sympathise with that.

Hours pass and my thoughts take me down every rabbit hole in my mind. This, that, the other, what ifs, fear, anger, downright rage, and then I come to a settling of the waves. There is nothing I can do, nothing can change what happened.

Mrs Mallow was a great believer in God and Heaven and Hell. She must have lived in dread of dying and facing her Maker. But what I do know is that if only we could have talked to each other, explained our feelings instead of letting them fester and poison us we might have had a better life. When you live so closely together, even a slight couldn't be forgotten. Out of sight out of mind, is true, but so is, never out of sight never out of mind.

And then I realise I am going to have to make a decision about all this, and soon. My family will know about Tom's letter, Sarah will tell them. Why should she not? They have no idea of what that letter contains. It's just a fun thing for a grandfather to do. A mystery they assume they will be party to.

Do I tell them the truth or not?

Do I put my shame on show? The shame of the rape, of my sham of a marriage, of their grandmother being a murderer, of their father's weaknesses. My weaknesses.

If there was ever a time I needed to go to the rocking stone and sit and think and decide what to do it is now. But, if the truth is told, I am too old to climb up to it. What shall I do? How can I decide?

I imagine myself sitting there, on its hard, smooth seat of granite and I feel its presence seeping into me. I remember all the times I've sat there, alone, or with Tom. It's with me as I sit and think for hour after hour. Then I realise there is one other thing that can help me make a decision.

I get up from my comfy armchair, stiff muscles complaining, and pour myself a glass of sherry. I take it into my bedroom and put it down on my cherry wood bedside table, remembering my mother's apple box that served for hers and the hooks in the wall she had for her sparse clothing. I look around at my beautifully decorated and carpeted bedroom, my cherry wood wardrobe full of my clothes. An outfit for every day and two for Sundays! I've come such a long way from my beginnings.

I look at my mother's two pictures of Italy which are on the wall opposite my bed, just as my mother had them in her own bedroom. They have supported me throughout the years, the only memento I have of her. I love them. I trust them to help me in this.

I promise myself that by the time I've drunk the sherry, I'll have made my decision. I settle myself down on top of the eiderdown, propped up by my pillows and look at the pictures.

I take a sip of my sherry, just a small one as I don't want to rush this. I close my eyes and let my mind drift. I want instinct to take over.

I think of all the lives that have been lived in the world and are now lost and forgotten. Of how many loves, hatreds, good deeds and bad, have covered this earth. Countless – and after every generation they're forgotten.

I'm the only one left to remember our family's past. Would it be better for the present generation to know or not? Should I let the past die, like all the lives lived before, or do my family have a right to know the struggle and sacrifices their ancestors went through to enable them to be born? Could knowing all this help them to live fuller and better lives? Is that my destiny – to pass all this on?

I drink the last of my sherry and finally, finally, I know what to do.

I get up and go into my living room and pick up the phone. I ring Megan first . . .

* * *